THIN A

THIN AIR

KELLIE M.
PARKER

RAZORBILL

RAZORBILL

An imprint of Penguin Random House LLC, New York

First published in the United States of America by Razorbill,
an imprint of Penguin Random House LLC, 2023

Visit us online at PenguinRandomHouse.com.

LIBRARY OF CONGRESS CATALOGING-IN-PUBLICATION DATA IS AVAILABLE.

ISBN 9780593526002

Printed in the United States of America

2nd Printing

LSCH

Design by Tony Sahara
Text set in Sabon LT Std

For my four clever, funny, beautiful,
book-loving children—Isaiah, Nate, Ella, and Luke.
Words can't express how much I love you.
Proverbs 3:5-6

THIN AIR

1

MAYDAY, MAYDAY, MAYDAY

June 22, 12:06 a.m. CDT, seven hours after takeoff

The cabin is deathly silent except for the low, constant thrum of the airplane's engines beneath the wings. Like a wasp buzzing in my ear, the sound grates against my tattered nerves, unsettling me almost as much as everything that's happened since the flight attendants distributed those horrible letters. Almost, but not quite.

Feet sinking into the carpet, I wrap my trembling fingers around the heavy glass paperweight and pluck it noiselessly off the desk. The surface is burled walnut—my dad used to have a desk like this in his home office—just a *bit* nicer than a plastic tray table. Normally, that kind of luxury would seem out of place at a cruising altitude of forty-two thousand feet, except this isn't a normal transatlantic flight—not by a mile.

A curtain of hair escapes from behind my ear and falls across one cheek, obscuring my peripheral vision. My heart lurches as I tuck the strands back, the brief blind spot making my pulse race. I clutch the makeshift weapon at my side. Track lighting along the floor and dimmed lighting overhead create a soft yellow glow in the otherwise dark space. It would be cozy if not for the bodies tucked away in an upstairs compartment.

I'd never seen a dead body before this trip. Maybe because I've been at boarding school and had to miss relatives' funerals. Or maybe my mom's fractured relationships mean she and I don't get invited.

You always hear about how stiff and cold and waxy a corpse is, but nobody talks about those first moments when the skin is still warm and it looks like all you'd have to do is give the person a good shake and they'd blink. It's the eyes that give it away—the way they glass over and go hollow. Nobody's in there anymore.

My throat closes up at the thought, but I force myself to swallow. Nothing can be done to help the ones we've already lost, but I *can* save the rest of us. Maybe.

The sense of betrayal stings deeper than that sea nettle that wrapped around my leg last summer on Cape Cod. My grip on the paperweight falters, and I tighten my fingers before it can drop to the floor with a telltale thunk. The evidence is clear, and no matter how I feel, I have to do this for the rest of us. Maybe this is my punishment, my moment of redemption, in which I finally pay the price for my mistakes.

Maybe that's why the killer chose me to frame. I know all about betrayal.

Tears sting my eyes. I swipe them away as I pass through the sliding doorway and into the next dimly lit space. Plush chairs and computer workstations rise like black ghosts from the floor, ready to swallow anyone looking for a place to hide.

The glass paperweight is smooth beneath my fingertips, the mass of it satisfyingly heavy in my palm. Weapons aren't exactly easy to come by on airplanes, even private ones. The thought of hitting anyone on the head with this thing makes my stomach churn, but my intention isn't to kill—only to incapacitate.

I make it out of the workstation compartment alive and tiptoe past the door to the plane's galley and the storage space on the other side of the corridor. Images from the past hours flit through my mind, stuttering my steps and threatening my sense of purpose:

Lily's red hair draped against dull skin, her breathing too shallow. The bruises around her throat.

No, I can't think about that now. Instead, I focus on her last words before she slipped into unconsciousness: *We were wrong.*

I pause at the entrance to the dining room. Someone has cracked open a few of the plane's window shades, letting in narrow streaks of golden-hued early morning light. The large table, long since cleared from last night's dinner, gleams like a dark lake in the middle of the room. Probably the flight attendants would be setting it for breakfast now—if they weren't unconscious in one of the staff rooms upstairs.

A shadowy figure leaning against the far bulkhead glances at me as I enter. He straightens. "Hey," he whispers. "Where are the others?"

How can he ask that question? Doesn't he figure I found the bodies already?

I point my thumb over my shoulder, swallowing a hard lump in my throat, ignoring the pounding in my chest.

Like the rest of the plane, this room is ridiculously luxurious, but it isn't huge. It'll only take a few seconds to reach him. And then . . .

My fingers tighten on the paperweight. Now isn't the time to second-guess.

2

FINAL BOARDING CALL

Eight hours earlier, June 21, 4:04 p.m. **CDT**

My phone, buried in the pocket of my navy school blazer, pings with the thousandth text from Nikki. I ignore it, instead scooping up my messenger bag from the floor and slinging the strap over my shoulder. Our flight is on a private jet, but the clock over the gate shows we're already ten minutes behind schedule. Surely they'll call us to board any minute now.

Last time I counted, all twelve of us were here. Two students each from six private boarding schools across the US, our clashing plaid uniforms like a Scottish tartan factory exploded all over the hard plastic seats of the terminal. We came in on different flights from our respective cities to meet here at Chicago O'Hare, and the last pair arrived forty minutes ago.

I *should* be using this time to size up the competition, but when the dark-haired gate agent behind the desk picks up her phone to make a call, I give in and dig my cell out. I swipe past the lock screen with its picture of me and Nikki. She looks like a model, with her hair falling in beach-kissed waves practically to her waist, wide-set eyes a few shades bluer than my sea-green ones, and perfect skin. She's got one arm carelessly slung around my shoulders, pinning my too-straight strawberry-blond hair. Freckles splattered across my nose glare back at me, making me look more like the popular girl's project rather than her BFF since childhood. Sometimes I wonder if I'm only popular by proximity.

Girl, u talk to any hot guys yet?

Despite the nerves making my knee bounce like a jackhammer, a smile cracks my lips. That *would* be the most pressing concern on my best friend's mind. The other student from my school, Dylan, leans across the gray armrest between us and reads over my shoulder.

"You talked to *me*," he says, one hazel eye winking behind his wire-rimmed glasses.

"I'm pretty sure she doesn't mean *you*."

He's close enough that his shoulder presses into mine, and I get another whiff of his ocean-scented cologne, the same clean fragrance I've been treated to all day since leaving Hartford this morning. Only years of practice keep me from giving up the secret that I've had a huge crush on him since seventh grade.

That and the fact he's Nikki's boyfriend.

Before I can tap out a response, Dylan swipes the phone from my hand and shoots off his own reply. **OMG, the hottest guy is sitting next to me.** Then a string of kissing emojis.

"Dylan, give it back!" I squeal. Too many sets of eyes swivel my direction in the quiet waiting area. Apparently, nobody at the other schools has a social life, except maybe the girl from Lancashire Academy in Philadelphia. Olivia? Her wavy blond hair and flawless complexion match the profile picture on the bio sheet the Bonhomme Foundation sent out—practically Nikki's clone. She's been splitting her time between giggling over her phone, eyeing Dylan, and shooting me dirty looks. *Good.* If she's distracted by him, she won't be as focused on whatever the foundation's scholarship committee has in store for us.

Another text from Nikki pings. **Dylan, give Em her phone.**

He snickers, shaking his head, and hands it over. "How do you two always know?"

I shrug. "Best friends since fifth grade. What do you expect?"

The sharp click of heels on linoleum announces the arrival of a flight attendant, a middle-aged woman with blond hair secured in a tidy bun and dressed in a purple crepe suit. She exchanges a couple of words with the gate agent, and the woman with the bun proceeds down the ramp toward the plane.

The agent at the counter picks up her microphone. "Ladies and gentlemen, thank you for your patience. At this time, we will begin boarding the Bonhomme Foundation's private flight to Paris, France. Please have your passports and boarding passes ready."

I've been perched on the edge of my seat waiting for this announcement for the last two hours, but my mouth goes dry anyway. Maybe because my future depends on this opportunity.

It's not every day you get to compete for an award that will guarantee four all-expenses-paid years at an Ivy League college, experience working as a youth ambassador for a nonprofit, *and* a postgraduate mentorship, much less travel to Europe for said competition. Missing part of summer break back home is an added bonus, seeing as how I don't technically have a home right now.

Another secret I've been keeping.

Two weeks in a posh Paris hotel sounds a lot more appealing than living in my mom's Subaru Outback, no matter how you slice it. My neck grows hot. Not even Nikki knows how bad things have gotten.

Thankfully, my needs-based scholarship to Exeter guarantees my escape from homelessness in the fall *if* I can survive the summer. My mom always insisted that my time at boarding school would be the best part of my childhood—speaking from *her* experience, of course. She still gets misty-eyed when she talks about Windsor-Dalton, like the only thing she wants in life is to time-travel back there and keep reliving her four years of high school, even though Dad used to hint it wasn't all roses and homecoming dances. If only she'd put more effort into her classes and less into her social life, maybe we wouldn't be stuck living in a car right now.

"Sweet." Dylan rises to his feet. "Let's get this party started."

I take an extra moment to type out one last message to Nikki and get a grip on myself. **Boarding. Text soon.**

K. Take care of Dylan for me. Love u. Her answer flies back so fast I can almost picture her flopped out on her bed with phone in hand and nothing better to do than live vicariously through me.

Guilt lances through my insides like a flash of lightning, competing with the anxiety treading on my frayed nerves. The same feeling I've had to fight off ever since the scholarship candidates were announced. Nikki should've been here, keeping watch over her own boyfriend. But then I remind myself that she doesn't need this opportunity. Her family is loaded.

Love u too.

It takes an extra minute, but I open my Gmail app and send Mom a quick note to let her know we're boarding. Texting would be far more efficient, but she dropped her cell line to save money after she lost the house to foreclosure. She should've canceled my line too, but she insists she has enough stress without having to worry about me. Like most days, she's probably at the public library, using one of the computers to search for jobs. Six months hasn't been long enough for anything to pan out, but she's doing her best. It's hard when all you can put on your résumé is "high school cheerleader, stay-at-home mom, and failed MLM direct sales home-based business owner." Those boxes of hideous, stretchy leggings lasted longer than most of our furniture, which is rather fitting, considering they *cost* more than the furniture. I swear she was crying when she finally had to unload them on the poor, unsuspecting employees at Goodwill.

She should've tracked my dad down when he stopped making child-support payments two years ago, but at the time she just wanted to be done with him. Not that I can blame her. There's no better way to tell your family—your *daughter*—that she doesn't matter than to refuse to give financial help. He left home when I was in fifth grade, the year I enrolled at Exeter, like I was the only thing tying him to Mom, and since the divorce was "amicable" they opted out of court-mandated payments. I got to see him a lot for a few years, until Mom eventually made him so mad with her reckless spending he just sort of vanished—birthday cards and payments and everything. For a while, I'd tell her to ask her sister or my grandma for help, but she'd get all quiet and pinched, so now I don't say anything about it. And Dad . . . he's just a distant memory.

When I glance up, Dylan is halfway to the line forming in front of the boarding ramp. I stuff the phone back into my pocket and climb to my feet before remembering my boarding pass is still in my bag. Trying to fish it out while walking turns out to be a bad plan, because I promptly collide with one of my fellow travelers.

"Oof, sorry," I mumble into a dark-red wool blazer. My gaze tracks upward past an embroidered gray crest to the owner's face, several inches above my own. Clear blue eyes beneath tousled dark hair fill my vision as my brain stumbles through the list of competitors' names. I come up with nothing, because how can I think straight when he's grinning at me like this?

"No worries. I'm Liam." He taps the crest on his blazer. "Scoatney." As if that explains everything I need to know.

"Em . . . Emily." I stumble over my own name. *Really nice, Em. Way to underwhelm your competition.* "I'm from Exeter. In Connecticut. Just finished my junior year." My hands flail like they're attached to somebody else. "This is my first time traveling out of the country, other than one trip to Prince Edward Island when I was little." Good grief, now I'm babbling, as if that's going to compensate for not knowing my own name. Why should he care about my travel history?

"Cool. I've never been up there." Graciously, he points toward a TV out in the hallway, where the Red Sox are taking on the Yankees in Fenway Park. I'd forgotten that game was on today. "Sorry for standing in the way"—he smiles apologetically—"but I got caught up watching the game."

In an attempt to regroup, I glance at the TV in time to see the Sox third baseman field a grounder and sidearm a stellar throw to first, making the double play. My fist pumps almost on its own. "Did you see that?"

A bemused grin flits across his face, and he pulls back like I'm contagious. "Oh no. Don't tell me you're a Red Sox fan."

"I'm from Connecticut." I hold up my hands. "What can I say?"

"You can say the Red Sox are losers and you regret your life choices." Despite his words, the way he's still smiling at me is, quite frankly, adorable. And for once, Nikki isn't here to steal the attention. Or tell me how boring baseball is.

"Whatever." I shake my head. "Why on earth would you like the *Yankees*? Isn't Scoatney on the other side of the country or something?"

"Seattle." Merriment dances in his eyes at my obvious lack of geographical knowledge.

Though how should I know where all the other schools are

located? Besides, I *used* to be a straight-A student, back before my family collapsed like a poorly built skyscraper.

"My family lives in New York," he goes on. As he's talking, the next Yankee at bat winds up and swings at a fastball. We both stand watching as the ball sails into left field, clearing the Green Monster. Home run.

Liam's smile straddles the border between smug and pitying. "Besides, why shouldn't I root for the best team?"

My mouth opens, but my brain utterly fails me. Where's the snappy retort? The witty comeback? Why am I standing here in slack-jawed silence, staring at this good-looking guy who's just bested me?

"Em, come on!" Dylan—bless him—waves to me from the line.

I flash my boarding pass at Liam and force my flaming cheeks into a smile. "Guess I should get in line. Nice to meet you."

His fingers brush against the small of my back as he gestures with the other hand to allow me to go in front of him. "After you, Emily from Exeter."

A casual touch that doesn't mean a thing, but my heart hammers anyway as I turn to join Dylan. When I glance back, Liam is locked in conversation with Olivia. Why isn't she with her own classmate?

While I'm scanning the crowd for another forest-green Lancashire blazer and tie, Dylan nudges me with his elbow. "Flirting with the enemy?"

"Of course not." I give him a look. It's not like there's room for relationships when I'm competing against all these people for the same prize.

He cocks an eyebrow and flashes his cutest grin, the one normally reserved for Nikki, and I'm reminded again exactly why I've had a crush on him for so long. I would never say a word about it to anyone in a million years—*especially* him. That dream died a slow and agonizing death when Dylan asked Nikki to the middle school spring formal his first year at Exeter. They've been on and off again ever since, but mostly on. As far as Nik knows, my feelings evaporated back when we were twelve, and she's never going to hear different.

"Good thing," he says. I start to wonder if he's magically reading my mind until he adds, "Because I've got to look out for my Exeter girl."

Obviously, I'm not actually his girl, but something about the way he says it makes me almost believe it. I'm so used to living in Nikki's shadow it's weird suddenly being on the receiving end of Dylan's charm. And he has a *lot*.

The students ahead of us start to move. A fresh wave of jitters courses through my body. Outside the large glass windows, thunder crackles as if even the sky knows what's at stake.

Everyone lines up more or less in pairs, hauling book bags and small totes. Our larger luggage was checked, to be transferred through to Paris. Two students from Waterford in North Carolina are at the back of the line. The guy's cropped blond hair and sturdy build shout "football player," and the girl, with her bubbly laugh and curly brown hair tied up with a ribbon, could've been pulled off any school's cheer squad. They're holding hands and gazing into each other's eyes like they're never going to see each other again.

Some of the tension eases in my shoulders. If they're this absorbed in each other, maybe they won't be much of a threat.

Standing in front of them is the pair from Saint Peter's, a Catholic school in San Francisco. The girl is the shortest of us all, with red hair and enough freckles she could be Anne of Green Gables' clone if it weren't for her sun-kissed bronze skin. The guy with her is a wall of solid muscle, but less bulky than the football player. Not tall enough for basketball, so I'm going with baseball. Especially because he keeps darting glances at the Red Sox–Yankees game. Between his dark hair and thick brows, he's got that hot broody look. I wonder if he has a girlfriend.

When he glances up and catches my gaze, his full lips curl into a lazy smirk. I jerk and turn away before he gets any ideas. I don't have time to invest in boys right now, especially ones who are my competition.

Olivia has finally found her classmate—Simon Walker—but she's got her back to him. He's reading something that looks an awful lot like a textbook. What on earth? From the slew of equations visible on the page, I'd guess . . . calculus? Physics? I might break out in hives just looking at it. At least I know who's got the brains on this trip—a useful bit of information to tuck away in case we need to work in teams.

He's not exactly unattractive, with spiky dark hair and black glasses over pale skin—kind of the geeky I-could-be-hot-if-I-tried look—but he's clearly not interested in Olivia. At all. Probably the first time that's ever happened to her.

My attention snags on a dark-red blazer out in the corridor, where people are scurrying past, towing bags and crabby children. It's Liam, stooped down, picking something up off the scuffed linoleum floor. A head of curly brown hair bobs nearby, and when they both stand, my insides grow warm and fuzzy. He was helping a little girl, no more than six years old, judging by her height. Liam hands the kid her backpack, waves at her and her mom, and turns back to our line. I whip around before he catches me staring.

Dylan tugs my sleeve, and we walk toward the gate agent. She scans my boarding pass and mumbles, "Enjoy the flight," and I thump down the long, echoing ramp to the largest private jet I've ever seen. Dylan's parents own one—a Gulfstream, I think—and I've flown on it a couple of times with him and Nikki, but it only seats twenty.

Nothing like this plane. Engines on the wings, white exterior, with THE BONHOMME FOUNDATION painted in ginormous blue letters between two rows of windows.

Yes, two rows. Apparently, the foundation is loaded. The upper row stretches all the way to the tail, like the Flying Palace—the huge plane that rich guy owns in the Middle East.

At the bottom of the ramp, the blond flight attendant I saw earlier stands to one side of the open plane door, only now she's wearing a cap to match her suit and a gold name tag that reads JENNIFER O'CONNOR. Her face is molded into the perfect professional smile, and she extends one hand toward the open door like we're filming a TV commercial.

"Welcome," she says. "Please enter and turn right to head aft, which means toward the tail."

Not kidding—my eyes nearly pop out of my face when I cross the threshold into the plane. Behind me, Dylan lets out a gasp that falls somewhere between *Who is this freaking rich?* and *Where do I get one?*

We're standing in a literal entryway. Dylan, who's pushing six feet, doesn't have to duck. And instead of being dark and cramped and plasticky, like you'd expect on an airplane, light bounces at me from every angle. A crystal chandelier hangs over a pedestal holding a vase of fresh-cut flowers. The floral scent helps mask the smell of stale recirculated air and jet fuel. Beside the vase sits a gold mesh basket full of cream-colored envelopes. Mirrors line the walls, and every surface that isn't crystal or mirrored is gilded.

A staircase sweeps upward through the glitter to the second level. It's hard to see what's up there, but I'd guess access to the flight deck. Maybe also space for the staff, or private quarters for the foundation's CEO. Will he be on the plane? The thought terrifies and excites me at the same time. I've only seen him on the videos our headmaster showed to introduce the competition prior to taking the first round of qualifying exams. Sir Robert Hamlin, British expatriate living in Paris, benefactor of humanity.

If he wants to share some of his excessive resources with me, I won't complain.

At the base of the stairs, another flight attendant stands beside an open door leading to the right. She's younger than the blond one, maybe late twenties, with shiny black hair and deep-brown skin. "Right this way, please. Straight through the entertainment salon, and on to the guest seating."

We pass through a short corridor with a coat closet on the left and a lavatory on the right, and then I nearly collide with the boy in front of me, who's standing with his mouth open in the entrance to the next compartment.

"Sorry," he says. "It's hard not to stare." He's shorter than me, but with his ruffled dark hair, his brown skin, and his wide grin, he's cute. In fact, everyone here is rather attractive. Did they factor in our appearance? Maybe because the winner will have so many publicity events for the foundation?

I'm guessing he must be Amir, the tech genius and the youngest competitor. Another person who could be a real advantage on a team.

The girl in front of him turns to flash a wide smile at both of us, her curly black hair swishing across her shoulders. A pair of gold eyeglasses complements her brown skin and frames her eyes, and a tiny diamond sparkles on one side of her nose. "I can't believe we're here!" she says. She must be Taylor, the one who loves theater and singing. If the gray-and-blue tartan skirt matching Amir's tie didn't give it away, her silky, resonant voice would. Her vibrant yet polished manner is going to be hard to match if we're evaluated on public speaking.

So far, I'm losing to Simon and Amir on brains, and Taylor for interview skills. Then there are all the athletes . . .

Who, exactly, do I have a shot at beating? A band tightens around my chest.

Behind me, Dylan lets out low whistle. "Get a load of this place," he murmurs, so close he's practically breathing in my ear. His nearness sends a tremor zigzagging down my back, which I attempt to hide by hoisting my bag strap a little higher on my shoulder. I take another step to put some distance between us.

A giant flat-screen TV fills the bulkhead wall next to us, and the rest of the space holds a tasteful assortment of cream-colored seating and wooden side tables. Along the back wall, a smaller screen hangs above shelves full of books and board games. It looks remarkably homey, for an airplane. Certainly better than a Subaru Outback.

I cross the compartment to the far side, where the other bulkhead conceals two sliding doors into the next section. Finally, we've reached something that resembles a traditional airplane, albeit maybe the first-class section. Between the two bulkheads stand three rows of seats, six in each row. Two aisles separate the seats into pairs, and overhead bins wait to receive our carry-on bags.

A third purple-clad flight attendant, this one with light brown hair, directs us to choose seats. Taylor and Amir stuff backpacks into the bins in the center of the last row.

I glance back at Dylan. "Where do you want to . . . ?"

He shrugs and points at the seats in front of Taylor and Amir. We stow our bags and plop down. The seats are cushy and comfortable. A little sigh escapes my lips as I lean my head back and close my eyes. Dylan and I had to be at the airport—the same one, since we both live close to Hartford—at six this morning to catch our first flight, which meant Mom dropping me off a half hour earlier so Dylan wouldn't see how packed our car is. It's even worse now, since the term ended and she had to pick me up from the dorm two weeks ago. At least the school lets returning students keep some of our things on campus. Otherwise, she'd have to tie the trunk shut.

The funny thing is, when she had to sell most of our stuff, I pretty much took it in stride until the day she emailed that last picture of my bedroom set, a pink-and-white canopy bed and a matching dresser with little flowers painted on each drawer. She sold it to a father and his six-year-old daughter, the same age I was when Dad took me to the furniture store to pick it out. Sure, I'm way too old for that bed now, but I broke down bawling anyway. Probably because it drove home the truth I'd avoided ever since Dad left—things are never going to be the same.

I am *so* not a morning person, and now that I'm safely on this flight, the adrenaline that carried me through the morning is wearing off. Rustling in the aisle to my right forces me to pry my heavy eyelids open. It's Liam's classmate, Ann—a Chinese American girl with black hair contained in a fabulously thick fishbone braid. Her orange-tinted lipstick would look atrocious on me, but it's gorgeous on her.

I steal a glance at Liam, the unapologetic Yankees fan I ran into while boarding, who's waiting in the aisle with both elbows propped on the seats to either side. He's staring at a point on the floor, his eyes dull, like he's lost in his own world. Then he glances up, his gaze landing on me, and his expression clears. My toes curl as one corner of his mouth hitches up. He's got this little cleft in his chin, just like Henry Cavill, which somehow escaped my notice earlier.

"Comfortable?" he asks.

We're all from exclusive schools, of course, but there's something about him that shouts "not prep school material." Like he doesn't fit the mold. I wouldn't be surprised to learn he rides a motorcycle or has a hidden tattoo.

I shift deeper into the seat, clearing my throat so my voice doesn't squeak like a mouse. "Very."

"Did you rethink your life choices yet?"

I shoot him a scowl, but I can't keep my face straight for long, not with his mouth curved like that in a lazy half grin. We can agree to disagree about baseball.

Ann takes the seat by the window, and as Liam waits for her to settle in, he stands next to me, close enough I can feel the heat emanating from him. I catch a whiff of something light and fresh, like cotton and citrus, as he moves. Nothing like Dylan's heavy ocean cologne. Liam hoists his messenger bag into the overhead bin and then proceeds to confirm my suspicions about breaking the mold by stripping off his blazer, tie, and button-down shirt, leaving only a white undershirt and a whole lot of ripped arm muscle for me to admire. Judging by the giggles, I'm not the only one to notice. Did it get hotter in here?

"Dude, that's what I'm talkin' about!" someone calls from the cabin doorway. It's the football player with the cropped blond hair. He points at Liam and pumps his fist.

Liam shrugs. "Might as well relax, right?" He pulls a fine-gauge gray sweater from his bag and accidentally knocks out something else, which lands with a little thump near my feet. As he slips the sweater over his head, ruffling his thick brown hair, I reach down to pick up what he dropped.

It's a spiral-bound sketchbook, and since it landed open, I don't feel as bad about looking at his drawings. They're character studies—the same person's face sketched multiple times—but there's one that reaches right into my chest and squeezes my heart. It's the eyes—the way they're looking straight at me with this perfectly captured, haunting expression of sorrow.

"Wow. These are amazing." I let the words slip out before I realize Liam is patiently waiting for me to close his private sketchbook and hand it back without gawking. Dylan leans over to see what I'm looking at but only grunts noncommittally.

"Thanks." Liam shrugs, and I could swear his cheeks glow with a hint of pink. "I like to draw. Just for fun."

I feel like I owe him, now that I've embarrassed him, so I lean away from Dylan in hopes only Liam will hear. "I can't do anything that realistic"—I nod toward the sketchbook, securely closed in his hand—"but I try."

"Yeah?" He turns away, stuffing the book into his bag and shutting the overhead bin. "That's cool. What do you draw?"

"Just doodles," I say, hoping Dylan isn't listening. "Sometimes a little fan art or a landscape."

I shrug like it isn't a big deal, because the last thing I want is to admit how much I really love drawing. The reality is I'm terrible at it and don't have the guts to show anyone my work, so no one needs to know.

His eyes light up, and I can tell he's going to tease me before he opens his mouth. "So, your sketchbook is full of guys from *Outer Banks?*" he asks, a whole lot louder than I would've liked.

Heat scorches my neck as I steal a glance at Dylan, but, thankfully, he's immersed in something on his phone.

"Well, I . . . It's . . ." I say it so quietly I'm practically mumbling. My Exeter bow tie has been digging into my neck since five this morning, so I tug it loose as I fumble for an answer.

Liam folds his tall frame practically in half, one arm leaning against the back of my seat, as he ducks closer. "I'm just messing with you. I'd love to see your stuff if we have time later."

Only one time have I managed to pull off a drawing that didn't make me cringe—Nikki's family cottage on the Cape. By some miracle, I managed to capture the light dancing on the waves just the way I wanted to. It's the only thing I'd even consider showing him.

Next to me, I can sense Dylan leaning closer, like he's wondering what we're discussing. So instead of giving a real response, I tuck a strand of hair behind my ear and smile.

"Dude, are you sure you should ditch the uniform?" he asks Liam. "Maybe professional appearance counts."

Liam straightens. "We've got like eight hours on this flight. There's plenty of time to put it back on."

Dylan frowns, glancing at me as I finger my bow tie. For a moment, I feel caught between them—like I'm choosing whose side to take. Which is ridiculous, but I still compromise, stuffing the bow tie into a pocket but keeping the blazer.

"Besides," Liam adds as he sinks into his seat, "it's not like Sir

What's His Name is judging us before we even get there."

His words bring back full force the reason I'm here, the price I paid for this chance—what I forced *others* to pay—and what's at stake. My fingers fold around the bow tie in my pocket. I hope to God Liam is right.

3

CARRY-ON BAGGAGE

5:11 p.m. CDT

Takeoff and landing are my least favorite parts of any flight. I hate the way the plane shudders and bounces, the compression as inertia forces you into the seat. Even before everyone is settled, I rummage through the mini storage area separating me and Dylan to make sure there's an airsickness bag. There's something reassuring about knowing one's there, just in case.

By the time all of us are buckled into our seats, the echo of pouring rain drifts faintly in from the outside, over the cycling of the air circulation system and the hum of the engines. Thunder crackles intermittently, but the storm must be far enough away not to interfere, because the plane eases back from the gate.

I think about digging out my phone again to text Nikki—after all, this will be my last chance to have cell service this side of the ocean—but I decide against it. Honestly, it's kind of refreshing to be here without her, though I feel horrid for even thinking that. Like, worst friend *ever*. But I'm always glued to her side, and for once, I'm the one having the adventure.

As the plane completes its turn and rolls forward, an announcement comes on overhead. "Ladies and gentlemen, this is your captain speaking. For your safety, the door to the flight deck will remain closed and locked for the duration of the flight. Questions or concerns should be addressed to the flight staff. Flying with us today are Ms. Jennifer O'Connor, Ms. Sarita Kumar, and Ms. Camille Allard."

The three women stand in the aisles toward the front of the compartment, each waving as they're introduced. The blond one, O'Connor, reaches for a handheld radio and reads the standard safety information off a card while the other two demonstrate how to put on our oxygen masks and use our seat cushions as a personal flotation device—because if the plane goes down in the middle of the Atlantic Ocean, it's going to be a real consolation having that seat cushion.

"On behalf of the Bonhomme Foundation and the Goodwill Merit Award Committee," O'Connor continues, "we'd like to welcome you aboard. Please stow your electronic devices and remain seated through takeoff. When the captain turns off the seat belt sign, you'll be free to move around the plane until dinner is served."

At this pronouncement, I exchange a quick glance with Dylan. His eyes gleam.

"We'll be playing a message shortly from Sir Robert Hamlin," O'Connor continues, "but in the meantime, please relax and enjoy the flight."

By this time, our plane has taxied into position at the end of one of O'Hare's long runways. The flight attendants vanish behind the bulkhead, and before I'm quite ready we're hurtling down the runway and jostling into the air. The clouds are ominously dark as we fly up into them, and I have the sudden horrible thought that maybe it's a sign.

I've been dreaming about this trip for weeks—not only because of the scholarship and Paris, but because I'll have a real bed. Three hot meals every day. A shower I don't have to operate using quarters. And my mom won't have to stress about taking care of me, on top of everything else. She's got enough on her plate as it is.

But what if it's not the escape I was anticipating? What if somebody figures out the truth?

My stomach, already doing gymnastics, fills with lead. Thick clouds envelop the plane for a few long minutes until we break through to brilliant afternoon sunshine and blue sky. The tops of the clouds, fluffy and white, look far more innocent, like I should be able to spot angels playing harps. Some of the tension eases out of my gut.

The interior lights lower, the window shades close by some invisible magic, and a large flat-screen TV on the forward bulkhead turns on. Sweeping orchestral music pours from the speakers as a promo video for the Bonhomme Foundation plays, showing clips of various projects the foundation has funded over the past twenty-five years, since it was created. Clean water in Liberia, rural schools in Nigeria, medical aid in Bangladesh, reconstruction in the Caribbean after a hurricane.

Sir Robert Hamlin comes on at the end. He's an older man, maybe in his sixties, with thinning gray hair, glasses, and an English accent that's remarkably soothing despite his nasally tone.

"It's my pleasure to welcome you to the twenty-first Goodwill Merit Award competition, and congratulations on your achievement in making it this far. Hundreds of boarding school students applied for our program, but only you twelve finalists were selected, based on your test scores, accomplishments, talents, and potential. I look forward to meeting you in person in Paris, but until then, let's discuss the rules."

A chorus of frustrated voices rises to greet this pronouncement, but I sit up a little straighter. Knowing how the competition works will give me the chance to strategize.

"First, since our goal is to choose the best possible candidate to further the foundation's mission of goodwill toward humanity, consider every moment from here on out as part of the competition."

Apparently, Dylan was right. More than one person around me fumbles for their blazer and tie, but not Liam. He leans in close to Ann, fully engaged in whatever she's saying to him.

Hamlin goes on. "As you'll see shortly, there's a touchscreen in the entertainment salon that will display the current rankings for all participants. Application essays and test scores were used only for initial selection, so you'll all be starting with a clean slate. During the flight, you'll be permitted a total of either three upvotes *or* downvotes to add or subtract fifty points from another participant. One may be used at any time once the system is activated. The other two, you'll be informed when to use."

Dylan glances at me. "Upvote each other?"

"Of course," I whisper. As if there's any question. Clearly, it pays to make friends on this flight.

"The selection of the winner," Hamlin continues, "will be decided at the end of the two-week period based on a comprehensive evaluation of character, intelligence, leadership skills, teamwork, and talent as displayed in contest events. These events will be divided into three areas."

A chart appears on the screen, and we all shift forward in our seats to study the text. My chest tightens. Does that last column say # OF STUDENTS CUT?

"First, social skills and negotiation abilities will be tested on this flight. As you can see on the chart, the three students with the lowest ranking when the plane touches down in France will be cut and their return flights booked for the following day."

A collective groan breaks out. "They don't even get to see Paris?" the Waterford football player asks. "That's a load of—" He cuts himself off before something pops out that could count against him.

No pressure, anybody.

Hamlin, of course, is oblivious to our reaction. "The nine of you who are left will embark on week one's competition in Paris. Your formal communication skills will be assessed by the Goodwill Merit Award committee through a series of writing and public speaking activities, with one competitor cut at the end of each day based on rankings. Finally, during the second week, the top two students will be evaluated for leadership and project management skills by accomplishing a final task with the help of a team composed of two of your former competitors. Anyone not selected to participate in week two will return home early."

He smiles warmly, his expression at odds with the death knell he's tolling over our heads. "If it sounds confusing now, don't worry—it'll all make sense once you're here.

"As a side note, other foundation members, outside persons, and staff will not be involved in this decision, nor are they privy to details regarding tests, interviews, or other data used to evaluate candidates, so please don't ask them for information.

"Third, and last, success in life takes many forms. But no path will be truly satisfying for those who can't find contentment. Enjoy yourselves and this once-in-a-lifetime opportunity. Best of luck, and I look forward to meeting you in Paris!"

The screen goes black. There's a moment of stillness before everyone starts talking—a low whisper punctuated here and there by a slightly more frantic question or exclamation.

Three students are heading home *tomorrow*. My stomach

clenches, and I suddenly wish I hadn't eaten that bagel for lunch. Oh, to feel some level of confidence. Thankfully, the committee doesn't know what I did to get here, but still . . . Surely somebody's going to notice the guilt scorching through me. Then there's the fact all these other people *earned* the right to be here. How can I ever beat them?

Beside me, Dylan straightens the lapel of his blazer and contorts his face into the pinched lips and frown of our headmaster. "Exeter students are always prepared." He mimics what plays across our school speakers every morning.

I want to laugh, but my throat is so dry only a cough manages to escape. There's too much riding on this competition for me. Instead, I pull out my red-and-blue bow tie and loop it back under my shirt collar. "Do you really think they're watching us right now?"

"My dad said to think of it like a two-week job interview. Maybe Hamlin isn't spying on us, but somebody on this plane is. How else are they going to assign points and rank us after the events?" He pats down his blond hair, though none of it is out of place. "I, for one, don't want to blow my chances over something foolish," he adds. His gaze flits past me toward Liam, still relaxed in his seat.

"You'll get into Harvard regardless," I tell Dylan. "It's practically in your blood. I mean, your dad's on the board, isn't he?"

A faint smirk tracks across his features. "Yeah, but that doesn't mean I don't care about victory. Besides, I'd make an excellent youth ambassador for the foundation."

He *does* like to win, even more when there's an audience. Nikki has dragged me to more of Dylan's lacrosse games than I can count. His drive to be the best is something I've always admired about him, although in this situation it's decidedly inconvenient. After all, I need this scholarship a whole lot more than he does.

But it's not like I'm going to explain my situation to him. He and Nikki both know about my dad and how he moved out right after I started at Exeter, but they don't know he stopped making payments. Or about how Mom's quest for the perfect stay-at-home job turned into a lose-your-home job, because she forked out so much cash to that MLM company, for inventory nobody in their right mind would buy.

I must have a weird expression on my face, because Dylan's hand finds mine on my armrest. He's not exactly known for his compassion. Do I look pale or something?

"Hey, you're going to do great too," he says. "We're in this together, right?" His eyes find mine and hold, then he gives my fingers a squeeze.

"Of course," I say, fighting to keep my tone even.

He glances down, smoothing out his blazer again. "Honestly, I was a little surprised Nikki didn't get the other slot. She usually nails her exams."

Heat steals across my face. Is he insinuating I'm not as smart as Nikki? Does the entire world only see me as Nikki's sidekick?

"Maybe it's better for her to be home, though," he goes on, "what with her mom and all. But she would've loved seeing Paris."

My brows pull together. "What do you mean, her mom?" Now that I'm thinking about it, there was something on her application about her mom and medical issues, wasn't there? And at least a few times last year she abruptly changed plans on me at the last second.

"She has cancer."

Cancer. My mouth drops.

Confusion flickers across Dylan's face. "Didn't Nik tell you?"

I clench the armrest, wishing the seat could swallow me up, as an unwelcome sense of betrayal fights with my guilty conscience. To be going through something like that with her family and not say anything to me . . . How bad is it? Is her mom going to die? When was she planning on telling me?

"I . . . had no idea," I stammer.

Did she think I wouldn't be there for her? That I couldn't be trusted with her family secrets? The sense of hurt rips me up inside, but even worse is the reality of what I've done to her.

I *can't* be trusted. But if I'd known, I *never* would have—

"I'm sorry, Em. I shouldn't have brought it up." He picks at imaginary lint on his blazer. "I figured you knew."

"No." My mouth is pasty-dry. But as much as her silence hurts me, haven't I done exactly the same thing to her?

I should have told her what was going on with my parents and the house. I wanted to tell her, at first, when Mom couldn't make her payments. But every time I came close to bringing it up, the timing felt all wrong. *Yeah, Nik, I love that sweater on you. And, by the way, I'm homeless now.* How exactly do you bring that up? And once enough time passed, it seemed too late. Too awkward.

Did Nikki feel the same way about talking to me?

Truth is, I guess talking about that stuff makes it more real. If I keep it locked away inside and nobody else knows, I can almost pretend things are normal. That *I'm* normal, not homeless and pathetic and struggling to make something of my life.

"You know how she is." Dylan shrugs. "Has to keep up a good face, even with us. She probably wouldn't have told me either, except I happened to be with her when her parents called with the news."

"I'll talk to her about it as soon as we land," I say. After a pause,

I add, "Sometimes I wish it were her here instead of me, Dylan. But I'm really glad to get this chance." It's as honest as I can be.

"Me too. You're a good friend to her." His gaze flits back to my face, lingering a bit longer than usual, as if he's truly noticing me for the first time. I shift uncomfortably in my seat, but then the captain comes on over the loudspeaker.

"We've reached our cruising altitude of forty-two thousand feet, and it should be smooth sailing from here on out." The fasten-seat-belts sign shuts off with a *ping*. "Feel free to move about the cabins and use your portable electronic devices at this time."

Taylor stands first. "Wait, can we do introductions before everybody bolts? I know we received the info sheets and bios, but it'd help to hear names. Cool?"

When a few of us nod, she goes on. "I'm Taylor Lewis from Wells Prep in Boston, and I'd like to be an actor on Broadway." Her eyes glow, like the mere thought of her cherished dream warms her from head to toe.

A sharp stab of envy spikes through me. Not because I want to be center stage, but because she knows what she wants. My life suddenly feels purposeless, narrowed down to the interior of my mom's car and surviving the summer.

I ball one hand into a fist, my nails digging into my palm, then steel my spine. This scholarship is going to change everything for me. With a mentor's help, I'll figure out what I'm good at, what career will provide for my mom and me and make a difference in the world.

Amir stands up beside Taylor, his laptop in one hand and a pair of earbuds dangling from his neck, and gives his name. "I want to go to MIT and become a cybersecurity hacker. And, yes, I skipped two grades and I'm fifteen. I know you're all wondering."

A few of us laugh. His smile is infectious. He's going to be tough to beat.

The red-haired girl from California goes next—her name is Lily Hernandez, and she wants to be a novelist. She seems too soft-spoken and sweet to fit in with this overachieving crowd, but that means she might be a good target to win over for an upvote.

I was right about her classmate, Evan Randall. He *is* a baseball player, and from the way he pretty much ignores Lily, he's carrying around an attitude that could be a helpful liability.

Liam and Ann go next. Then it's my turn. I get my name out properly this time, with no trace of the nerves that've been tying my tongue since I set foot in O'Hare. Everyone else has shared their postcollege goal, but I'm pretty sure *I'd like to not be homeless* isn't exactly what I'm supposed to be going for.

Besides, there's the little issue of my bio, which I had to write to match my application. "I'd like to be a lawyer."

Dylan scrunches his brow, and since it's his turn next, everyone watches his reaction. "Really?" he says.

I screw up my nose. "Yeah, of course. You know that." He doesn't, but I'm hoping he'll roll with it.

He shakes his head slightly, then introduces himself. When he's finished, he turns back to me. "You and Nikki are like clones or something. She keeps going on about becoming a world-famous litigator. You know, if she can't get on a remake of *The Vampire Diaries*."

"She *does* like to be the best." Probably why she and Dylan make the perfect pair.

His hazel eyes scan my face again, as if I'm some mystery he's just discovered and has to puzzle out for himself. "Gotta admit, I'd never peg you for a lawyer."

I'd act offended, except he's right. Confrontation makes me want to run and hide. But my bio says I want to be a lawyer, so that's what this crowd needs to hear. "I'm thinking about family law. Maybe working for a nonprofit." That sounds slightly more believable, doesn't it? Emily the do-gooder. I hope Hamlin is listening.

Only two pairs left. There's a momentary lull as the two girls stare each other down, until the cheerleader stands up with a loud huff. Any trace of irritation vanishes as she flashes us a winning smile. "I'm Paige Hall from Waterford in North Carolina, and I want to be a professional cheerleader."

Nailed that one. Not to be stereotypical and all, but she and her boyfriend must've made it into the competition based on athletic talent. I'm not exactly picking up Mensa vibes. Hopefully, I can rule them out as serious competition. That only leaves nine others. My mouth goes dry.

Paige pulls her boyfriend to his feet. "And this is Blake Adams," she says, drawing his name out like she's announcing the team for the next Super Bowl. "He's going to be a quarterback in the NFL." She squeezes an arm around him, her face glowing with pride, and he shrugs and winks at the rest of us.

"Thanks, babe," he says. Then he dips his face to give her a kiss, which rapidly turns into something the rest of us do *not* want to watch.

Just when I'm thinking we'll need a pair of pliers to separate their faces, Olivia stands and loudly clears her throat.

She waits until Blake and Paige drop sheepishly back into their seats, then flips her hair behind her shoulder. "Olivia Mitchell from Lancashire Academy. I'm already a part-time model." Of *course* she's a model. "And after college, I'm going to start my own fashion design business."

She bestows a perfect smile on us before turning to the scowling dark-haired boy standing next to her. He's still holding that textbook in his hand, and this time I catch a glimpse of the cover. *Differential Calculus.*

Just what *I'd* want to read on a long flight. On the other hand, if he knows the foundation is paying attention . . . it could be a smart move.

"Simon Walker," he mutters. "Anything else isn't your business."

Well, then. He's got some ground to make up in terms of tact.

As the others stand and trickle out of the room, Dylan reaches for my hand to help me up. The move catches me off guard, and as I slide my palm against his, it takes serious effort not to smile as warmth flutters through my insides. Thankfully, he doesn't seem to notice as he tugs me into the entertainment salon.

My gaze flits automatically to the small flat-screen on the back wall above the bookcases, but it's still black. No rankings yet.

Relief eases the tightness in my chest until I notice Olivia staring at my and Dylan's interlinked hands. He's only dragged me into the room, but I feel a wash of guilt all the same. She raises her eyebrows and gives me a haughty smirk before waving Ann and Liam over to join her and Evan.

My cheeks burn, and I drop Dylan's hand under the pretense of stopping to turn and take it all in. As if by magic, Olivia manages to shake Ann and wrap her hand around Liam's arm, pulling him after Evan toward the entryway and the staircase to the second level. Apparently, she's decided Dylan is taken, and either Evan or Liam is going to be the lucky recipient of her attention. Or victim.

A few minutes later, the blond flight attendant, O'Connor, appears near the lavatory door by the entryway. She speaks into a handheld radio to broadcast a message throughout the plane. "At this time, the Wi-Fi will be turned off for the remainder of the flight."

Groans echo in the room. I hadn't even tried to connect yet.

"The committee wants to help minimize distractions and provide the best setting for your success. Please proceed aft to the dining room on the far side of the seating compartment, but don't open the envelopes until instructed to do so. Dinner will be served shortly."

She shoots us a broad smile as she hangs up the radio. "This is fun, isn't it?" she asks, dropping the professional tone and sounding much more conversational. "Reminds me of my own days in private school. There's something really special about your group this year."

She sounds just like my mother. But what was that about envelopes?

My nerves buzz with energy as we head back through the seating compartment. Light streams in through the partially open window shades, but it has that late-afternoon feel, like it'll fade to burnished orange and pink any minute now. The last, dying gasps of daylight.

Night is coming. Each minute, each mile, brings us closer to Paris and my best shot at changing my future. But I can't shake the feeling that whatever is in those envelopes holds the key to this competition.

4

LET THE GAMES BEGIN

5:54 p.m. CDT

Like the rest of this plane, the dining room is jaw-droppingly luxurious. A monstrous wood table, its surface polished to a gleaming sheen, takes up the bulk of the space. Twelve padded leather chairs surround the table. The top is set with taupe place mats, each with a large square charger plate, a drinking glass, and actual metal utensils wrapped in a fine linen napkin.

Just a *bit* nicer than the plastic silverware and paper sacks I've been eating from lately.

Three crystal vases hold the green stalks of tall white lilies. The faint scent tells me the flowers are real—no surprise on a plane like this one.

On each charger plate rests a cream-colored envelope, perhaps the ones we passed in the entryway when we boarded. The people who've entered ahead of me silently circle the table, scanning the envelopes before taking seats. Our names are written on them in perfect calligraphy, with gold curlicues embellishing the corners. I find mine and slide into the seat between the red-haired girl—Lily—and Dylan.

Dylan and I exchange a glance. "What's inside?" he whispers.

I shrug and run a finger across the elegant gold ink. What did Hamlin say about the flight? We'd be tested on social skills and negotiation? Honestly, after years of navigating friendships with Nikki, Sam, Ava, and the rest of our group at school, I should be well qualified for whatever test the committee has come up with. But somehow that fact isn't translating from my head to my gut. Expectation hangs in the air, like that moment in a softball game when you're up to bat in the last inning, staring the pitcher in the eye as she winds up, and you're either going to crush the ball past the fence for the win or strike out.

I'm really praying for past the fence, because I've been striking out a whole lot lately.

The head flight attendant, O'Connor, who followed us in, skirts around us to the far end of the room, where the other two materialize at the doorway. After an eternal minute of soft conversation, she turns to us with a warm smile. "We'll be serving the meal momentarily. You may open the envelopes."

My fingers tremble as I lift my envelope. As much as I want to shred it to get to the contents, I force myself to slow down and observe everyone else. My gaze collides with Simon's across the table. He's the only one of us leaning back like this isn't a big deal. His lips twist to one side in an expression I can't quite read, and then he looks down.

The envelope isn't sealed. The flap isn't even tucked in, but the linen paper feels crisp and thick beneath my fingers as I open it. There are only two things inside—a folded square of paper and a blue Bicycle playing card.

The ace of hearts. I scrunch my eyebrows together in confusion, then slide the card beneath the paper.

"What the . . ." Down the table, Evan trails off with a muttered swear word. A band tightens around my ribs. That can't be a good sign.

The folded paper isn't the same material as the envelope, it's lined notebook paper. Wide-ruled, like we're in second grade. Very much at odds with the luxury we've experienced so far. A chill prickles my arms.

Next to me, Dylan crumples his sheet into a ball. "Is this some kind of sick joke?" Thin blue lines tangle with the white of the paper—his sheet is also from a notebook. The vein on his neck bulges like he's just run the length of the lacrosse field in blistering heat.

In fact, the temperature in the room does seem to have risen ten degrees.

On my other side, Lily presses her hands together in her lap. White edges of paper stick out from between her fingers.

Liam's face goes slack as he glances between his card and the paper. Blake, who's used to being pummeled on the field, slumps in his seat like he's having a hard time holding himself upright. The only person who seems utterly unfazed is Simon, who merely tucks the paper into his textbook as a bookmark.

My shoulder muscles go taut. I can't put off the inevitable forever.

The paper rustles as I lift the bottom edge to open it. Scrawled blue ink fills the lines, barely legible. Certainly not like the elegant calligraphy on the front.

Three numbered items are listed beneath a title that reads *Two Truths and a Lie*. I vaguely recollect filling out something like this after being selected for the competition.

Only as I read the messy cursive, a tremor of fear pummels my system. These are *not* the things I wrote.

And worse, they're all true.

⁘ ⁙ 5 ⁙ ⁘

ENJOY YOUR MEAL

5:58 p.m. CDT

My mouth goes dry like I've eaten too many saltine crackers without water. I glance again at my page, holding it close so no one else can see the painful truth.

Two Truths and a Lie
1. *My mom lost our house, and now we live in our car.*
2. *I nearly failed math in 9th grade and have a 2.75 GPA.*
3. *The only way I managed to get into this competition was by cheating.*

Shame burns hot inside my chest, and, like Dylan, I ball up the paper before anyone else can read it.

Fourteen-year-old Emily thought dealing with family drama was more important than studying, but by the time sixteen-year-old Emily had survived academic probation and realized she was going to end up just like Mom if she didn't fix her GPA, it was too late. Two years already wasted.

GPAs are terribly unforgiving. Even with near straight A's last year and solid test scores, my application was never going to stack up against the other students' from my school. Especially Nikki's.

I swear I never planned on cheating. I still don't know what came over me that day in our dorm room. I'd had my application prepped and ready for weeks, but I'd waited to submit it to give myself one more chance to read over my essays. Then Nikki had some mysterious emergency, so she asked me to create her profile and submit her forms when I did mine. In hindsight, now I realize her emergency was probably related to her mom's illness.

I fully intended to do what she asked, but then Mom called and told me she'd taken a part-time job at a fast-food restaurant because it was the only way to pay for my cell phone, and that I'd better not get injured, because she couldn't make our medical insurance payments anymore and I'd get stuck with the debt. *Thanks for the encouragement, Mom.* Especially coming on the heels of how hard I'd been busting my tail all semester to bring up my GPA for such minuscule results.

Society doesn't offer a lot of second chances, does it? The line between success and failure is razor-thin sometimes.

What I did next was entirely impulsive. Thoughtless. Horrible. When I created Nikki's profile, I swapped our student ID numbers and submission packages. In a matter of seconds, she became me, and I became her. Someone with stellar test scores, excellent grades—even if the classes weren't the most difficult—well-written essays, and a legitimate, important-sounding life ambition.

And every day since, I've lived with this awful, gnawing panic that someone is going to find out. But no matter how much I regret what I did to my friend, I can't undo it now. There's nothing left but to move forward, make the most of this stolen opportunity, and hope she never finds out.

But if Robert Hamlin knows all this about me, why would he ever let me set foot on this plane? Or if it isn't him—if this isn't part of the competition—then who is it?

A sharp voice cuts into my thoughts. "Who did this?" Olivia demands, shaking the piece of paper in her hand at the head flight attendant as she reappears in the doorway with baskets of dinner rolls. "It wasn't the scholarship committee. This isn't what I wrote."

O'Connor's brows pull together in confusion. A sea of angry faces stare at her. "I'm sorry. All I know is that I was instructed to set them out just before dinner."

Blake bursts out of his chair like a firecracker, his face so red it reaches his ears. "This isn't what I wrote either." Both fists are balled up at his sides. The rest of us pull back a fraction at the sudden display. "Lies. It's all lies."

His girlfriend, Paige, lays a hand on his arm, mumbling something to him, but he shakes her hand off with a such a vehement scowl she wilts against her seat.

A loud whistle right next to me breaks the clamor, and we all turn toward Lily.

"Everybody, calm down." Her voice is surprisingly resonant for someone who appears so meek. "Ma'am," she says, addressing the flight attendant, who is now setting the baskets on the table, "are these papers part of the competition? Or did somebody else stick them in as a prank?"

"They've been sitting on the table in the entryway since before takeoff," she says, as if that answers the question. "We placed them on the table in here about ten minutes ago."

"I'm pretty sure the scholarship committee wouldn't use paper ripped out of a notebook." Lily waves hers in the air. I like her—she's bold and smart. She could be a valuable ally.

O'Connor sets down the last basket of rolls and walks over to take a closer look at the paper Lily clutches in her hand. "You're right. That does seem odd."

The others are still muttering among themselves, some of them half ignoring Lily, and even though my normal MO is to avoid confrontation like the plague, I decide to throw some weight behind her words. In a situation like this, someone *has* to step up. You'd think her classmate Evan would help her out, but he's too busy massaging his shoulder and staring at the ceiling. Besides, my gut tells me I want Lily on my side.

"Lily's right," I say. "It must be a prank. Something to throw us off our game."

"But that means it was one of us," Ann says with a frown.

But *who*? Somebody here knows far more about me than they should. Of all these people, the person who knows me best is Dylan—but he appeared just as shell-shocked about his paper as I felt, and there's no way he would have treated me the way he has this entire time if he knew I stole Nikki's application.

One hundred percent out of the question, with the way he wears his feelings on his sleeve. But if I mentally cross him off the list, that means it had to be one of these near-total strangers.

Who wants to win badly enough to dig up dirt on the rest of us and use it as leverage? And are there more nasty surprises to come?

The thought makes me shiver.

"I can certainly contact the committee to ask," O'Connor offers.

"Please do. What about the playing cards?" Lily asks.

"I believe you'll find out shortly. I'm sorry I don't have any other information to share at this time." She heads for the corridor, which must lead to the plane's galley.

Blake sinks back into his seat, muttering something under his breath to Paige. I glance at Dylan, but he's talking to Taylor, so I turn to Lily. "Hey, thanks for speaking up," I say quietly. "That was wild."

"Yeah, it was." Her red eyebrows pinch together, crinkling the freckles on her nose.

On her other side, Liam tucks his playing card into his pocket and turns to us. His face is still pale. "The last thing we need is to turn on each other."

"It had to be one of us, don't you think?" I ask softly. "But who would've had time to tamper with the envelopes?"

"Probably any one of us," Lily answers.

Points for honesty. I'd love to cross her and Liam off my mental suspect list, but I can't yet. Not until I know more.

"I didn't watch everyone after the introductions," Lily says. "Is there anyone who never left the entertainment room?"

"Blake and Paige?" I offer. "They were sitting on the couch when I entered. But I came in last."

"Evan, Olivia, and I took the stairs to the second-floor lounge," Liam adds.

"Is it cool up there?" I ask, then clamp my mouth shut. Totally off topic. And the fact I'd like to be the one spending time in the lounge with Liam has nothing to do with figuring out who knows our secrets. I've got to assess him fairly—I can't just write him off because I like him.

"Very," he says, his lips hitching up on one side. "We didn't see anybody else in the entry area, but we just passed through. I'm not even sure the envelopes were still there or if the flight attendants had already moved them. How long do you think it would take to slip all those papers in?"

Lily frowns. "You'd have to match each paper with the right envelope. At least a couple of minutes."

"Evan went back downstairs before me and Olivia, but I don't know if it would've been long enough," Liam says. "And somebody else was already down there, because I heard them laugh."

As we talk, the flight attendants weave around the table, depositing salad plates in front of us. They serve Taylor last. Her salad is the only one covered in plastic wrap, as if they have to keep it separate.

"Nut-free," says the dark-haired attendant as she sets the plate in front of Taylor. She's got a separate roll too.

I lean forward slightly, glancing her way, and Taylor shrugs. "Peanut allergy."

Before I can turn back to Lily and Liam, Dylan taps my arm. "Who do you think did it?"

I bite the inside of my cheek, shaking my head. "Do you have any ideas?"

He shrugs. "It wasn't me."

"Duh." I roll my eyes at him, and he laughs. I'd love to ask him about his paper—if his three statements are actually true—but that's impossible. Not unless I'm planning on an epic confession and crushing my hopes of winning. Instead, I pull the playing card out of my pocket and flash it at Dylan. "I got the ace of hearts. What did you get?"

He rummages inside his blazer, then lays his card on the table between us. "The king of diamonds. What does that mean?"

"Maybe it's for a game." Hopefully, I'm wrong, because I've never been good at cards. Not since my days of playing Old Maid as a preschooler. "An ace is good, right?"

"Yeah." Dylan smiles in his aren't-you-so-cute way that melts my heart whenever he gives it to Nikki.

But why is he giving that look to *me*? I've gotten it a few times, but always as an extension of Nikki, like that time the two of us broke down laughing in the middle of dinner and couldn't stop to save our lives. Never to me alone. And after what I've already done to Nikki, the look sets me on edge. Like there's slime coating my insides.

I'm in the middle of buttering a roll when the cabin lights dim, the window shades lower, and the flat-screen TV on the forward bulkhead flicks on. Sir Hamlin's weathered face appears on the screen.

"Ah, dinner. My favorite part of an overseas flight," he says. "I hope you're enjoying your trip so far. By now, you've received your envelopes containing your team designations."

Teams? Oh, this could be critical, especially if it's one of those situations where the losers have to vote someone out, like Tribal Council in *Survivor*. I sit up a little straighter, scanning the faces around the table. Who would I handpick to be on my team?

For brains, Amir or Simon. Ann, for her leadership skills—she's been class president for three years, according to her bio. Lily or Taylor could be solid choices. Dylan? Friendship dictates he *should* be a choice, but in all honesty, I wouldn't mind a break from the emotional drama he unwittingly creates for me.

Now, Liam, on the other hand . . . A smile cracks my lips as Hamlin keeps going.

"You've been divided into three teams of four based on playing card suit. After the meal, each team should meet for the first game—a chance to get to know each other with Two Truths and a Lie. The answers you filled out on your information sheets have been printed onto these pages, as you've already found in your envelopes."

He holds up a piece of fine stationery, which looks nothing like the notebook paper we received. I glance at Lily and Liam. Confirmation it wasn't the committee.

The thought curdles the ranch dressing in my stomach. Someone here knows far more about me than they should, and if I don't figure out who, my chance at this scholarship could vanish in a heartbeat.

At the end of the table next to Taylor, Ann flags down the third flight attendant, the one with the French name. Camille Allard? Clearly, I'm not the only one who's worried. Does that mean Ann didn't do it? Was it one of the quiet ones, who don't seem to care? Like Simon or Evan or Amir? Or is someone here just an excellent actor?

In the background, Hamlin is droning on about the virtues of camaraderie and teamwork, but I lean forward to watch as Ann shows the attendant the slip of paper. I can't catch what she says, but the way Allard holds her hands out apologetically is unmistakable.

"I believe Ms. O'Connor sent a message," she says, "but I don't know if she received a reply yet." She apologizes, and I'm reminded of a bobblehead doll repeating "I'm sorry" again and again.

The video ends, and the window shades roll open as the cabin lights come back up to full strength.

At the end of the table, Olivia's face splits into one of those laughing smiles straight out of a Hollister ad. What does she have to be happy about?

Then I realize she's looking at Liam's playing card. They've got to be on the same team.

"Lily"—I lean toward her—"what card did you get?"

"Let's see . . . Ace of spades." She stares at it for a moment, as if she hadn't really looked at it before. "That's the highest card in most games."

"Most games?" I repeat, because I know nothing about card games, and what else am I going to say? *You must be the favorite to win?*

She sets it down firmly on the table. "Games where aces are high. Aces can equal ones sometimes. Spades are the highest suit. I take it you don't play poker or anything?"

I shake my head. My family can't afford for me to pick up gambling. "Do you?"

"It's a thing at our school, in the dorms. The teachers act like they don't know, so long as no scuffles break out." She glances at my card, which is lying facedown on the table. "What's yours?"

"Ace of hearts." I flip it over. "Too bad we're not on the same team."

"Yeah, it is," she says, and from the way her brow crinkles, she looks like she means it.

The recirculating plane air fills with the scent of cooked chicken and sautéed vegetables as the three flight attendants reappear and whisk away our empty salad plates. I'm dying to know who *is* on my team, since it isn't Lily or Dylan, but the conversation drops as the attendants return with loaded trays.

My expectations are pretty low—I mean, even a luxury plane has to reheat the food, right? Besides, most mass-produced meals, like the ones our cafeteria churns out for special occasions, aren't anything to text home about. But when every meal comes out of grocery packaging or a drive-through, even the smell of airplane chicken cordon bleu is enough to make a person's stomach growl. The sides, garlic mashed potatoes and sautéed asparagus, look far more appetizing than anything I've had to eat since school got out.

I'm about to dig in when I realize Taylor hasn't been served yet. A few of the less tactful members of the group are already busy chewing, but most of us wait patiently until her plate arrives.

As with her salad, an attendant brings a separate plate out for her. Though the food appears identical, it must've been prepared on different equipment. A couple of kids at our school have severe allergies too, something our school handles by forcing them to sit at a separate table in the dining hall. It looks lonely to me, sitting there with people who probably wouldn't be your friends if you had any say in the matter.

Taylor accepts the plate with grace but doesn't make eye contact with us this time, as if she's ready to drop it.

The attendants vanish into the recesses of the plane as we dig in. The food is hot, salty, and satisfying, though I can already feel it settling like a rock. I should probably back off, but it'll be hours until they serve breakfast—probably just prior to landing—and I've barely eaten all day. Across the table, the small windows behind Evan's shoulders glow in shades of pink and lavender and soft yellow as we eat in near silence.

After a few minutes, Paige sets down her fork and nudges Blake with her elbow. He nods at her, then says to the rest of us, "What playing cards—"

A fork clatters onto a plate a few seats away from me. I lean around Dylan, trying to see what's going on. Taylor's face has paled to a dull gray, and both hands are clutched at the base of her throat, but it's the look in her eyes that makes the food congeal in my stomach.

Utter terror.

▦ ∷ ⋮ **6** ∷ ⋮ ▦

FASTEN YOUR SEAT BELT

6:37 p.m. CDT

"*Taylor!*" someone shrieks.

My lungs freeze as she leans forward in her seat, making horrible wheezing sounds, like a cat coughing up a hairball, like there's not enough air. Her mouth opens and closes as she tugs at her shirt, even though the collar isn't what's choking her.

Dylan swivels in his chair, blocking my view, but by now we're all scrambling out of our seats. Everyone yells at once.

"*Somebody get help!*"

"*Is she choking?*"

"*Where's her EpiPen?*"

I'm about to dash back to Taylor's seat to search her bag, but Ann beats me to it, her dark braid flying behind her as she vanishes through the doorway.

The youngest flight attendant, Allard, stands with her back pressed to the far bulkhead, hands clasped over her mouth. Her face is pale, and she's crying. Her obvious lack of emergency preparedness is seriously disconcerting. Aren't flight attendants trained for this kind of stuff?

She's not the only one breaking down. Paige stands behind her chair, flapping her hands like a manic chicken. Her boyfriend has his hands over his mouth, like he's trying very hard not to puke. Olivia has managed to bury her face into Liam's shoulder, clutching his sweater.

Simon, though . . . he's had the decency to stop eating, but the slight frown on his face makes him look more like a scientist observing a lab animal than someone who's truly concerned.

I take in all of this in a matter of seconds before touching Dylan's shoulder. "Give her some space. Ann's looking for the EpiPen."

Taylor makes more horrible wheezing sounds as she arches her torso and slams her shoulders against her seat. I run past her toward the flight attendant. Behind me, Dylan barks, "Stay back. Give her room, okay?"

When I reach the attendant, I have to pry her hands off her face. I glance at her name tag. "Camille. Ms. Allard. Where are the others? She needs *help*." My hand trembles as I point at Taylor, struggling to breathe.

The attendant is worse than useless, her eyes wide as saucers, cheeks streaked with tears and mascara like dribbling ink.

I'm about to search for a radio myself when Ann shouts, "Got it!" from the other room.

Thank God.

Everyone parts like the Red Sea to let her through. The precious yellow EpiPen flashes in her hand as she slides into Dylan's chair and faces Taylor.

"Do you know how to use that thing?" Dylan asks, worry crinkling his forehead.

Ann yanks off the cap and touches Taylor's arm with her free hand. "I'm going to give you the injection. Try to stay still, okay?"

Taylor manages to nod as she forces her body to relax in the seat. After pressing the orange tip of the device against Taylor's thigh, Ann counts slowly to ten.

When the time is up, she carefully withdraws the huge needle and turns to Dylan. "My little sister is anaphylactic to bees. I've seen a gazillion training videos."

Taylor slowly stops wheezing and pulls her hands away from her neck. It feels like forever before she can breathe without the air whistling down her throat, but it's probably only a matter of minutes.

"Feeling better?" Ann asks when the desperate tension finally leaves her face.

Taylor's hands shake, and she looks jittery, but she squeezes the armrests and manages a slow nod. Then scowls at her plate of food.

"Here." I hold out a hand. "I'll take that away."

Ann hands it to me, and I practically shove it into the face of the lone flight attendant, who manages to get enough of a grip on herself to take it.

"Now can you call for more help?" I ask. "Is there a medical kit on board?" It's probably too much to hope one of them has medical training.

Allard nods and fumbles her way over to the corridor leading to the galley. Still holding the plate, she swings open a panel and pulls out a radio. After what feels like an eternity, the senior attendant appears with a white plastic kit bearing a red cross, followed close behind by the dark-haired one, Kumar.

O'Connor's face is unreadable as she perches on the seat on the other side of Taylor. She pushes aside the place setting and sets the medical kit on the table, then turns to Ann. "You administered the epinephrine?"

Ann nods. "She had an EpiPen in her bag. There's a second if we need it."

"Good. Your quick thinking probably saved her life." O'Connor smiles, her tone reassuring, and the tension lifts a little in the room. Finally, someone who knows what they're doing. She opens the kit, revealing a large assortment of bandages, ointment, rolls of gauze, and vials. She lifts out a tray to find a blood pressure cuff and one of those fingertip things doctors use to check your oxygen.

"I'm only trained in first aid," she says to Taylor, "but I'll be able to monitor your vitals until we land."

"Do we have to turn back?" Taylor's voice trembles.

"One of the foundation's doctors in Paris will have to make that call." Her tone is soothing and calm, a perfect bedside manner for a distraught teen. She pulls out the automatic blood pressure cuff and slides it onto Taylor's arm. "How's your breathing? Your oxygen's getting better."

Taylor relaxes into the seat, relief written in the slump of her shoulders.

The gadget beeps, and O'Connor glances at the numbers, then writes them down in a small notebook in the kit. Next she checks Taylor's pulse.

"Better," Taylor says, though her skin is still dull and dark circles have popped up beneath her eyes. She could be part of the cast of *Les Misérables*. Yet despite nearly dying, she's afraid we'll have to turn around.

How badly does *she* want to win this scholarship?

Any odds in my favor feel like they're slipping away in the face of my competition's determination.

Which leads me to wonder . . .

How did Taylor's set-aside, specially prepared meal provoke an anaphylactic reaction?

Is she allergic to something else besides nuts? Or is there more going on?

The thought makes me shudder. Figuring out secrets is one thing, but intentionally trying to hurt somebody? Surely not. Surely this was coincidence.

A bit of natural color is returning to Taylor's cheeks, and she manages to sip her drink, though her hand is trembling so badly water sloshes out.

"As soon as you're strong enough," O'Connor says, "I'd like to move you upstairs to the staff quarters. That way I'll be able to monitor your vitals easier."

Taylor shakes her head. "I can't leave the competition. I don't even know who my teammates are."

"Taylor . . ." Ann's tone carries a hint of reprimand. "Your health is more important." Certainly, the rest of us only stand to gain if she drops out. But does a medical emergency count as dropping out?

She tugs at her lower lip. "Is there somewhere I can rest where my team can still visit me?"

O'Connor's mouth tightens into a frown, but finally she relents. "I'll take you to one of the semiprivate cabins in the nose. Just as soon as I contact the foundation." She packs up the kit and carries it to where the other two attendants wait, by the wall at the back. "Keep an eye on the situation, please," she tells them. "And you can clear the plates once everyone is finished. Be sure to lock up the cutlery."

Although a few people manage to choke down a couple more bites, I hand off my half-eaten dinner to one of the attendants. It's the best meal I've had in days, but my appetite is shot after witnessing someone's near death. We watch in silence as the attendants work.

Whispers arise around the room as the minutes grow long

and the group restless. We're only an hour and a half out from Chicago. Maybe they'll make us land in New York City. Or worse, Hartford, and I'll be right back where I started.

Finally, O'Connor returns, smiling broadly. "I'm sure you'll all be happy to hear that the foundation's chief doctor says the flight can continue to Paris as long as Taylor remains stable over the next hour." We let out a collective sigh of relief.

"What about the slips of paper?" Ann asks, waving her envelope. "Any news?"

"Yes, thank you for the reminder." She smiles warmly. "The committee gave permission for you to make up your own answers for the game, rather than using the papers, and they'll investigate what happened when you arrive."

A pit opens in my stomach. I mean, that's good they're going to investigate, but what if they want to collect the papers as evidence? They might decide to dig deeper into my application.

Maybe I can "lose" mine before we land.

"At this time, you'll be dividing into teams based on the suits of your playing cards," O'Connor says. She points to different sections of the room as she talks. "Spades over there, Hearts here, and Diamonds there. Feel free to move about on the plane. There's a workstation compartment farther aft, as well as the entertainment salon toward the front and another lounge upstairs. You'll have approximately thirty minutes to play Two Truths and a Lie before meeting again in the entertainment salon for the first challenge."

She and Ann help Taylor to her feet. As they shuffle out of the room, Ann says, "Don't worry, I'll tell your team where to find you."

The head flight attendant's departure leaves a lingering air of uncertainty in her wake, but it only lasts a moment, until Blake holds up his card. "Time to get this party started?"

Before he and Paige separate, she rises on tiptoe to kiss him. As she walks away, they stare at each other with the kind of dreamy longing that makes the rest of us want to puke.

When I turn back to Dylan, he rolls his eyes and I do my best to smother my laugh.

"Good luck," I say.

"Thanks. I'm gonna need it." He says the words so quietly he's practically mouthing them, and when I give in and laugh, he winks.

Sigh. That boy is cute. I feel like I've swallowed an entire package of fizzy Pop Rocks as he walks off to join Paige. Evan, the baseball player from Lily's school, stands there too, but they're missing a fourth. Taylor?

Closer to the forward bulkhead, Olivia still clings to Liam—not by holding on to him, but hovering close by, like she wants the rest of us to know he's taken.

Simon stands a few feet away, that textbook open in his hands, but he's not really reading it this time. He keeps glancing over at Olivia, a crease filling the gap between his dark eyebrows.

She scowls as I approach. "Great. Are you a Heart too?"

I nod, my breath catching as Liam flashes a warm grin at me. But just as quickly, he checks himself, his face going neutral. Maybe he has a girlfriend. In fact, it's kind of hard to imagine a guy like him *wouldn't* have one.

"I've got the ace." I hold it up for their benefit, and I could swear Simon groans from behind his book. But two out of three from *my* list of picks isn't bad at all. Between Simon's intellect and Liam's easygoing personality, we've got a strong group. Maybe even Olivia can prove to be an asset.

"I'm the queen, and Liam is the king," she says.

Or maybe not. She latches on to Liam's arm and shoots me a smug half grin. Liam gives her the same politely neutral look he offered me. *After* that glimpse of a smile.

"And Simon?" I practically whisper the words, jerking my thumb over at him. From the way he blinks, he heard me.

Liam seizes his chance to break free from Olivia's tentacles. He turns to Simon and says, "Hey, man, do you have a heart?"

The question comes out all wrong—especially directed at somebody who's been reading a calculus textbook the entire flight instead of engaging with any of us—and this time Olivia and I both break down laughing. I manage to stifle it pretty fast with a fist to my lips and by clearing my throat, but Olivia practically collapses onto one of the chairs. When our gazes meet, I nearly lose it again. To be fair, we're amped up over Taylor's near disaster. Maybe this is how Olivia handles stress, which means we might have more in common than I thought.

Liam glances at us, but instead of frowning, humor dances in the crinkles around his eyes too. A guy who knows how to laugh at himself. I knew I liked him for a reason.

Simon's lips press into a frown. But he holds up the jack of hearts, confirming my suspicions.

"Awesome," Liam says coolly, unfazed by the scowl. "Guess we have a team. Shall we find a place up front?"

"How about the upstairs lounge?" Olivia says. When we all nod, Liam heads for the next compartment.

Behind us, the room fills with chatter as the others finish dividing themselves into groups. The Spades—Lily, Blake, Taylor's classmate Amir, and Ann—cluster together in animated conversation.

That leaves the Diamonds—Dylan, Paige, Evan, and Taylor,

who's waiting for the other three in some compartment up front. Paige keeps stealing glances at Blake, like she can't stand being this far away from him. Evan's full lips protrude in a definite pout. Is he worried about having a teammate who's somewhat out of commission?

Then there's Dylan, the picture of long-suffering patience. He's gazing past Paige, out one of the plane windows, where the sunset is deepening into fuchsia and violet.

I can still see traces of the boy who walked into our seventh-grade class for the first time just before Christmas and threw our entire social world into chaos. Nikki and I talked about him all the time at our sleepovers. I told her I liked him, but that wasn't a big deal—heck, half the girls in our grade had a crush on him. After he asked her out to the dance, I never said anything about it again. But even those six months I spent last year dating Braden, one of Dylan's friends, weren't enough to eradicate my feelings.

As I chew the inside of my lip, Dylan turns away from the window and glances my way. His eyes widen slightly as he catches me staring. Whoops. Heat creeps up my neck, and I offer what I hope is merely a friendly smile before fleeing after my teammates.

When I pass through the doorway into the entertainment salon, I find them on the other side of the bulkhead, staring at the small flat-screen above the bookshelves.

Olivia glances at me and points. "Look, it's on."

My throat goes dry. There we are, all twelve listed in alphabetical order on the left side of the screen, each name with a 1 in front of it under RANK. On the right side, a blank column is headed POINTS. And in the bottom right corner, a thumbs-up and thumbs-down wait for upvotes and downvotes.

I swallow. "How do we vote?"

Liam lifts an eyebrow. "Why? Eager to get started?"

"Not really."

I must look green, because his expression softens. "I'm just messing with you. We tried pressing the screen already but couldn't get it to do anything."

Simon shakes his head. "The touchscreen is locked."

Regardless of how it works, one thing is clear. The game is on.

7

THE FIRST GAME

7:03 p.m. CDT

"Who wants to go first?" Olivia asks, pinning each one of us in turn with her crystal-blue eyes.

Our team has successfully claimed the upstairs lounge for the first game, and it's every bit as spectacular as Liam said. There's a semicircular bar at the center, which unsurprisingly has been stripped bare of all alcohol. But in the soft overhead lights, tall drinking glasses gleam on shelves behind glass doors, and the mini refrigerator cases lining the back are stocked with every brand of soda a high schooler could wish for. The shelves under the counter hold a dizzying array of chips, trail mix, granola bars, and fruit snacks. With the flight attendants busy elsewhere, we've already deemed the operation self-serve.

I take a slow sip from the can of Diet Coke I snagged and try not to squirm on my cushy seat. We've bypassed the high barstools and low benches beneath the windows in favor of plush lounge chairs grouped along the back wall. Behind the bulkhead, there's a short hallway with two lavatories flanking a single closed door, perhaps the staff quarters or guest rooms the foundation doesn't want students snooping through.

After several long moments of staring each other down, Simon neatly sets aside his textbook, pushes his drooping glasses higher, and announces, "I will." When he pulls out the paper scrap from his envelope, I nearly spew Diet Coke across the carpet.

"We're not reading those, are we?" I manage to choke out between coughs. "I mean, the committee said we could make up our own answers, right?"

Simon shrugs. "I don't mind." Before any of us can object, he reads his list in a dull monotone, perfectly at odds with the words rolling off his tongue. *"Number one: I may be brilliant at math and electronics, but I have no friends. Number two: I sit alone for every meal. Number three: The teachers argue over who gets stuck with me in their classrooms."*

When he finishes, he folds the paper in half, slides it neatly into his textbook, and gazes at the polished back panel of the bar. The rest of us stare at him, mouths agape. How could he not be embarrassed to admit any of that? Unless none of it's true.

"Aren't you supposed to say which one is the lie?" he finally asks. "Isn't that how this pointless game works?"

"*Is* one of them a lie?" Olivia leans away from him, giving him the same look she'd give a piece of gum stuck on the bottom of her shoe.

I'd say her behavior was wrong, except . . . Simon hasn't exactly put in the effort to make himself likable.

"Does it matter? We're all only pretending to care. *I* don't care. Do you care? No, all we care about is winning a scholarship." He huffs out a loud sigh. "Just so you know, I prefer being alone. And since no one else could reasonably ascertain my teachers' feelings about having me in class, that one must be the lie."

Liam coughs, a pointed gesture meant to stop Simon's mini tirade, which surely will be noticed by the committee if anybody is actually watching us. It's good of him, considering Simon is competition. "Somebody might be listening," he whispers.

Simon's eyes narrow. "Thanks, Big Brother. I'll keep that in mind."

Olivia laughs. "*You* watch TV? I'm surprised you can squeeze it in between doing math for fun and antagonizing everyone else."

He presses his lips together, then says, "No, I meant George Orwell. *1984?*"

Olivia scowls, then flips her hair over both shoulders and strikes a Miss Teen USA interview pose. "I'll go next. But I'm not reading that paper. One: I was homecoming queen last year. Two: I have a 3.9 GPA. Three: My family spends the summers at our second home in the Hamptons."

Ugh, it's like being on an episode of MTV's *Cribs*. We sit in silence, until I venture, "Two?"

She glares at me. "What, do you think I'm an airhead? I earned that GPA fair and square."

"Copying other people's work is fair?" Simon breaks out in uncharacteristic cackling. It's then that I remember he and Olivia both go to the same school.

Olivia's face turns scarlet, and she shoots Simon a look so venomous I'm surprised he doesn't wither in his chair. Is it anger at an unfair accusation, or does he know something the rest of us don't? She tries to cover by taking a sip of her drink, then says, "Three. We visit the Hamptons home at Christmas. Summers are for the yacht."

Ah, the yacht. Right.

"Wow, that was tricky," I blurt.

Liam's mouth puckers behind his water bottle, and the liquid sloshes as his hand shakes. When his eyes find mine, it takes a concentrated effort not to convulse into a fit of giggles. Maybe he *doesn't* return Olivia's interest.

He covertly wipes at his eyes. "Guess it's my turn?" When we all nod, he goes on. "I think I'll pass on reading my paper too. Number one: I was a state champion in swimming. Number two: I'm saving up to buy my own motorcycle. Uh, let's see . . . Number three: My best friend, James, died in March." He sobers, rubs the back of his neck, then adds, "Sorry. I'm not sure why I said that."

Something inside my rib cage sinks. That third one has to be true, because nobody would make up something that awful for their lie.

"Oh, Liam, I am so sorry," Olivia gushes. She leans closer to him, resting a hand on the khaki twill covering his knee. "What happened?"

Liam stares at his hands, as if he's lost so deep in memories he didn't hear. That picture in his sketchbook, of the boy with the haunted eyes—was that James?

"Swimming," I say a little too brightly. "Number one is the lie. You play some other sport. Or two. Or three." My gaze wanders appreciatively over his broad shoulders and his arms, where the muscles are evident even beneath his sweater.

He looks up, brows pinching together, as if he's just noticed me. "Yeah. How'd you know?"

I shrug. "I guess I can picture you on a bike." Leather jacket, blue jeans, black helmet tucked under one arm . . . Did it suddenly get hotter on this airplane? I push my blazer cuffs up my forearms.

He fixes me with a grateful smile. "Come visit me at home in New York next summer, and I'll take you for a ride. Maybe we can go to a Yankees game."

My stomach is now doing an entire gymnastics routine, because I can't imagine anything I'd like better than sitting behind Liam on his motorcycle, arms wrapped around his waist. Even if we *are* going to Yankee Stadium. He's probably just being polite, though, so I casually slip off my blazer and try to redirect the conversation. "So what do you play? Baseball?"

He nods. "And basketball and football, though football's my weakest. Pretty much the regular set."

"I play softball," I offer, then check myself. "Or I used to, anyway." Back before I quit the team partway through last season. I'd been putting nearly all my evening hours into studying, in an effort to fix my wrecked GPA, and then when softball started, I had almost no free time left. Nikki and our other friends never said anything, but I got the distinct impression I was missing out. After all, lacrosse is a spring sport too, and Nikki needs an entourage to go to Dylan's games. No one wants to get left behind by their friend group.

"No way. I play softball too!" Olivia's mouth twists. I can't tell if she's serious or making fun of me, but I can kind of see her on the pitcher's mound. She's got this competitive air lurking beneath the glossy surface.

Time to test the waters. "What position?"

"Shortstop." Her eyes flash, and a vision pops into my mind of her throwing out a runner at first with a nasty gleam in her eye. "What about you?"

A dull ache spreads across my chest, almost like that feeling I get when I see old Christmas pictures of my family from before my dad left us. I hadn't realized how much I missed playing.

I swallow. "Catcher." At the center of everything that happens in the game.

The coach tried to talk me into staying, but Nikki had come along for moral support, and I could see her face through the glass office door, nodding at me, giving me the thumbs-up. *You can do it,* she'd said. *Think how much more time we'll have together this spring. We can go to all the lacrosse games and check out the guys. We'll be able to shop for spring formal dresses after school.*

Suddenly, that stuff feels pointless. Resentment bubbles up deep inside, competing with my sense of loss, even though she didn't make me quit. I can't blame her for my choice.

Though I *can* question past Emily's judgment, prioritizing making her friends happy over doing what she loves. And even if I never was a good enough player to earn a college scholarship, it would've looked good on my applications. Why did I listen to Nikki? What was I *thinking?*

"That explains a lot," Liam says, interrupting the war going on inside me. "Though I still fault your choice in MLB teams. So why'd you quit? Injury?"

"No, I just . . . didn't have time anymore. Schoolwork and stuff." That excuse sounds as hollow as it feels. I clear my throat. "Should I do my two truths and a lie now?"

"Yeah. Good idea." He glances around the room like he's checking for a clock, even though he's got a watch. The dying sunlight outside the plane windows fades rapidly into deepening twilight. Lights flash at the tip of a wing. "I wonder how much time we have left."

Good question. And an even better one—what happens next? As I'm scrambling to think up three statements, Simon stands abruptly and tosses his textbook in his seat.

"Where are you going?" Olivia demands.

He doesn't glance back as he heads for the stairs. "Lavatory. Feel free to carry on without me."

"Isn't there one—" *Back there?* I point toward the short hallway behind us but give up when he keeps walking.

Olivia rolls her eyes. "Whatever. Go on, Emily."

"Okay. I guess you already know about softball, so I won't include that one. So . . ." How come every sentence coming to mind is something I can't share? *My dad divorced my mom when I was in fifth grade, and now he won't pay child support. The only reason I can afford Exeter is because of financial aid, something I almost lost sophomore year because of my rapidly tanking GPA. My mom spent our entire savings on ugly leggings and lost our house, and the car is probably next.* It's so pathetic I feel like gagging over my own sob story.

Instead, I clear my throat. "Number one: I started going to boarding school in fifth grade. Number two: I'm an only child. Number three: I've never been out of the country before."

Seriously, could I sound more boring? But the truth is, I don't really know what to say. My life at Exeter is pretty normal. Modern versions of the stuff my mom tells stories about when she was in high school—breaking curfew to chill with friends, playing pranks on the guys, sneaking off campus for midnight pizza. I'm not an exceptional student. I don't have any sparkly talents or fifty million TikTok followers. I had to cheat to get here.

I realize I've been staring into space when Liam says my name. "Em?"

My nickname. And the way it rolls off his tongue turns my insides into melted ice cream.

"So which one is the lie?" I ask, infusing my voice with brightness to cover up the fact that even I think I'm boring.

He glances at Olivia to see if she wants to answer, but she's flopped back in her seat, staring out the window like she's hopelessly uninterested. "Easy," he says. "Number three is the lie. You told me you went to Prince Edward Island."

My mouth forms an O, and I freeze, hands in midair like some ancient Greek sculpture. Apparently, he was paying attention to my little spiel earlier at the airport. "Yes, I did. Forgot about that."

Olivia sits up, her gaze darting suspiciously between the two of us as if we've had a secret rendezvous. I'm pretty sure nearly knocking him over in the terminal doesn't count.

"Where's Simon?" she asks. "And are we done yet? I want to join the others downstairs."

"Guess we might as well be done." Liam stands and stretches. Then, like a true gentleman, he offers us each a hand. His fingers close, warm and strong, around mine, and he pulls us both up.

I give his hand a squeeze before I let go. "Thanks."

Olivia doesn't let go—because she has to beat me, apparently. Not that Win Liam is even a game when we're all competing against each other. She tugs his hand toward the stairs, giving him an impish grin that must win over every boy she uses it on. "Come on. Maybe we'll be able to vote for each other now."

Has she already made an agreement with Liam to upvote each other? The thought makes my stomach twist, but I can hardly begrudge her when I've made the same arrangement with Dylan. Especially when she's not going to get any help from Simon.

For a moment up here, hanging out with them and talking about our lives, this flight almost felt like a normal class trip. But now the fact that three of us are heading home right after we land stares me straight in the eye. I *can't* let my name be in that bottom three.

I'm so focused on what's at stake I nearly slip when we get halfway down the stairs and an earsplitting burst of feedback screeches out of the overhead speakers.

8

TURBULENCE AHEAD

7:19 p.m. CDT

I clap my hands over my ears, hunching my shoulders in a futile attempt to block the awful noise.

When it finally dies into silence, Olivia, two steps in front of me, shrieks, "What the *hell*?"

The captain's voice blasts out of the speaker. "Sorry, everyone, looks like we're having an issue with the sound system. Just hang tight while we—" His voice cuts out in a burst of static, like there's a short in the speakers.

The loud intermittent crackling grates on my strung-out nerves as I follow the others down the stairs. If there's something wrong with the audio, could there be other issues with the plane? The thought freaks me out. When we reach the marble floor of the entryway, one of the mirrored doors opens and another group spills out from a hidden forward compartment. Dylan slings an arm around me in a surprise hug.

"You okay?" he asks between bursts of sound, tucking my head under his chin. He's tall and strong and very real, and his attention sends a thrill dancing up my back, but uneasiness competes with the sensation. *Uh, your girlfriend is my BFF?*

And then there's Liam standing three feet away. The last thing I want is for him to think there's something between me and Dylan. His gaze flits over us as he turns toward the entertainment salon, his expression unreadable.

"Yeah, I'm fine." I wriggle free, putting a hand to his chest in a stay-back gesture I hope Liam recognizes. I turn to follow Liam and Olivia into the lounge, but the lavatory door flies open into Olivia's face as we pass through the short corridor.

"Ugh, Simon," Olivia screeches, her voice just audible above another burst of static. "Watch what you're doing!"

"Don't worry. I was." A smug smile crosses his face as he latches the door shut behind him and turns his back on her.

The senior flight attendant, O'Connor, stands by the controls for the intercom system, fiddling with the dials. "Please be seated, everyone," she says. Her tone carries the same reassuring sense of authority as when she helped Taylor. "We'll get this fixed right away."

Those of us who are still standing look for places to sit. As Dylan heads for one of the love seats, I slow my pace, hoping for some way to end up next to Liam instead.

Another squeal of feedback blasts over the audio system, and I scrunch my face and cover my ears. This time when the sound clears, there's glorious silence. O'Connor heads aft, and, for a minute, we think the problem's been fixed. Dylan drops into a seat, and I stand nearby, rolling the tension out of my shoulders.

Then a voice comes on, a slow and soothing female computer tone, like Alexa or Siri. It sounds like it's in the middle of a recording. I strain to hear familiar expected words for an airplane, but the voice doesn't say "seat belt" or "oxygen mask" or "flotation device."

We exchange puzzled glances. Everyone talks at once.

"What's she saying?"

"Can you hear it?"

"Shh!"

The volume, which started out low, swells into a tidal wave of sound until we have no choice but to hear the words.

The disembodied voice says:

"Blake Adams.

"One: I'm on the brink of flunking out of school.

"Two: The only reason I'm a football All-American is because I use anabolic steroids.

"Three: Last summer, I spent two months in juvenile detention for nearly beating a fifteen-year-old to death."

Goose bumps pop up on my arms, and I slip my blazer back on for some warmth.

"Blake?" Paige's faltering voice fills the sudden, oppressive silence when the recitation ends. "You said you went to Florida with your—"

"Paige Hall.

"One: I've hooked up with more than half the football t—"

Blake jumps to his feet. "Shut this freaking thing off!" he bellows over the voice as it rattles off humiliating things about his girlfriend, who's already keeping more space from him than I've ever seen between them.

". . . first abortion at sixteen."

"Paige?" Blake's tone shifts from anger to confusion and hurt, but it's the look of betrayal on his face that makes me squirm and turn away, like I've invaded what should've been private.

"Three: I'm addicted to painkillers."

Paige buries her face in her hands. Her shoulders shake as she sobs into her palms. At this point, does it even matter if the things are true? Hasn't the damage been done?

"It's going in alphabetical order, isn't it?" Liam asks from close by.

"Lily Hernandez.

"One: I was suspended last year for violating school rules."

That's not *so* awful. Nikki and I nearly got suspended that time we rickrolled the headmaster during the morning announcements instead of giving him the right link for our winter banquet promo video. But it was *so* worth it. My lips curl at the memory, and for a second, longing to have Nikki here with me stabs at my insides.

"Two: I failed my driver's test twice and still don't have a license.

"Three: When I was eight, I attacked my stepfather with a knife."

Lily? The seemingly least violent person ever? No one makes a move or says anything to her, but whispers track across the room.

The voice drones on, spilling "facts" about Taylor Lewis and Ann Liu. Taylor spent a semester in treatment for an eating disorder and poisoned the lead in the school musical when she was the understudy. Ann only became class president because she rigged the election. Two years ago, doctors pumped an entire bottle of Advil out of her stomach.

The knot beneath my ribs tightens with each name.

Liars. Cheats. Abusers. And as much as I don't want to hear the allegations, there's no way to stop myself from listening.

The dark-haired flight attendant appears halfway through the "facts" about Amir Mehrotra, who hacked into Boston's utility network and caused a three-day power outage but was never caught. "I'm so sorry," she announces, "but we can't shut it off. We think somebody wired in a device with a preset recording, and we haven't found it yet."

Dylan leaps to his feet. "Let's go look for it, then!"

Kumar shakes her head. "Absolutely not. It isn't safe for you to wander the plane while we can't make announcements. We'll find it." She disappears into the entryway, leaving us alone again, and Dylan slumps into his seat.

"**Olivia Mitchell. One: My father bought all those awards I've received from Lancashire.**"

She inhales sharply but otherwise stays still, staring at a spot on the floor. "It's not true." Her voice trembles.

"**Two: My older brother had better grades, more accolades, and better athletic stats than I do.**

"**Three: I lied about what happened in the car accident that killed him.**"

My heart aches for her, and I shift my weight from one leg to the other to avoid giving in to the impulse to hug her. Somehow, I'm pretty sure Olivia's pride wouldn't let her appreciate sympathy.

Evan Randall unleashes an ear-scorching stream of expletives when his name is called. "This is a bunch of—"

"Dude," Dylan yells over him and the droning voice. "What if the committee is still monitoring us?"

"**. . . shoulder injury but haven't told my coach.**"

"They can't count this against us, can they?" Ann asks, her gaze darting between Dylan and Evan.

"**Two: The only reason I haven't been expelled for my low grades is because of baseball.**

"**Three: I faked my medical approval to play.**"

The scholarship is probably the farthest thing from my mind at this moment as the voice pauses between names. Dylan is next, and it'll be me soon after.

No matter how horrible the others have been, I still don't want to hear my own name. Don't want everyone else to hear the truth about me. Or the scholarship committee, for that matter.

"**Dylan Roberts.**"

My fingers fumble for his, where they clutch the armrest. I can't help myself, even if it makes us look like a couple. We need solidarity at a time like this. He squeezes back. Doesn't let go.

"One: I took out a rival team's top-scoring lacrosse player with a cheap shot in the championship game."

I frown, trying to remember last year's tournament. He does love to win, but would he cheat to do it?

"Two: Last fall, I ran over my neighbor's dog and never admitted it."

I glance at him, my grip on his hand going slack. "You did?"

"Of course not," he hisses.

"Three: I have a second girlfriend in my hometown."

This time, I let go completely. Of course, it isn't fair to assume that any of these things are true, but the seed of doubt is hard to combat. Especially with Dylan's flirty personality.

"Em," he says, "none of it is true." Is that a hint of pleading in his tone?

I open my mouth to reply—what can I possibly say?—but stop myself when the next name is announced.

"Liam Scott. One: I invite my father to all my games, but he never shows."

Beside me, Liam stiffens, like he's bracing himself for a hurricane.

"Two: I went to jail for theft."

He clasps his hands behind his back and stares at his feet as the words cut like a knife.

"Three: My best friend's death was my fault."

A sharp inhalation, and he shifts his stance, releasing his hands from behind his back and running them across his face and into his hair.

"Liam . . ." Pain twists my voice as I whisper his name. He doesn't look at me, just keeps staring at the floor. It's not like there's anything I can say that will make this better.

I'm so caught up in his grief I forget it's almost my turn. There are only two of us left—me and Simon—and since I can't remember his last name, I have no idea how much time I've got before everyone hears what I did.

My heart and lungs feel like they've hardened into concrete as I wait.

"Simon Walker."

I exhale through pursed lips, trying to rid my chest of some of the tension. The voice drones on through the same list Simon read to us earlier, confirming my suspicions: whoever was behind the notes in the envelopes is behind this prank too.

But which one of us could've pulled it off? There are more than a few geniuses in this group with the technical know-how to hook up a recording into the plane's audio system.

From the way Simon is casually polishing his eyeglasses on his shirt, he makes a pretty darn likely candidate.

But does he want to win this contest *that* badly? Or is it a ploy for revenge against someone here?

"Emily Walters."

I'd be swearing right now if it weren't for my Catholic upbringing. Any second and the game will be up. Sir Robert Hamlin and the entire merit award committee will know that I cheated to get here, and I'll be disqualified.

"One: My mom lost—"

The feed cuts out. Just like that, silence descends over the low, steady hum of the jet engines. No more feedback squeals, no static.

We all hold our breath. Then the captain's voice comes on,

blessedly normal. "Sorry about that, folks. The flight staff appear to have resolved the issue, so you're free to move about the cabins again."

Tension ebbs out of my back, and I'm about to collapse into a chair when I realize nearly everyone is staring at me.

The only one who wasn't publicly humiliated.

Their expressions walk the line between slightly suspicious and downright hostile. The chaos breaks loose a few seconds later.

9

THE SECOND GAME

7:28 p.m. CDT

"It was you, wasn't it?" Paige says, her lips trembling beneath puffy, red eyes. The trace of venom in her voice makes me feel like inching backward into a hole to hide. "You set this up. That's why it cut out before it said anything about you."

Liam's the only one who isn't looking at me—instead, he stares at the floor, apparently lost in painful memories.

"It wasn't Em."

When Dylan speaks up for me, I could kiss him. Instead, I scooch a step closer, and he drapes an arm around my waist, warm and comforting.

"She wouldn't do something like that." His eyebrows pull together as he looks at me. "Would you even know *how*?"

"No, of course not. Besides"—I raise my cell—"my phone's right here."

"Burner phone?" Evan not-so-helpfully offers. He's standing off to one side, behind Olivia's seat, throwing invisible baseballs with a shoulder that looks decidedly stiff. Especially when he winces.

"It wasn't me," I repeat. I'm tempted to ask him if the recording was right about his injury, but the potential conflict isn't worth it.

"What about Taylor, then?" Blake suggests. He leans so far forward on the edge of his seat I'm surprised he doesn't fall off. "She's had plenty of time alone to figure out a way to hack the plane's sound system."

While I appreciate the redirect, why's he pointing the finger at Taylor? Because she's on Paige's team and he thinks bringing her down will help Paige? Or because he's behind this and wants to mislead the rest of us? Surely not, though—not with how upset it made Paige.

What would anyone here stand to gain by revealing that stuff about themselves? Unless whoever did it just made up something false about themselves, trusting the scholarship committee to sort it out later. Whose reactions were genuine, and who might have been acting?

Dylan squeezes his arm a little tighter around my waist as he rolls his eyes. "And Taylor tried to kill herself at dinner too?"

Blake's jaw hardens. "It'd be a good way to avoid suspicion, don't you think?"

I witnessed her near death close-up. No one is *that* good of an actor.

Liam rolls his neck and looks at the ceiling, as if he's debating whether to get involved. Then, with a little sigh, he steps into the center of the room, holding up both his hands. "Guys, guys. Wouldn't it be best to assume what we heard was false? Or at least a misinterpretation of the facts? You know, give each other the benefit of the doubt?"

Blake sits in silence for a long moment, then rises to his feet. "Agreed," he says. Paige is huddled into a ball alone on the love seat, her knees tucked beneath her chin, the fire she was directing at me long gone. "We've still got, what—six hours until we reach Paris? And as far as we know, there's still a scholarship on the line."

"What about you, Simon?" Olivia asks, like she hasn't heard anything Liam or Blake just said. "Were you really in the bathroom that entire time?"

That *is* a good question.

Simon glares at her but doesn't answer.

"Drop it, Olivia," Liam says. "Unless somebody wants to fess up, we could stand here all night accusing each other. I don't see any choice but to let it go."

Amir breaks out into Elsa's theme song from *Frozen*, and despite everything, I jump in on the harmony until laughter gurgles out of my mouth. Too bad Taylor isn't here to join in. All that tension torquing my insides has to get out somehow. Dylan shakes his head as I collapse onto an empty chair and lean my head on my arms to hide the tears springing into my eyes.

Clearly, I'm losing it. I'm exhausted and hungry, and my nerves are way beyond fried. More like burnt to a crisp. And I have no clue how to figure out which one of us is lying. But I do know this—somebody here knows *way* too much about me.

When the radio kicks back on, in a burst of static, I jolt upright, but this time it's only O'Connor, who has reappeared at the front of the cabin. "Thank you for your patience, everyone. We seem to have fixed the problem. You can rest assured the committee will handle the situation in a way that's fair to everyone. In the meantime, I believe"—she fiddles with some buttons on a console—"you have another video to watch."

The window shades close, the lights drop, and several people sink into seats. Now that the crisis has passed and I've laughed out all my stress, my body goes limp like a rubber snake. It's only seven thirty at night, but after the day we've had, I'm ready to crash. Too bad sleep isn't the next thing on the agenda.

Hamlin's face lights up the big screen. His forehead shines like it's been freshly polished. "Welcome back, competitors. I hope you're enjoying yourselves and seizing the opportunity to showcase your best traits." More than one listener lets out a loud snort, and I have the sudden urge to wipe that irritating smile off Hamlin's face. Sure, he might've worked his way to the top of the nonprofit food chain, but he has no idea the trauma we've been through today.

"You've had a chance to meet as teams," Hamlin continues, "and now it's time to kick off the true competition by working together to accomplish a goal. Leadership, teamwork, communication, and negotiation are all critical skills for achieving success in life. Here's your chance to show the committee what you've got."

On-screen, he holds up a small black pouch—about the size of a grapefruit—tied with a gold string and embroidered with a gold spade, just like a playing card. "We've hidden three of these bags on the airplane, one for each team. They're located in public, accessible areas, but they're well hidden. Each bag contains what your team needs to accomplish the task, except for something hidden in another team's bag. Your goal is to work together to find your team's bag, identify what's missing, figure out which team has it, and use your negotiation skills to get it back. First team to complete their task wins this round, and each member will be awarded two hundred points. Losers will each choose one team member to downvote. Remember, you also have one free-choice vote. But only one—I recommend you use it wisely."

Huh . . . I exchange a glance with Dylan. Is that what we're supposed to use to negotiate? Our votes? Maybe he and I *can't* just go upvote each other.

"One last thing. To help you find your bag, each team will receive an envelope with a clue. You have a one-hour time limit. Best of luck, competitors!"

The lights come back up, and despite my exhaustion, a surge of adrenaline washes through my body in a prickly wave. O'Connor walks over to us with another stack of cream-colored envelopes. Hopefully, nobody has found a way to tamper with this set.

Before she's even had a chance to hand them out, Blake tugs on Paige's arm and gestures to the screen. "Come on, let's try it."

Paige blinks up at him, shakes her head, and then drops her face back into her hands. Despite the fact she accused me, my heart goes out to her. Whether or not those messages contained any truth, she's obviously shaken. Pretty sure I can rule her out as the culprit. Blake too—because why would he do that to her?

"Well, I'm going to," he insists, until Ann stops him.

"Hey," she says gently, "I'm one hundred percent for you promoting Paige, but we might need those votes for this next game. Can you give it a bit?"

"Sound advice," O'Connor says as she passes out the envelopes.

Liam accepts ours when she calls out, "Hearts."

As I start to follow him, Dylan grabs my hand. "Hey," he says, his voice low, "you holding up okay?"

"Yeah." I swallow. Deep down, I know he's asking because he's my friend. Not because he has feelings for me. But then why is he searching my face this way?

I drop my eyes, flustered at the unexpected intimacy. "How about you?"

"I'm okay." He slides his arms around my back and pulls me into his chest. Again. That insistent and annoying little worm of doubt eats into my insides.

I can't decide if he's genuinely worried about me or if he's hitting on me, but something doesn't feel right. No—that's ridiculous.

He's not hitting on me. He's Nikki's boyfriend. Sure, they've gone through their share of temporary breakups, like a leading couple on a daytime soap opera, but it only lasts a few days before they make up. As Nikki's bestie, I'm always the go-between, carrying messages from one side to the other, so I've had plenty of private conversations with Dylan. Only a handful of times have things deviated from Nikki into territory that might make me question his feelings. But then they always get back together, so . . .

But now, with Dylan acting touchy-feely all of a sudden, I'm not sure what he's thinking. After everything I've done to her, keeping away from him sounds like a solid plan. I pull back and look up at him, but he keeps his arms draped loosely around my back.

"You know that stuff about me isn't true, right?"

"Yeah, of course." I mean, I'm going to give him the benefit of the doubt.

He smiles, and the unwelcome thought flits through my mind that maybe he's playing me. Putting on a show of affection to make sure I don't report any of this stuff to her.

"Em? You coming?" Liam asks. Simon and Olivia are already waiting near the forward doorway on the right side, ready to retreat to the space we claimed earlier up in the lounge. When Liam glances at Dylan, his gaze hardens ever so slightly. Or is it my imagination?

"Yeah." I turn away from Dylan and don't look back. For somebody who's spent her whole high school career as an accessory—like a nice handbag or pair of earrings—it's hard to fathom how I'm suddenly caught between *two* hot guys.

Unless, of course, this is all in my head. Maybe Dylan's just being friendly, and Liam only cares about me because he wants our team to win.

My nerves clearly disagree, because when Liam's arm accidentally brushes against mine as we walk, a jolt of electricity sizzles across my skin.

"So . . ." He glances at Dylan. "Is he your boyfriend?"

"No." My lips curve into a smile almost on their own. He wouldn't ask a question like that without being interested, would he? "He's not."

His lips tilt up, and his blue eyes linger on my face. My heart is doing more funny flips, and any trace of the exhaustion I felt earlier has vanished.

It takes me an extra second to realize Olivia is staring us down with a full-on glare. "Come on, let's get this over with," she grumbles. "We only have an hour."

We traipse back up the fancy staircase to the lounge, but this time we bypass the snacks in favor of creating a plan. Liam holds up the envelope to reveal the red heart colored on the outside, then opens the flap. He pulls out a single sheet of paper, which, thankfully, matches the envelope this time.

He stares at the page, eyebrows bunched, then lays it on the coffee table in the middle of our group of chairs. It's a string of numbers, typed in a standard font.

12 21 21 18 24 22

"Great, just great." Olivia groans. "That's *real* helpful."

I squint at the numbers for a minute, then shrug. "Maybe it's a phone number."

"Too many digits." Liam chews his lip. "Or you're thinking with a country code?"

"Yes, like this." I draw imaginary parentheses around the numbers to group them. **12 (212) 118-2422.** "What country is twelve?"

"It's not like it matters." Olivia flops back in her chair, rolling her eyes so hard I'm surprised her pupils don't vanish. "We couldn't call it anyway. Airplane mode, remember? They wouldn't expect us to break the rules, even *if* we had cell service up here."

"Right," I say, tapping my chin. "Forgot about that."

She glances at Simon, who's ignoring us and the message completely, in favor of jotting something down in the margin of his textbook.

"Simon," she hisses. When he doesn't respond, she whacks his arm. "A little help here? Or do you not care at all about winning?"

He's certainly giving off that impression. Or is it an act?

"I don't care about helping *you* win, that's for sure," he shoots back. "Of course, we all know there's little chance of that happening."

We've been staring at the numbers in silence for too many minutes when footsteps thump on the stairs at the far end of the lounge. Almost automatically, I snatch up the sheet and fold it again to hide its contents. Not that prying eyes would learn anything useful.

Liam stands and peers around the edge of the central bar. "Hey, guys," he says to whoever's coming, waving a hand. "Did you decipher your clue already?"

"Ha." Lily laughs, a welcome breath of fresh air compared to Olivia's and Simon's icy stares. She and two of her Spades teammates—Ann and Blake—stroll up to our chairs, and she flings a thumb over her shoulder. "Amir is working on it. The rest of us decided to start searching. You haven't seen any black pouches around here, have you?"

"I wish," I say.

Ann sits on the armrest of Liam's chair, perfectly at ease next to him. In the background, Blake wanders around the lounge, scanning the various seats, tables, and shelves.

"How about you guys?" Ann asks.

"No. But we'd rather argue than work together anyway." The snarky answer pops out before I can stop myself.

She quirks her eyebrows, glancing between me and Liam.

"Not us." The tips of my ears grow hot, and I play with a strand of my hair.

Olivia lets out a loud sigh. "Excuse me, but can we get back to work? I'd prefer not to just give up already."

"Right." Ann rolls her eyes but gets up. "Good luck!"

"And feel free to share your secrets if you figure it out," Lily adds.

"Will do." I give her a mock salute, ignoring the way Olivia's eyes narrow and her lips pinch together.

After the others have wandered out, I set the paper back on the table and turn to her. "It's not like I'm *actually* going to tell her. I was just being polite. After all, we might need to get our missing item from them."

"I suppose." Olivia leans against her armrest until her elbow nearly touches Liam's. She turns her bright eyes up to him. "What do you think about the clue?"

"Maybe," he says after a moment, "it's a combination for a lock. Are there lockers on board? Some kind of storage room?"

Seems plausible to me, but Simon, who's been doodling in his book this entire time, starts laughing. It's a quiet, grating sort of sound, and when combined with the self-satisfied look on his face, it practically shouts "I'm making fun of you."

"Get the chip off your shoulder already and tell us what you're laughing at," Olivia snaps.

But Simon merely chuckles over his book, like derivatives are so entertaining. Is he naturally this mean? Or is it all part of some genius plan to ensure his victory?

"Hey, man," Liam says, "do you have any ideas about the numbers? We're wasting a lot of time up here."

Simon surveys him coolly. "It's fairly obvious, don't you think? Code."

I swallow my irritation with his smug intelligence and pick up the paper. "Like, each one of these numbers represents something?"

"Obviously," he mutters. "Isn't that what a code is?"

It wasn't obvious to us, and I feel a flash of the same annoyance that's pinching Olivia's face. She keeps her mouth shut, for a change.

"So," I say, "we need a decoder . . . like out of a cereal box." An image of better days flies into my mind—Mom and Dad talking softly in the kitchen, the comforting smell of brewing coffee, me eating Lucky Charms in front of *Dora the Explorer*.

"Or an Enigma machine." Liam's lips hitch. "From World War Two."

At this, Simon lets out a loud you-guys-are-totally-dense sigh and practically throws his book on the table. "It's not even complex. I solved it on the second attempt."

"Are you going to tell us?" Olivia presses.

"That *would* be helpful," Liam adds.

"Fine." Simon sets down his pencil and book and tents his fingers beneath his chin like he's Benedict Cumberbatch's understudy for *Sherlock*. "You three agree to upvote me, and I'll tell you."

"We can't do that." With a dramatic huff and a rustle of plaid, Olivia rises to her feet and hovers next to Liam. "I'm going to start looking on my own. If you two want to sit around wasting time with him, go right ahead."

"So much for teamwork," I mutter. "How much time do we have left?"

Liam checks his wristwatch. "Forty-eight minutes, by my reckoning." He turns to Simon. "She's right. We can't promise those votes to you, because we might need them to negotiate."

Simon taps his fingers together, looking over us again as if assessing his options. "Very well. Then you'll promise *not* to downvote me if we don't win."

We glance at each other, then nod. Was this his plan all along? Or is there more to it?

"Agreed," Liam says.

Simon points at the paper. "It's a simple letter cipher. Each number represents a letter."

Liam raises both eyebrows, his blue eyes widening. "Ah, that makes sense! Anybody have a pen?"

Simon scowls but hands over his pencil—an old-school yellow wood Ticonderoga with a pink eraser. I'm pretty sure I haven't used one of those since third grade. Liam hunches over the coffee table as he scribbles down the alphabet. He assigns a number to each letter, starting with one for the letter *A*.

A-1, B-2, C-3, and so on, to Z-26.

The whole thing now seems painfully obvious, until he unscrambles our string of numbers and comes up with:

LUURXV

"Oh my word, this is stupid." Olivia waves toward the stairs. "If you need me, I'll be searching the plane."

"Wait a sec," I say. "Can you be a little more patient? Maybe we need to shift the code one direction or another. Or run it backward."

Simon's knuckles tighten around his book ever so slightly at my last suggestion.

"Backward. Try it backward," I say again to Liam, pointing at the paper.

He takes a moment to jot out the new code, then uses it to translate our numbers.

OFFICE

"Bingo." Liam taps the pencil on the table with a loud thwack.

Simon glares at him and snatches it back up. "Took you long enough."

Liam and I scramble to our feet, and even Simon closes his book and stands.

"We've got forty-four minutes," Liam says, checking his watch.

I lead the way toward the staircase. "What kind of plane has an office?"

Behind me, Liam chuckles. "Apparently, the crazy one we're stuck on. Let's go find it."

10

SCREECHING HALT

7:50 p.m. CDT

Lily and her teammates are nowhere in sight as we rush down the stairs into the empty entryway.

"Should we split up?" I ask.

"Good idea," Olivia says, practically jumping on my words. "You check the forward compartments. The rest of us will head farther aft."

Trying to ditch me?

She slips a hand into Liam's and tugs him into the entertainment salon without even waiting for a response. Typical. Simon trudges after them, so I obediently turn to the mirrored wall and search for the door handle that will let me into the front. My reflection stares back at me, rumpled navy-and-red plaid skirt, blazer sleeves rolled unevenly over my wrinkled white dress shirt. Dark circles are forming under my eyes, and my hair could use a serious combing. The bow tie is totally crooked, so I give up and pocket it again.

Good thing we aren't being judged on appearance.

After finding the right panel and pulling the door open, I step into a central open hub surrounded by six smaller compartments, accessed by frosted glass doors. I peek inside the first one on my left. Four seats face each other, two on each side. Nothing here shouts office to me, but I check the other compartments just to be safe.

In the second to last one on the right, Taylor reclines in one of the seats, her feet propped up on a raised footrest. She opens her eyes and glances at me.

"Sorry," I mutter. "I forgot you were in here."

She waves at me. "Don't worry about it. That bossy flight attendant won't let me leave."

"Are you feeling any better?" The ticking clock nudges me to get moving, but I don't want to be rude.

"Yeah, just tired. What are you doing in here? Dylan's searching the plane."

Why does she assume I'm looking for him? I press both hands against the cool metal door frame. "Did you guys decipher your clue?"

A frown curls her lip. "Well, let's see. Paige wouldn't come back here to help, and Evan and Dylan gave up trying and went to search without it. I'm sure we could've gotten it with a little more work, but they were so impatient. Maybe you could find Paige and tell her I need her?"

Part of me—the generous, selfless part—considers telling her the secret, but then I remember that I'll probably be spending the summer sleeping in a car, while Taylor will no doubt be touring Europe or enduring some other such trial of the rich. "I will if I see her. Good luck," I say, offering her a weak smile.

She calls after me as I head across the hub for the door. "Did you guys figure it out?"

"Sorry, gotta go." I slip back out into the entryway and pull the door shut slightly harder than necessary, just to make sure she knows I'm gone. Her situation sucks—being stuck all alone with your fate in the hands of a bunch of bickering strangers—but I can't let pity cloud my judgment.

I stride through the lounge so fast I almost miss Paige hunched in a ball on one of the love seats. My team needs my help—we're running out of time—but I can't just walk by and do nothing. Besides, I promised Taylor.

"Hey." I gently touch her elbow where it's draped around her knees. She's got her head buried in a mass of curls. "You okay? Taylor wants your help."

When she glances up, I pull back, balling my fingers into a fist. Her cheeks are tear-streaked, her face red and puffy, and the hollow look in her eyes radiates fear and distrust. Nothing like I'd expect from the effervescent cheerleader. Does she still think all of this is my fault?

"Stay away from me," she mumbles, sinking deeper into the seat like she can make herself disappear. "Don't you have a team to help?"

I stumble to my feet, backing away a step like she's an injured animal I shouldn't have messed with. "You do too," I manage to squeak out. "What about the scholarship? Hamlin said the losing teams will have to downvote one of their members."

You're not exactly being helpful, I want to add, but I keep the thought to myself. The way things stand on my team now that we made that deal with Simon, we *have* to win. Otherwise, we'll have to choose me, Olivia, or Liam.

"After what happened, how could I give a—" Her voice cuts out with a sharp cry as a sob racks her body, shaking her shoulders. She stuffs a fist against her mouth and drops her head back down.

My cue to leave.

I tried, didn't I? It's more than a lot of people would've done. Part of me can't help wondering how many more of us will break before this competition ends.

Our seating compartment is empty, though the overhead bins

now hang open. Somebody searched in here. I press my lips together and waste a precious minute closing the bins. Why can't people be a little more considerate? My messenger bag has shifted, and the flap is askew, but a quick glance inside shows everything is still there.

I pause when I hear a crinkling noise as I close the buckles on the bag. Stretching up on tiptoe, I can just see it, a blue wrapper tucked beneath my bag, near the back of the overhead bin. Trash from a previous flight?

That hardly seems likely, with how meticulously clean the rest of the plane is, and I could swear this bin was empty when I stuck my carry-on in it. Pulling on my bag, I manage to drag the wrapper close enough to reach. Blue-and-red plastic crinkles in my hand, but when I get a good look at it, I nearly shriek.

It's a small package of Planters peanuts. And it's empty.

I glance up and down the compartment, but nobody is there. Nobody to witness me standing here with a bag of something that could've killed Taylor. In all fairness, none of us knew she had a nut allergy. We weren't told not to bring peanuts on the plane.

But this trash is *not* mine, and I can't think of a single good reason why it'd be up here with my bag. Unless someone is trying to make *me* look responsible for what happened to Taylor.

The thought sends a chill skittering down my back. Especially after what happened with the voice recording, how it had cut off on *my* name. I'd assumed it was a coincidence, but could it have been intentional?

And if so, who's behind all of this? Did they hurt Taylor on purpose? As much as I'd like to believe no one here would do something like that, what are the odds she just happened to react to her food, and someone else just happened to shove their empty bag of peanuts into a random overhead bin?

I clench my teeth and ball the wrapper up in my hand. It'd be irresponsible to leave it lying around where Taylor might inhale the dust, so I stuff it into my blazer pocket until I can find a trash can.

Lily's team has taken over the dining room. They're seated around the big table, sorting what looks to be puzzle pieces—which must have been the contents of the black velvet pouch lying nearby. A new ripple of panic flies through my system. My team is behind.

When I enter the room, both Lily and Amir smile and wave.

"A puzzle," Lily says with a shrug.

"You solved the clue?" My voice cracks on the way out.

Amir waves their paper in the air. "It was a letter cipher. Told us to search in here."

"Are you sure you should tell her?" Blake asks from across the table, but Ann rolls her eyes.

"You blurted it out to Evan. Besides, they already solved theirs," she says. "She's on Liam's team."

I point aft toward the kitchen. "Are they back there?"

When Lily nods, I mutter a quick thanks and practically run for the next compartment. There's a narrow hallway with doors on either side—one labeled GALLEY for the kitchen, another marked STORAGE. It's darker here, and the walls of the passage press close, giving the space a claustrophobic feel.

I nearly jump out of my skin when the galley door flies open behind me. O'Connor steps out with an empty trash bag.

She smiles. "Sorry, didn't mean to startle you."

"No, that's okay. Is there an office back here?"

"In the tail." As she closes the galley door, one of her sleeves pulls up, revealing a tangled web of old purple scars above her wrist. What happened to her? The fabric falls back into place, and as she turns, I hold out the wrapper, balled up in my hand tightly enough that she can't see what it is.

"Oh, here's some trash." The last thing I need is the senior flight attendant telling the merit award committee I tried to kill off one of my fellow competitors. But she opens the bag without even glancing at what drops inside.

A few paces later, I step through an open doorway into a new compartment. It looks like the love child of the entertainment salon and the seating area. The same cushy chairs are here, but instead of facing forward, they're clustered in groups around tables, forming workstations. The window shades have been drawn, keeping out the vast, black night sky and the lonely flashing lights on the wings.

Nobody's in here, but the remains of potato chip bags and drinking glasses give evidence to its recent use. I pause to scan the trash. *Bingo.* One of the papers is there, along with the same thing Liam wrote out for us—the alphabet with numbers assigned to each letter. Their code reads BEDROOM. My chest squeezes a little tighter, but I force in a deep breath and try to relax. Must be Dylan's group, who managed to solve it after Blake told them how to break the code.

With a rustling of plastic, O'Connor follows me and tosses the empty wrappers into the trash bag. That peanut bag is history now, and I can't help feeling like I've dodged a bullet. But how many more will come my way if I can't figure out who left that wrapper near my bag? And why would anyone here choose *me* to frame?

Again, I think of Dylan—he's the only one who knows me—but I'm positive it's not him. He couldn't act to save his life. If he knew how I got here, that I stole Nikki's application, there's no way he'd be able to play nice.

No, it must be one of the other competitors. Maybe picking

me was a matter of convenience. Maybe it's as simple as my name being at the end of the alphabet, allowing the recording to play through everyone else's names. Regardless of why, I have to figure out who, and soon.

I find my team in the next compartment—an office, with a big, burled walnut desk and bookcases lining the walls. They're crowded around one end of the desk, their shoulders hunched in concentration. Even Simon.

The tension pinching my ribs eases a little, and the grin that lights up Liam's face when he sees me is like the sun popping out after a thunderstorm. He holds up a black bag with an embroidered gold heart. "We found it. It was hidden in one of the desk drawers."

"I saw the Spades—they've got theirs too."

"Evan and Dylan are back there." He tips his head toward the aft bulkhead. "There's a bedroom suite in the tail."

A couple of containers on the desk appear to be permanently bolted into place: a penholder, a paper sorter, and a wooden tray holding a desktop calendar pinned down by a large glass paperweight. The green-and-brown logo—a W intertwined with a D, embedded in the bottom of the glass—looks vaguely familiar, but I can't think where I've seen it before.

My team has dumped out the contents of the bag onto the large, glossy desktop.

"Here, help us sort." Olivia shifts so I can squeeze beside her. Simon stands at the end, moving around tiny bits of colored cardboard with his index finger.

"Ugh, what is this, like, a five-hundred-piece puzzle?" I can't keep the grimace off my face. I've never liked puzzles. They take forever to finish, and the payoff is hardly worth it when you can find a better version of the same picture online in a matter of seconds. "I expected something less . . . anticlimactic."

"It's two hundred." Simon's lips press together, his silent reminder that I'm hopelessly dense, because—duh—it should be clear at one glance there are only *two* hundred ridiculously small pieces, not five. "And obviously the task isn't about the puzzle—it's about teamwork."

Does that explain why he's actually helping now? Where was this "teamwork" when we were trying to unscramble the clue?

"There's no box to show the picture." Olivia groans. "How are we supposed to assemble a two-hundred-piece puzzle in the next twenty-seven minutes?"

They're separating the pieces based on color—blue, green, multicolored, and a bunch of gray ones, some solid, and some with either curving or straight bands. A separate area holds the corner and edge pieces. Suddenly, I'm eight years old again, sitting at the kitchen table with my dad. He loved puzzles. The slow, rhythmic pace. The time to talk. My heart twinges at the memory. Sometimes I forget how much I miss him.

But time is something we *don't* have, so I scan the piles looking for a place to start. A picture pops into my head as I survey the disjointed bits of imagery. "Maybe it's the Eiffel Tower. We're headed to Paris, after all."

"Hey, I think you're right!" Liam slides over the section he's been working on—six pieces connected to form a frame. It could definitely be part of the base of the Eiffel Tower.

Simon raises his eyebrows over his black frames, glancing at me with the closest thing to respect I've ever seen on his face. Despite the fact he's mean and he possibly orchestrated revealing all our secrets, it makes my chest puff out just a bit. Nobody ever notices me—not with Nikki around to claim the attention.

When we're down to fifteen minutes left, there's still a too-large pile of pieces remaining, and a couple of them don't remotely match our picture of the Eiffel Tower on a bright Paris summer day.

"Maybe those are for other teams," I suggest. "Didn't Hamlin say we'd have to negotiate? We must be missing some too."

Liam separates out the ones that are obviously wrong for our picture. They're gray, like some of our pieces, but the shade is darker and the texture appears grainy—like stone, rather than metal.

I stare at the six pieces. "Do you think they all belong to the same team? Or do we have to negotiate with more than one?"

He shrugs. "And it might not be the same team who has our missing pieces."

"Should we start bargaining, though?" Olivia asks. "We're running out of time."

"I'll go," Simon offers. When we all turn to him and Olivia shrieks, "No," he bursts out laughing at his own joke.

"How about me?" I ask. Definitely we shouldn't send Olivia—she'd make enemies of the other teams. And Liam . . . Let's just say he's a million times better at putting together this puzzle than I could ever hope to be *and* keeping the other two on task. "I can be diplomatic, and you three are making great progress."

He drops the extra pieces into my hand, his fingers brushing against my palm and sparking warmth up my arm. I wish I could just sit and talk with him for half an hour. You know, a regular conversation, like during a boring class in school. Maybe I'd even dredge up the courage to show him some of my artwork. But there's nothing normal about this situation.

"Good luck," he adds. "Don't give these up lightly. We don't want to waste our votes."

Right. Because I literally hold another team's fate in my hand. I slip them into my blazer pocket. "I won't."

My best bet is probably to check back in with Lily's team, as they've got to be further along than Dylan and Evan, but it's more efficient to head aft first, so I slide open the lone door in the bulkhead and peek my head in.

The opening leads into a short passageway, maybe five feet long, with glossy faux-wood paneling for walls. Voices drift from farther inside. When nobody says anything to me, I invite myself in.

The space is, indeed, a bedroom suite, complete with two huge closets on either side of the doorway—these account for the paneling—a nightstand bolted to the wall, a built-in dresser, and a huge bed covered in a fluffy down comforter and pillows. It's clear I've reached the tail of the plane, as this room narrows significantly toward the back, though there's one more door that presumably leads to a bathroom.

The voices are coming from this door, which is partially open.

I cross the empty bedroom and stick my head in. "Wow . . ."

It's one of the fanciest bathrooms I've ever seen, with tile floors, gold fixtures, and a massive walk-in shower next to a Jacuzzi tub taking up the far back. Dylan and Evan sit hunched in the center of the floor around their puzzle, which is noticeably less finished than ours.

Dylan's face is a mask of tense concentration, but he offers me a crooked grin when he looks up. Evan glances up but then turns back to his work.

"Here to help us?" Dylan asks.

"Um, no." I hold out my handful of puzzle pieces. "I'm here to see if you need these, and if you have any of ours."

He gives me a rueful smile. "We haven't even figured out what picture we've got yet, so I'm pretty sure we won't know if those are ours."

"This is *stupid*. I told you we should've taken this up front so Taylor could help," Evan mutters. "We can't afford to lose this task."

Dylan frowns at him. "Dude, the flight attendant said to let her rest. Weren't you listening? Besides, it's not like this would've fit on the slide-out table in that little compartment."

"Yeah, well, if Paige wasn't too busy sulking to help, maybe we'd actually be making progress." Evan balls his fist around a handful of pieces, then lets them trickle out slowly to the ground. He looks at me. "How far ahead are you guys?"

The bathroom floor looks pretty darn uncomfortable. They could've at least gone back to the entertainment salon, but I keep my opinions to myself and instead say, "We've got a lot left. The Spades are probably in the lead."

Evan grimaces but returns to moving pieces around until he clicks another one into place. "Hopefully, the committee will recognize we're a little shorthanded here."

I lean over, studying their picture. They've got little clusters of pieces fitted together, but not enough to make the image obvious. A lot of the pieces have the same grainy dark-gray color as the ones in my hand, but I'm not about to hand these over without finding ours first. None of their pieces scream "Eiffel Tower," and I've squandered enough time here already. After all, you can hardly negotiate when you don't know what you need.

"Well, good luck," I say. Then I turn and walk out of the bathroom.

"Hey, Em, wait up." Dylan scrambles to his feet, catching up to me halfway across the plush carpet of the bedroom.

"Yeah?"

I stop, and he stops, and we're standing a whole lot closer than we should be. Time slows, measured in the too-loud thumps of my heartbeat and the breaths I can barely draw in. Is there less oxygen in this room?

He swallows. "If we find the extra pieces, I'll check with you first."

"Thanks." I don't move. I just keep standing there too close to him, like my feet have been bolted to the floor to keep me in place during takeoff and landing. Obviously, the part of my brain responsible for logic is misfiring.

His blond hair is all tousled from running his hands through it, and his wire-rimmed eyeglasses sit slightly askew on his straight nose. I reach a hand up to adjust them, stopping just shy of touching the frame. Practically touching his face.

What am I doing?

One of his eyebrows lifts, and his lips tilt into a small, knowing grin.

Great. I've just blown it—years of keeping my feelings a secret— and now I've practically made an announcement over the intercom system.

Heat flares in my cheeks, and I start to drop my hand—this is *not* what I'm supposed to be doing—but he catches it in one of his. Calluses from lacrosse press into my skin, and my heart rate skyrockets as we somehow interlock our fingers.

Feet. Move. Now, I tell them. But my brain still isn't working the way it's supposed to. The way I *want* it to.

Because instead of stepping away like he should—like I should— he leans closer. There's no doubt what he's thinking as his gaze drops to my lips.

Warning bells go off inside my head, but the part of me that's had a crush on him for years ignores them. Has he wanted me too, but never found the right time to say something?

No, this is wrong—

But as I start to pull away, he leans down, his lips find mine, and my brain goes utterly, uselessly blank. All my carefully tended reasoning flies out the window as I melt into his touch.

He kisses me softly at first, maybe waiting to see how I'll react, but my senses have abandoned me completely, because I kiss him back. Not gently either, but like a girl who's pined for this moment since she was thirteen.

Dylan lifts our intertwined hands and drapes mine around his neck. As his hands find my waist, the puzzle pieces I was clutching fall noiselessly to the floor and I lift my other hand to his shoulder.

The sane part of me objects, scrambling to come up with a reason why I shouldn't be wrapping my fingers around the back of his neck, where the soft ends of his hair tickle my skin. But passion's voice is far louder than that niggling worm of guilt, and Dylan's mouth moving against mine has removed any rational thought.

He murmurs something against my lips. *Cass?*

But that makes no sense, and when his fingers dig into my waist the thought slides away like dirty laundry down a chute.

What finally pulls me out of the moment isn't my own better judgment, it's a soft cough from the short hallway behind me. I break apart from Dylan, reluctantly at first, until the haze in my brain fades and I realize it's someone clearing their throat.

I press a hand to my burning lips and turn, dread filling my insides, all the way to my toes.

Liam stands in the doorway between the two closets, his lips slightly parted, eyes wide. The passion of a minute before vanishes like I've been doused with ice water.

His gaze hardens as he glances from me to Dylan and then to the floor, where the puzzle pieces lie.

I'd forgotten about them completely.

And the game. My team. The scholarship . . .

Nikki.

I'm a horrible friend. Scratch that—a truly horrible *person.*

I blow out a breath against my fingers, and my knees tremble.

Wasn't stealing her place in this contest enough? Do I have to steal Dylan too?

Does he even *want* to be stolen, or was he just playing me?

When I glance back at him, he gives me a half shrug. His lips are red, the skin around them irritated from the contact, but his eyes are dancing. Like he's ready for round two.

What was it the message said? *I have a second girlfriend . . .*

Is that what this was? A chance to cheat with somebody new? And a way to prevent my team from completing our task?

Disgust churns in my gut. At him. At myself. At what we've just done to Nikki. Regardless of his motivations.

I turn away from him to face Liam. "I'm sorry, Liam. I . . ." *Forgot? Got distracted? Found something better to do?* Everything sounds stupid. I bend down to swoop up the puzzle pieces, but he beats me to it.

The colored fragments vanish into his hand, his knuckles whitening as he tightens his fist. "No problem. I'll take care of these."

I pry my eyes off his clenched hand and force myself to look at his face. His nostrils flare slightly, but then his expression shifts from anger to disappointment. If only I could slink into one of the closets and hide for the rest of my life.

Before he can vanish into the next room, a loud chime sounds over the intercom system, followed by a woman's voice. "Time."

We failed.

11

SECURE YOUR OWN MASK FIRST

8:35 p.m. CDT

Liam doesn't say anything, doesn't even look at me as we rejoin Simon and Olivia.

"Please return to the entertainment salon for a video from Sir Hamlin," O'Connor's voice continues.

Behind us, in the bedroom suite, angry voices fly back and forth like a tennis volley. I have no idea if Evan saw what happened, but it doesn't change the fact Dylan ditched him.

Or that I did the same to my team.

I feel as low as an earthworm—maybe even one preserved in formaldehyde and laid out on a dissecting tray in biology class—as I glance at our puzzle. In the time I lingered with Dylan, they nearly finished it. Only a few pieces remain off to one side.

The Eiffel Tower stands tall and striking against a bright-blue sky, surrounded by green gardens and tiny multicolored tourists at the base. Suddenly, the thought of seeing it in person makes me feel ill. I haven't earned that privilege, not with the things I've done.

"What on earth?" Olivia's nose crinkles as she gives me a once-over. "Where have you been? Did you get our pieces?"

I open my mouth to say something, anything, but Liam cuts me off.

"Come on, we need to go." He doesn't look at me as he slips the extra pieces into his pocket.

"Dylan and Evan weren't even close to being done with their puzzle," I say to Olivia, loud enough that Liam can hear, in case he's remotely interested in knowing I did more back there than kiss Dylan. "I scanned their pieces, but I didn't see any that looked like ours."

The dining room is empty by the time we reach it. Lily's team's puzzle, a picture of the Arc de Triomphe, is nearly complete.

But not quite.

A wild flash of hope springs into my heart. Nobody won. Maybe we'll all come out of this on equal ground.

But then I remember the harsh truth—Hamlin said the losing teams would have to pick one team member to downvote. Maybe we'll all have to do it. And who is that likely to be on *my* team? Not Simon, because we promised. Not Liam or Olivia.

No, they'll pick the girl who wandered off during the game for a quick make-out session with her BFF's boyfriend. The one who can't manage to accomplish even the simplest of tasks. And that mysterious person who's out to get me? Here, have some more ammunition to fire.

I set aside my self-scathing until later as we reach the entertainment salon. Lily's team is already in here, perched on armrests and coffee tables. O'Connor still must have Taylor resting up front. Paige is noticeably absent, but the lavatory door on the left is latched shut, with the red OCCUPIED sign in place. I hope she's pulling herself together in there. This situation is stressful enough without people coming unglued.

Olivia picks a love seat near the back of the room, and Liam sits beside her without so much as glancing my direction. A heavy weight settles on my chest, like he's grinding me beneath his heel.

And, what's worse—I absolutely deserve it. She flashes a wide grin at him, darts a quick smirk at me, and then flips her hair over her shoulder with a flourish. Victory.

Whatever. I never deserved to win.

And it wasn't a game anyway. I stand a little straighter. These people just met me. They have no right to judge.

Dylan and Evan show up a few minutes after us. Evan takes a seat near Blake, leaning in close to tell him something. Hopefully, not a story about how I tried to hook up with a guy from another team.

I stiffen when Dylan stops next to me, torn between the same sense of longing that drove me to kiss him back and the knowledge that I'm 100 percent certifiably the worst friend ever. How on earth am I going to break this to Nikki? Stealing her application was bad, but kissing her boyfriend . . . ? That's, like, an entirely different level of awful.

He glances at me, his lips quirking in that small, knowing grin that makes my insides feel squishy and warm, despite the epic vat of shame roiling in my stomach.

My head is still reeling from the reality that the kiss even happened. And yeah—not gonna lie—it was everything I'd hoped it would be. Except I have no clue what's going through Dylan's mind, behind those clear hazel eyes. I mean, he's Nikki's *boyfriend*. Doesn't he feel guilty *at all*?

The broadcasted message said he's been two-timing Nikki, but surely that was a lie. Wasn't it? I can't have been wrong about him all these years, can I?

When he tries to take my hand, his fingers fumbling to grip mine, I squeeze once, then shake him off. His eyebrows lift in question, and I whisper, "We need to talk." There's too much to think about, too much we should discuss, before I can stand here like we're . . .

What, exactly? We're certainly not together, nor are we ever going to be.

Friends, then? But how is that going to work now that we've kissed?

What in the world was I thinking?

The problem is, I *wasn't* thinking. Like when I stole Nikki's application. And now I have to deal with the consequences. For a second, I glance wistfully at the closed lavatory door with its metal toilet, like it's a sanctuary where I could hide. And throw up this guilt.

Dylan shrugs, then stuffs his hands into his pockets and turns to face the front. But there's something about the set of his shoulders that rubs me the wrong way. Almost like he feels smug. Like he got what he wanted.

So I take a deep breath, ditch Dylan, walk past him to Liam's end of the love seat, and stand a foot away from the armrest. Liam glances at me but, just as quickly, averts his eyes.

The lights dim, and the TV springs to life. Sir Hamlin's face glows down on us like a benevolent deity, but the more I see those beady eyes and that wide, shiny forehead, the more I loathe the sight of him.

"Well," he leads off, "how did it go? Let me guess." He raises both hands, like he's about to make some astonishing pronouncement. "Nobody accomplished the task. Am I right?"

We all groan. Why would the committee assign us a task they knew we'd fail? And does that mean they'll let us off the hook and there won't be a penalty?

"Now, we didn't give you this assignment for the purpose of

making you feel bad, but we wanted you to learn a valuable lesson. In life, and especially in the business world, there are things you can't accomplish on your own. You had to work together to find and assemble your puzzle in the allotted amount of time. But sometimes even when we do everything right, things still don't work out. In this case, the other teams also had to have their puzzles assembled to be able to identify the extra pieces. Even if all of you reached the point of finding your extra pieces, you still had to figure out which team you needed to trade with and negotiate an agreement. That's a tall order for a single hour, especially after a long day of travel."

At his words, weariness washes through me. This whole competition is starting to feel more like a punishment than a golden opportunity. And here I thought we'd be sipping hot chocolate and eating croissants between rounds of taking tests and doing interviews.

Hamlin's drone isn't helping my exhaustion, so I brace one hand against the back of Liam's love seat to give my tired legs a rest. When he flinches, the heavy weight on my rib cage presses down harder.

"Unfortunately," Hamlin continues, "when we fail in the real world, there are real-world consequences. Even when the task is impossible, or failure isn't our fault." Now we're coming to the point. My fellow competitors perch on the edges of their seats, like a line of birds on a telephone wire. "A failed negotiation or a blown opportunity for a major nonprofit often means *somebody* has to face the consequences, even if it's only to set an example for the rest of the team. No, it isn't fair, but in a high-stakes world of big profits and bigger losses, you have to be prepared.

"Now it's your turn. You're switching from negotiation to the boardroom."

My heart sinks. It sounds like an episode of that old reality show *The Apprentice*. So much for another chance.

"This is ridiculous," Ann mutters, her hands clenched around the end of her braid.

"As I mentioned earlier, every team that failed must select one person for each team member to downvote. For this special case, you'll also need to downvote yourself in the event you are selected by your team. The downvotes must be entered on the screen behind you within the hour, or else the entire team will lose one hundred points apiece."

Fantastic. Sweat breaks out on my back as I quickly run the math. No points were awarded, so we're all still equal. There are three teams. When each team downvotes one member, that'll mean three of us sitting at negative two hundred points. That's a *huge* deficit.

And the bottom three get the guillotine in Paris.

I'd have to get four upvotes just to make it back to *zero* if they choose me, and others will be bumping up to fifty or a hundred or even higher if they get upvotes or win another game.

"That's a bunch of bull!" Blake erupts from the couch, full-on shouting at the TV and nearly making me jump as he apparently reaches the same conclusion I have. Whoever gets picked now is basically done for. "We didn't go through all this to get sent home—"

He shuts up when Hamlin keeps going, but there's a low buzz of grumbling voices. "You'll have an hour to reach your decision, finish your negotiation, and complete your puzzles to earn fifty points apiece. Good luck, teams. I have faith in you and your decision-making abilities."

When the lights come back up, silence hangs over the space for a heartbeat. The others look the way I feel. Overwhelmed. Exhausted. Wondering why they thought this competition was a good idea.

Well, for the most part. Simon carries an air of sharp serenity, like he's got things under control no matter what happens. Is it because he's already extracted a promise of immunity from us?

Or because he's got more intimidation tactics planned?

At least with him on my team, I can keep an eye on him. But what if the person behind the messages is on another team?

A swirl of purple near the lavatory draws my attention. It's O'Connor. Her smile is sympathetic as she announces, "Teams, you have another hour, starting now." She pauses. "Please remember that the flight staff have no say in the competition. I'm sorry."

She replaces the intercom handset and disappears into the entryway. I glance at the time on my phone. 8:44 p.m. Chicago time. Just over halfway through this flight.

The others start to disperse, returning to the puzzles, but my feet stay rooted to the ground as I watch Liam and Olivia stand. Liam casts me a quick glance, his face pale, and something unreadable flashes in his eyes.

Worry?

Olivia's haughty frown is a little more obvious.

They're going to choose me.

I lead the way toward the tail, my shoulders slumping. Is it anything more than I deserve? I might've been the one to figure out our puzzle was the Eiffel Tower, but how else have I really contributed?

Simon solved the code, and, well, he's out anyway because we promised. Olivia . . . She's kind of worthless, but why would Liam side against her after what I've done?

And Liam . . . Nobody will vote against him, because he's a natural leader.

We file into the office in silence, stand around the desk, and start moving puzzle pieces into place.

"I think the Spades have our pieces," I offer. "It's not the Diamonds."

From the hostile look Olivia shoots me, it would've been better to keep my mouth shut.

Liam runs both hands over his face, then up through his thick, dark hair. For someone who's been so laid-back this entire time, he's more tense than I've ever seen him. "Are we going to vote first? Or finish this puzzle?"

"Finish the puzzle," I blurt. Because, hey, that buys me an extra ten minutes. Maybe I'll think of something brilliant before then.

Three sets of eyes settle on me, but I pretend not to notice. Instead, I shift a few pieces around, sticking in a blue one to fill in a gap in the sky. A jewel-toned one from the border of a flower bed.

"We have to pick someone," Liam says. His tone is flat, defeated. "Otherwise, our whole team takes a hit."

"Well, obviously it should be Emily." Olivia crosses her arms across her chest. "Whatever she was doing back there"—she jerks a thumb toward the bedroom suite—"it didn't involve getting our missing pieces."

Did Liam tell her about me and Dylan? I can't stop myself from searching his face, hoping to read a trace of guilt written across it. He meets my gaze—the first eye contact we've had in what feels like hours—and shakes his head the slightest bit.

No. I let out a slow breath, fully aware that I've done nothing to deserve his kindness.

"I think we should pick Olivia." Simon smiles, the fake kind meant to make her mad. From the way her lips thin, it's working.

Huh. I thought it could very well be Simon trying to get me out, but if he's the one who knows my secrets, why didn't he say my name? Maybe he thinks that peanut wrapper will get me disqualified.

If he planted it.

We grow silent as someone passes through the room. It's Blake. He points to the bedroom door as he skirts the far end of the desk. "Is Paige's team back there?"

I nod. "Hey, do you guys have any of our pieces?"

He stops and scans our puzzle. "Maybe . . . Do you have ours?"

Liam holds out the stash of extra pieces for Blake to inspect. He frowns and shakes his head—they must belong to Dylan's team, like I thought. Which means those guys probably have the Spades' pieces, and the Spades must have ours.

"Who did you vote for?" Liam asks.

"We're still working on it." There's something evasive about his answer that leaves me wondering what they're planning. Are there more options I hadn't considered? Like demanding upvotes as part of the negotiation to compensate for the points lost by the person the team picks?

It would take some serious camaraderie and selflessness to pull that off—otherwise, the remaining teammates could keep any negotiated points for themselves.

He stops at the bedroom door and turns. "Paige never came back here, did she?"

We glance at each other and shake our heads.

"I think she's still in the lavatory," I offer, though it isn't much help.

Blake frowns and walks into the bedroom suite. Is he here to negotiate with Dylan and Evan, or is he worried they'll choose Paige?

We find out within minutes, as his voice carries despite his attempt to speak in a hoarse whisper. "That isn't fair, and you know it. Taylor's not back here either."

The four of us stop all pretense of working and listen instead.

"Dude"—Evan's tone is cool and calm—"she hasn't helped us. Like, at all."

He's got to be talking about Paige.

"Taylor helped with the clue." Dylan, this time. Normally, his low rumble would make my heart race despite my better judgment, but this time all I feel is guilt. And anger, if I'm being honest. What right did he have to kiss me like that? "And the only reason we didn't bring the puzzle up front to her is because that flight attendant told us not to."

"And why would Dylan and I vote each other out, after we've been working together?" Evan asks.

"It's not her fault." There's almost a pleading undertone to Blake's voice. "You heard that garbage the speaker system spewed out. She's really sensitive. She just needs a little more time."

"I'm sorry, but it's not like we have a choice here," Evan says. "We've got to pick *someone*, and she makes the most sense. Besides, don't you have your own team to manage?"

A pause, then Blake again, and this time he makes no pretense at being quiet. "Those messages that played over the speaker system weren't an accident. Someone on this plane did it to wreck this competition. It isn't fair for you to use that against her."

Someone sighs, and even from a compartment away I can tell

it's Dylan. "Blake, be reasonable. We have no clue who did it. And what about Taylor? It's not her fault the flight crew nearly killed her with whatever was in her dinner. We can't use an allergy against her."

"And it's not Paige's fault either!" Blake insists. "Don't you get it? It's the same thing. For all we know, someone tampered with Taylor's food to try to knock her out of the competition, the exact same way they used those messages to destroy Paige."

The image of that peanut wrapper flits through my mind, but I'm not about to bring it up. Not when they're facing off back there, probably with chests puffed out like rivals on a sports field. No reason to invite them to turn on *me*. It's so quiet in our compartment you'd be able to hear a puzzle piece drop if not for the steady vibrating hum of the plane's engines.

"Sorry, bro"—Dylan again—"but this isn't your business. You don't get to decide."

"Easy for you to say. The girl you love isn't about to get voted out of a scholarship she desperately needs, all because some *losers*"—Blake spits the word—"don't know how to be fair."

I grit my teeth and breathe in slowly through my nose, which makes a noise way too noticeable in the silence.

Liam glances at me. His brows pull together as he frowns. I can guess what he's thinking.

"Dylan's not my boyfriend," I mutter. "And he doesn't love me."

The words pop out automatically, but confusion and anger spiral through me. Why *did* Dylan kiss me? And . . . what was that he said while we were kissing? *Cass.* Another girl's name?

Olivia whips her head around to stare at me like a vulture eyeing fresh roadkill. "Wait—you're *not* Dylan's girlfriend?"

"No." Irritation flares hot in my chest, drowning out the

emotional dust devil inside me and the rising voices from the bedroom suite. Why does it even matter to these people? "My best friend, Nikki, is," I blurt. "Not like it's any of your business."

"Your best friend." Liam says it as a statement, not a question.

Oh, good Lord, did I really just reveal how I betrayed Nikki?

He pins me under his hard gaze, until I feel like scum in a corner of the school bathroom.

"Can we not . . ." I swallow, trying to get a little moisture into my too-dry mouth. "Can we not talk about this right now?"

Or ever? Because as much as I like Liam, clearly he has no reason to return the feeling, and seeing as I'm about to get eliminated and lose my shot at going to a decent college, why even bother with trying to explain why I was kissing my best friend's boyfriend?

Then there's Dylan. How many girls is he stringing along? Or am I being unfair by even considering those messages about him as true?

Regardless, I deserve to be someone's first choice. Judging by the look in Liam's eyes, I've blown my chance at that too.

The whole thing is an utterly hopeless mess.

"I vote for Emily." A smug smile parks on Olivia's face.

"Second." Simon doesn't even bother looking up from the puzzle pieces he's putting together.

Liam sighs heavily, running his hands through his hair again. He frowns as his blue eyes linger on me, disappointment tracking across his features like I let him down.

Which I 100 percent did. I swallow.

"Third." His jaw clenches. "I'm sorry, Em," he whispers.

My heart sinks into my shoes. Here I'd had such good intentions to put boys out of my mind and focus on this competition, and now what?

I've blown my shot.

A loud thump comes from the back of the plane, yanking me out of my moment of self-pity.

"The least you could do is hand over my team's pieces." Blake's angry tone drifts from the open door. He must've slammed his hand against the counter.

"Do you *see* your pieces back here?" Evan asks. "We can't make any progress because you won't leave us alone to work."

"Dude," Dylan says, "go back to your own team. When we figure out which pieces aren't ours, we'll tell you."

We hold our breath as the stomping comes our direction. Blake appears in the doorway, his face flushed. He doesn't make eye contact as he heads straight for the next door.

He barely makes it out of our compartment when a scream from the front of the plane splits the air.

12

EMERGENCY EXIT

8:55 p.m. CDT

It's coming from somewhere far forward in the plane, this unnatural wail, which seems like it's bouncing and echoing off every surface between its source and our ears.

Even Simon's eyes widen as we glance at each other, then take off through the various compartments toward the front. Footsteps behind us mean Dylan and Evan have heard the screaming too.

We tumble into the entertainment salon just behind Blake. One of the flight attendants, Allard—the useless one who panicked while Taylor nearly choked to death at dinner—hovers in front of the open lavatory door. Both hands are clamped over her mouth, and she's trembling. Was she the one who screamed?

Taylor, Ann, and Lily stand next to her, clutching each other, and Amir presses against one of the seats, his eyes wide. Blake, who's a few paces ahead, gets there first. He takes one look past the flight attendant into the open lavatory, his face goes as white as a piece of notebook paper, and he backs away, spinning in circles and muttering incoherently.

My chest tightens as we push closer, because it's clear something awful has happened.

The flight attendant's eggplant-hued suit obscures my view as we approach, but nothing blocks the stream of blood flowing from the tile floor of the bathroom, soaking into the low-pile carpet of the salon.

That's a lot of blood.

Close behind me, somebody gags. I look over my shoulder to see Dylan nearly doubled over, covering his mouth with his hand. Thankfully, he manages to choke the bile down before anything comes out. Behind him, Evan clutches the back of a seat with one hand, the other pressed to his face.

Footsteps pound in the forward entryway, and a second later O'Connor appears, followed by Kumar. "What's going on?" O'Connor asks, her alert gaze sweeping over us. "Who screamed?"

Allard glances at her and points into the lavatory. When she tries to speak, only strangled sounds come out. O'Connor pushes past Lily and nudges Allard aside. Her eyes go wide as she surveys the scene.

I slip around the circle until I'm standing between Taylor and Lily, but I can't see past the flight attendants into the tiny space. "What happened?" I murmur.

"Paige," Lily says. "It's Paige in there."

"Is she . . . ?" I let the question trail away.

"I don't know. We just got here, seconds before you."

I turn to Taylor, whose face is a frozen mask of horror. She shakes her head.

Before I can press, O'Connor turns to Allard. "Clear some space. I need to move her out. Then we'll notify the pilots and the foundation."

The younger flight attendant merely stares at her, like she can't register what she's saying, and a flash of sympathy rakes my insides as frustration crosses O'Connor's face.

"I will," Kumar says, though a slight tremor in her voice betrays her fear. "Move back, everyone, please." She holds up her hands, pushing against the air to show us what to do, as if we're too stricken to understand. Maybe we are.

Collectively, we stumble backward a few paces, except for Blake, who's still wandering in random circles that bring him closer to the door on each pass. Finally, Evan and Dylan grab on to him and hold him still.

Kumar takes Allard's arm and guides her toward the entryway. There's a pause, then O'Connor grunts and squeezes out of the narrow lavatory doorway and into the short hallway. She's carrying Paige, arms beneath her knees and back, the way a parent cradles a sleeping toddler.

But unlike a blissful child, Paige's arms hang loose, flailing out at an awkward angle. Blood drips from deep gashes on both wrists. O'Connor angles Paige's body as she turns through the doorway into the entry, leaving a gruesome trail of red drops soaking into the carpet, and it's at that moment I see the full truth. Her skin color is close enough to normal she could almost be asleep, but her head lolls backward unnaturally, her eyes open and glazed.

She's dead.

Then the three attendants are gone, leaving us alone with a tiny room full of blood and a thousand questions. Shocked silence follows, in which we all stand there gaping, trying to process how this happened.

Blake moves first, wrenching loose from Dylan and Evan and pacing across a stretch of carpet running the length of the lounge from the lavatory door to the next compartment. Every time he gets to the lavatory, he looks inside, a sob hitching his thick chest. He is, understandably, a wreck.

"Anybody know what happened?" Evan asks finally, breaking

the silence. He gestures toward the open door but doesn't venture any closer, whether because of the blood or Blake pacing like a caged lion in front of it, I'm not sure.

"Was anyone in here?" Olivia asks.

Taylor opens her mouth, then clears her throat. "I came in here to use the bathroom, but it was locked for so long and nobody answered. So I asked the flight attendant for help, and she unlocked the door from the outside."

"It looked like she slit her wrists . . ." It feels like stating the obvious, like pointing out that the elephant in the room is gray, but I say it anyway.

Even though I said it softly, Blake stops. Stares at me. Then turns and punches the wall of the lavatory so hard the paneling vibrates. I jump six inches at the noise, and I'm not the only one.

"She didn't," he insists, his face going crimson. "She would *not* have hurt herself. That's not— No. She just wouldn't have."

"I'm really sorry," Evan mutters, and the rest of us nod. Though, honestly, I think we're still in shock.

"People surprise you sometimes." Liam says it so softly I almost don't realize at first that he's the one speaking. He's completely rigid, tendons straining in his neck, hands clutched to his sides.

"*What?*" Blake scrunches his face. Anger flashes in his eyes. "What do you know about it?"

"Remember the messages?" Liam laughs bitterly, shaking his head. "Well, they were right about one thing. My best friend killed himself three months ago. And I never saw it coming. I didn't even know something was wrong. I failed him."

"It wasn't your fault, Liam." I hate to see him in pain like this. Although I've only known him a few hours, I know this—he's a good person. "You would have helped him if you could have."

He doesn't look at me but stares straight ahead, eyes glistening more than usual in the room's dim lighting. His jaw tightens. "Good intentions won't bring him back, though, will they?"

I want to slide my hand into his, squeeze his fingers, and let him know he's not alone. But I'm not brave enough, not after what happened with Dylan.

Instead, I think back to how I found Paige earlier tonight, balled up on the love seat. My insides twist. I tried to help her, tried to talk to her, and she pushed me away. Would I have tried harder to get help for her if I'd known she was this distressed?

I'm not sure I want to know the answer after everything I've done to Nikki . . . My own head is the last place I want to be right now.

Blake slams the sides of the lavatory doorway again. "How did she even do it?" he demands.

This is something I *can* do—try to find answers to straightforward questions. Despite Blake and his intimidating temper, I weave around the others and approach the lavatory. "Can I look?"

"Don't touch anything," Amir warns. When we all turn toward him, he pushes away from the seat he's been leaning against. "You know, in case they need to evaluate it."

"Like a crime scene?" Olivia asks, her voice going high-pitched. Somehow, her words bring home what's happened. Somebody is gone. Forever.

Paige won't walk back out of whatever compartment they've taken her to. She isn't going to join Taylor up front, having her vitals checked while she waits to touch down in Paris. She'll never cheer at a football game again.

It occurs to me there would have been *two* bodies if we hadn't found Taylor's EpiPen in time. Goose bumps prickle my arms as that fact sinks in.

Blake moves wordlessly aside, and I peer into the lavatory, being careful to keep my feet on clean patches of carpet outside the door. It's a much smaller version of the ornate one in the tail of the plane, sans the shower and Jacuzzi. And coated with rust-colored liquid that makes my stomach turn.

I've seen blood before. I can handle it. But this much? I never realized exactly how much blood pumps through our bodies.

The urge to gag is strong as the tang of blood coats my mouth, but I swallow and suck in a few shallow breaths as I scan the sink and the floor. Something silver gleams on the counter beneath the bright vanity lights, lying partially hidden under what appears to be a paper towel. Then I notice the lines and the tattered edge, like it was ripped from a sheet of notebook paper.

The paper from Paige's envelope? Despite the sudden protests of the people behind me, I lean inside the doorway and manage to get two fingertips on the paper to snatch it up.

I wave it at Blake, then unfold it. As I suspected, it's got the three lines about her that we heard earlier, but someone has added extra notes in the same handwriting. It takes me a moment to realize it's a list of names. And above the list are the words *Last Year's Top Baby Names*. My heart hurts.

"This was on the counter." I hold the paper out to Blake, fingers trembling.

His eyes go glossy, and he blinks rapidly. Then he swallows. "Flush it. I don't care if it clogs their stupid toilet system. No one should've tormented her like that."

I nod and gingerly lift the lid of the toilet, which is just to the left of the door.

"Wait," Amir starts to object, "that could be"—I drop the paper in anyway—"evidence."

It starts to dissolve almost instantly in the remnants of blue liquid in the steel basin. It's a little harder to reach the flush button, but when I hang on to the doorway and lean inside, I can just get a finger on it.

"She volunteered every month at this homeless shelter for families," Blake mumbles from behind me. "She made me go with her sometimes. We'd play with the kids, or help organize the donations, or help a family move into their new place once they got back on their feet."

I press the button, and, with a noisy sucking sound, the "truths" about Paige vanish into an unseen tank in the bowels of the plane. It's hard to meet Blake's eyes when I'm done. "Paige's bright smile must've meant the world to those kids," I say, "when they had nothing else and nowhere to go. That's really cool."

"And the thing is," he goes on, "she did it because she *wanted* to. Not because somebody made her, but because she cared about people. After how hard her parents' divorce was on her, she knew how much those kids needed somebody when they were going through tough times."

I nod. Swallow. I know a thing or two about how painful it is to have your family break apart. I hate how easily I categorized Paige, labeled her, and blew her off.

Tears burn my eyes, so I turn to look in the lavatory one more time, at that silver object now visible where the paper used to lie.

A razor blade, like the kind we used in biology freshman year to cut open flowers to see their parts. And it's sitting on another, smaller sheet of notebook paper.

"There's a razor blade on the counter," I murmur. I just manage to tug the slip of paper out from under the blade without knocking it onto the floor. Several of the others edge closer to see. "She used a razor blade," I announce.

"Where'd she get it?" Blake asks, his forehead crinkling. "That's not something she would carry around with her. Does anybody?"

"Maybe she found it somewhere on the plane," I say. "Like in the emergency first-aid kit, or in one of the larger bathrooms? She *was* very upset."

Blake doesn't look convinced. I move off to the side to stand next to him as the others take turns looking in the lavatory.

"This was beneath it," I whisper to him. I open the paper and scan it, half-worried it will incriminate me somehow.

The all-too-familiar handwriting reads: *Thought you might want this. It's only a matter of time before everyone in your life finds out.*

How can one of us be *this* cruel? My gaze lands on Simon, who stands alone behind one of the lounge chairs, clutching his textbook and staring at the red-stained carpet. He looks a bit dazed at the sight of so much blood, but not as disturbed as the rest of us.

I turn a questioning face to Blake. "Did Paige find this in her envelope?" She didn't look *that* distraught at dinner.

He shakes his head, brow furrowed.

Maybe someone slipped it into her blazer pocket. Could it be the same someone who left a peanut wrapper near my bag? That last part of the note reads a whole lot like a threat, as if someone planned on sharing her secrets beyond our group.

I can't shake the thought that, of all of us, Simon comes across as the most antisocial. Coldhearted, even. Maybe he knew that, despite his intelligence, he'd have a hard time winning over the committee, so he created a backup plan.

Before we can discuss the note further, O'Connor returns with Kumar. She motions for us to sit, and I stuff the paper into my pocket. "I'm sure this is a very difficult situation for you," she says. Her voice is infused with warm concern, soothing my overwrought nerves the tiniest bit. "As you might have guessed, it appears that Miss Hall has taken her own life. We're far enough over the Atlantic that we'll be continuing to Paris. The foundation will notify Miss Hall's parents once we arrive. I've been asked by the committee to communicate the following to you." She holds out a piece of paper and reads it aloud. *"Given these unique and troubling circumstances, the Goodwill Merit Award committee has decided not to award or deduct points based on today's competitions. All scores will remain at zero and candidates given equal rank heading into week one, where additional cuts will be made to compensate."*

I let out a small sigh, but guilt follows hard on the heels of my relief. The committee's generosity won't save Paige.

O'Connor folds the paper and goes on. "Sir Hamlin has asked me to play his next prerecorded message. In addition, two of us"— she gestures at herself and the other attendant—"will stay with you at all times, for your safety."

Evan snorts. "I feel so much safer."

A few of the others manage weak laughs as the lights dim.

Before the video starts, Kumar stoops to say something to Taylor. Taylor frowns but stands and allows Kumar to escort her forward, presumably back to her compartment in the nose of the plane.

Seconds later, Sir Hamlin's face glows from the big TV. "Welcome back, teams! How is everyone holding up?"

Bad, obviously. His singsong voice is jarring after what we've just seen. I dig my fingernails into my palm. Why, exactly, did we have to watch this?

"I hope you've come to see how difficult it can be to make decisions when you're holding someone else's fate in your hands. Hopefully, your team found a fair and equitable way to choose whom to downvote. Now, by my reckoning, the hour has grown late, and you're probably exhausted from a long day of travel. Please take this time to grab a snack, relax, get to know each other without the stress of a game, and perhaps catch a little sleep. In a few hours, you'll be nearly across the Atlantic, and it will be time for breakfast and one last game before landing. Enjoy your break!"

The video ends, but the lights stay dim. O'Connor picks up the intercom handset again. "I realize Miss Hall's death must be shocking and traumatic for you." She pauses, as if collecting herself. "Please know that if you need someone to talk to, either myself or Ms. Kumar would be happy to listen. I can't promise we'll have the answers, as we're not trained therapists, but we're here for you. In case anyone wants to sleep, we'll be leaving the lights low for the next few hours. Snacks and beverages are available upstairs in the lounge, or you can ask one of us." She gestures at herself and Kumar, who has reappeared and now stands near the entryway door. "If you need to use the restroom, there are lavatories in the far forward and far aft compartments, as well as two upstairs, off the lounge. Your safety and well-being are truly our highest concern. Please don't hesitate to ask if you have any questions."

My mind buzzes with questions, but they're probably not the kind O'Connor wants to answer. *How did nuts end up in Taylor's meal? If there's a lavatory in the front, closer to where she's sitting, why did she want to use this one? How did somebody access the intercom system to play those horrible messages?*

And perhaps most pressing of all, given how things are going: Is anyone else going to die?

13

IN NEED OF A FLOTATION DEVICE

9:20 p.m. CDT

I shake off my disturbing thoughts as O'Connor hangs up the handset. The others stir and look around, like we're waking up from some evil spell. I almost consider telling them about that threatening note for Paige I found in the lavatory, but then I decide against it. Whoever is trying to frighten the competition doesn't need to know that *I* know. Blake shoots me a questioning look, but when I shake my head, he doesn't say anything.

Liam drifts toward the entryway, and I wish I could follow, find some way to explain what happened earlier, but Dylan is working his way over. It's probably wise to clean up the mess with him first.

"Want to catch a movie or something?" he asks.

Not exactly the "Let's talk" I was anticipating, but he *is* a guy, and they're not always the best at talking about feelings. And I do need to figure out what's going on behind those clear hazel eyes.

"Like Netflix and chill?" I ask slowly.

"Noooo . . ." He drags out the word as he rolls his eyes. "Seriously, Em, what happened before was a total lapse of judgment. This is a stressful situation, and I was caught up in the moment. So were you, obviously." He gives me a pointed look. "The seats have movie screens. I just want to get my mind off all of this."

A lapse of judgment. Somehow, I manage to feel both hurt and relieved at the same time. Does that mean he's never had feelings for me? Or that he does but he doesn't want to act on them? I wish

I could pry open his brain to see inside. Instead, I settle for another question.

"What about Nikki?"

His brows pull together. "What do you mean?"

Over his shoulder, I watch Lily, Ann, and Amir stroll out to the entryway after Liam. Heading up to the lounge? And where's Olivia? Ah, helping Evan comfort Blake. That's really decent of them, especially after the way Blake spoke to Evan in the bedroom suite.

I force my attention back to Dylan. "I mean, how are we going to tell her about what happened?"

The puzzled expression doesn't leave his face. In fact, the frown grows deeper. "Why would we tell her? It'd just upset her."

He genuinely seems like he doesn't get it. I, on the other hand, feel like rushing for the lavatory to unleash the disgust churning in my gut. "Dylan, she's my best friend. I can't kiss her boyfriend and not tell her."

Yet I managed to steal her scholarship application and not tell her. The thought nearly buckles my knees. How did we reach this place?

"Of course, you're her best friend, Em. You're awesome, and she needs you." He places both hands on my shoulders and smiles. "But sometimes looking out for her means not telling her things that will hurt her. You know what I mean?" One eyebrow quirks as he makes a face I'd normally find adorable, but not right now.

Right now, it makes me nauseated.

"She deserves better," I say firmly, shaking his hands off my shoulders.

"Totally. I'm so glad we had this talk," he says, like he hasn't listened to anything I've said. "What do you want to watch?"

Nope. It's time to be done with this stupid crush I've harbored for years, and that means hanging out with other people. Besides, how else will I figure out who's trying to undermine the competition? I point to the doorway leading upstairs to the lounge. "You go ahead. I'm going to grab a snack."

He frowns, and his lips part, almost like he wants to press me. But then he stuffs his hands into his pockets. "Okay, sure. Catch you later."

Olivia has abandoned Evan and Blake and now lingers a few feet off, scanning the bookshelves at the back of the room. *Ha.* As if she's going to spend her free time reading. I'm kind of surprised she didn't chase down Liam. Is it because I told her I'm not with Dylan? She flashes Dylan a bright smile as he approaches, and I shake my head. She probably listened to half our conversation. No reason to hang around and see what happens.

The one person who's missing, though, is Simon. Where did he go? On my way upstairs, I take the long route and pause by one of the doorways to the seating compartment. No one's back here. Did I miss seeing him go up front, or did he head back to the tail? Maybe to our puzzle? For a second, I consider checking there, but then Blake and Evan walk in my direction.

"Sorry," I say, moving aside to let them through. Slinking off alone might look suspicious, especially after I just told Dylan I was heading upstairs, so I turn for the entryway.

The third flight attendant, Allard, descends the stairs, and I move over to let her pass. She tugs at her short purple jacket and offers me a curt nod, but the skin is blotchy around her eyes—a reminder that there are much bigger problems than my feelings for Dylan.

By the time I get upstairs, Lily and the others have gathered around the bar. Liam stands behind the counter like a bartender, pouring a bottle of water into a glass, while the other three perch on stools. I pause at the top of the stairs. They haven't seen me yet—I could still vanish back downstairs. Try to figure out where Simon went. What if I'm not welcome up here?

Too late. Lily catches my eye and waves, making her red hair bounce around her shoulders. "Hey, Emily. Come join us."

"Where's Dylan?" Liam asks as I walk toward them. His tone carries just a hint of surliness, but nobody else seems to notice. He passes the glass of water to Amir.

With Olivia, I *almost* say, but I change my mind. No reason to be petty. There's been enough ugliness on this flight already. Instead, I slide onto the open stool next to Lily and shrug. "Watching a movie or something?"

"I'm glad they're giving us a break." Ann pries open a bag of mini pretzels. "Poor Paige. It's so awful."

Liam clears his throat, and Ann goes suddenly quiet. That's right—he lost his best friend to suicide. This has to have hit way too close to home. "Can I get you a drink?" he asks me.

It's late. I should probably give up the caffeine. But something bubbly sounds pretty darn good right about now. "Diet Coke, please."

"On the rocks?"

"Is there an ice maker back there?" I lean forward over the counter but can't see much beyond Liam's leather shoes on a nice-looking laminate wood floor.

He scoops up ice in a glass and sets it on the counter. "But of course. This is a luxury jet. We have everything you could possibly want."

I laugh, savoring this bit of normalcy. It feels like hours have passed since we sat up here playing Two Truths and a Lie. Is there a chance he'll forgive me? If only I could talk to him alone.

After pouring a can of soda over the ice, he slides the glass to me.

Amir, who sits a few seats down, leans in. "Did you guys ever figure out who had your puzzle pieces?"

"It wasn't the Diamonds," I say. "I'm pretty sure we've got theirs, and I didn't see anything that looked like part of the Eiffel Tower." Liam's gaze flicks to me from the Mountain Dew he's pouring, but he doesn't say anything.

"Then I bet we have yours," Lily says. She digs into her blazer pocket and lays a pile of pieces on the counter between Liam and me. "They're definitely not part of our Arc de Triomphe."

I lean in to study them at the same time as Liam, our heads coming within a few inches of each other. Between the blue sky and the dark metal framing, I'm sure they're ours. When I glance at Liam to see what he thinks, his blue eyes are already studying me. Butterflies let loose beneath my ribs, a lovely reminder that there are, in fact, more guys in the world than just Dylan Roberts and that I'm not doomed to singleness. So long as I don't keep blowing my chances.

"Hey, look at that. I think you're right." I tear my attention away from him to turn to Lily.

"The game's off. You can have them," Amir offers. He glances at his teammates. "Unless either of you object."

My fingers creep toward the pieces, but then I stop myself. What would they be getting out of the deal? "No, that wouldn't be fair. Dylan's team must have yours. We should get them to trade too, so you get your pieces."

"Maybe we should set a time to meet back up and trade," Amir says. "Make it a group effort."

We all look to Liam—somehow it feels like the natural thing to do that whenever he's in the room—yet he doesn't respond. Instead, he pushes the puzzle pieces around on the counter in silence. Is it because he's trying to give others a chance to speak up, or does he not want to lead?

Finally, he nods. "Good idea. We could use some redeeming in the committee's eyes, don't you think?" His eyes flick to me again, and I look at my hands on the counter, anywhere but at his incriminating gaze.

"Let's go tell everyone," Ann says to Lily. She checks her wristwatch. "Say, meet downstairs in twenty minutes? That'd be ten till ten."

Hope bubbles inside my chest. If they all go, maybe I can snag a couple of minutes to talk to Liam alone. I should be trying to find Simon and figure out if he's the one behind the threats, but right now all I want is to try to fix things.

"Sounds good." Lily takes a last sip of her drink and slides off her stool to follow Ann. She turns to me and Amir, her eyebrows raised in question, but I've already leaned forward, planting my elbows firmly on the counter. I'm aiming for casual, but when she glances at Liam and then back to me, heat creeps up my neck. "Come on, Amir," she says.

I wait in thick silence as the three of them leave the upper level, their footsteps echoing softly on the stairs. Liam turns his back on me, busy washing his hands in the tiny stainless-steel sink. I take an awkward sip of my soda. How on earth am I supposed to begin this conversation? Maybe I should've gone with the other three.

Deep breath. Better to just get it out there, off my chest. "Liam, I'm really sorry about earlier. I didn't mean . . . I never meant . . ." Argh. Finding a way to explain is a lost cause. How can a language so full of nuance and borrowed words be so utterly useless sometimes?

He turns around as he finishes drying his hands. "To get caught?" There's no trace of a smile.

Frustration wells up inside me until tears prick at my eyes. "No, that's not what I meant. Dylan is with Nikki, but I've liked him since middle school." Why does it sound so immature to say aloud? *Get over it already, Emily.* The new me is moving on, letting Dylan go. And admitting the facts is a big step in the right direction.

"So you took your golden opportunity?"

I drop my head into my hands, digging my fingers into my hair. When I look back up, Liam is walking around the counter. He takes a seat on the nearest stool.

I grope for any possible explanation that might help him understand. Help *me* understand. Maybe there's nothing for it but total honesty. "Nikki is a lot like . . . Olivia. Gorgeous. Popular. Smart. She gets whatever she wants. She *expects* life to be that way." Bitterness leaks into my voice, but I can't stop it. My heart hurts when I think about all the years of friendship between us, Nikki and me. Shared secrets and silly made-up songs. Passed notes and giggling late into the night. But somewhere along the way, everything changed. And it happened so gradually I didn't see it until now, when I have some space from her. In some ways, our friendship has become a shell, like an egg that's been blown out and painted for Easter. Pretty on the outside, empty on the inside.

It hits me all at once how much I *miss* her, and the relationship we used to have. Deep down, maybe I've been blaming her for all of the negative things in our friendship. I didn't realize how much resentment I felt toward her.

Is that why I keep taking things from her? Like her application and her boyfriend? Because I hate what our friendship has become and I'm jealous of how easy her life seems?

But how much of that is *my* fault? It takes two people to wreck a relationship.

Heaviness settles over my chest. But Liam is still waiting for me to explain, so I suck in a ragged breath and keep going. "I never meant to kiss Dylan, and I'm certainly not trying to steal him. I've spent years wishing I could erase my feelings for him. But when he made a move on *me* . . ." It's hopeless. Liam will always think I'm a jerk.

"You gave in." His expression is serious, but his eyes have lost the hard edge.

"I gave in," I repeat. Because it's true. Apologies have never been my strength, but some of the weight lifts off my chest as the words gush out. "But it was stupid of me on so many levels. Not only because of Nikki, but also because I hurt our team. And you. You trusted me, and I'm sorry."

For the first time in what feels like hours, a tiny smile cracks his lips. "Thanks for telling me. I mean, it's not really my business, except for the team stuff. But you're cool, and I hate seeing you getting tangled up with a guy like that."

Warmth spreads across my cheeks, and I swirl the ice around in my glass to give my hands something to do besides fidget. "I didn't know Dylan was like that until this trip. I mean, I know he's a thrill seeker, but I never thought he'd cheat."

Even if Dylan did have a stress-induced lapse of judgment, like he claimed, that's a horrible excuse. *He* made the first move.

Liam's expression is serious as he nods. "Yeah, cheating on your girl, letting people think you're honest when you're not . . . that's pretty much for the lowest of the low."

My spirits plunge like they've been dunked in my icy drink. Because all I've done since I stole Nikki's application for this scholarship is lie about who I am. Come to think of it, I've been lying ever since my mom lost the house. Trying to pretend I'm as rich and popular and smart as everyone thinks I am, instead of just fessing up to the truth.

And on top of it, I cheated my best friend out of her chance to be here. So, really, how am I any worse than Dylan?

"Yeah." I can't bear looking into Liam's clear blue eyes anymore, so I stare at my glass. Any second now, he'll see the truth in my eyes: I'm a liar and a cheat. For one brief moment, some wild part inside urges me to tell him the truth.

I could do it—come clean—and get the rest of the burden off my back. But when I open my mouth, other words pop out. "I'm sorry about your best friend."

Liam is silent for so long I give in and look up. Now he's the one staring down, tracing a finger in the condensation on his glass.

"I'm sorry. I didn't mean to . . . If you don't want to talk about him, I totally get it."

"No, it's okay." His gaze meets mine again, and he offers a small, sad smile. "His name was James. He entered Scoatney on an athletic scholarship. His mom was single, his dad long gone, and he was bristlier than a porcupine. We all practically worshipped his skills on the field that first football season, but nobody dared hang out with him." As he gets lost in the memory, a smile curls his lips, that adorable one that makes his eyes sparkle.

"What changed?"

"Basketball season, freshman year. He and I got into a bit of a . . . sparring match."

Liam in a fight? When my eyes widen, he shakes his head.

"No, not like that. Just words. I was a little cockier back then. More to prove. Anyway, the only way to solve it was staying late in the gym shooting free throws. First one to miss two in a row was out, but we were both on fire that night. I don't think I've ever hit so many threes." Laughter dances on the edge of his words as his gaze focuses on some invisible scene from the past. "We missed dinner, so I invited him back to my room to hit my junk food stash. After that, we were inseparable."

He pulls out his phone, taps in a password, and holds up a picture of himself and a good-looking guy with black hair, both wearing gray mesh tanks with SCOATNEY written across the chest. Sweat drips off both their foreheads, and Liam's hair is tousled, but their smiles are huge.

"You know that night in jail the voice over the intercom mentioned about me?"

"Yeah?" Curiosity prickles my insides. Was it true?

Liam laughs and nods at the image on his screen. "James and I stole a rival school's mascot. It was this scrappy little ferret, and not only did we have to spend a night in jail, but the thing bit me, and I had to get rabies shots too."

I laugh with him, then look at the picture again, at the wide smiles on their faces. "You're so happy here."

"That was in February, at states. Right after we won our Elite Eight game. Scoatney's first time advancing to the Final Four in over two decades." Liam pulls the phone back, a smile lingering on his lips as he glances at his friend once more. Then he pushes a button and the screen goes black.

"Was that drawing of him, in your sketchbook?"

He sucks on his upper lip and nods.

Maybe I shouldn't ask this question, but it's burning right through me. "What . . . happened?"

From the weight of Liam's sigh, he knows I'm not talking about the basketball tournament. "I wish I knew. Things were tough for him at home. His mom was dating somebody new, and he had this older brother, out of school, who picked on him. All. The. Time. James told me about it a little, but after Christmas break, he grew more and more thoughtful. Reserved. He was always super smart, a top student, but he started blowing off homework." Liam's shoulders drop, and his eyes grow sad. "I tried to get him to open up, but he'd always laugh and get me to shoot hoops or play Xbox. If I'd known how serious it was, I would have literally dragged him into a counselor to get help. I feel like"—one of his hands balls into a fist—"I should've known. I should've been able to stop it."

"I'm really sorry, Liam." Automatically, my hand reaches for his sweater-clad arm, as if my touch could *possibly* comfort him. I stop, with my fingers hovering inches away, then jerk my hand back, in the hope he didn't notice.

No such luck. He's staring at the space my hand occupied only a second before. I shift my weight on the stool. Maybe I could lock myself in one of those private compartments for the rest of the flight.

"You can't blame yourself," I insist.

He drags a hand through his hair, doubt eating at his features. "But shouldn't I have seen it coming?"

"That was his decision. You can't hold yourself responsible for it," I say gently. When he doesn't respond, I go out on a limb. "Is that why you're holding back? Here?"

His brow furrows. "What do you mean?"

I shrug. "You're a natural leader. Everybody looks up to you. But . . . you've been a bit quiet. Removed."

He shifts his glass, rotating its base on the counter, and for a minute I'm afraid I've offended him.

But when he looks at me again, a smile plays on his lips, and his eyes are warm. The way he looked at me before that horrible spectacle with Dylan. "You might be right." He lets out another sigh—a short, decisive one this time—and sits a little taller. "Thank you."

"Friends?" I stick out my hand.

He takes it, his grip warm and strong against my palm. "Friends." We shake, and I could swear he lets his hand linger around mine a fraction of a second longer than necessary.

We should probably go find the others, see if they're ready to finish the puzzles. But it's nice to just sit here with him, like everything is normal. Besides, when he's looking at me like this—like there's no one he'd rather talk to—I can't drag myself off my seat. That achy place inside that's cared about Dylan for so long and felt hurt by Nikki's seeming indifference—not that she knew— doesn't hurt around Liam. So I keep talking. "I've never been on a motorcycle."

He laughs. "Technically, I haven't either. Unless we're counting those video games at Dave and Buster's."

"For real? How do you know you want one?"

"I dunno. I just always have. It was our thing, me and James. When we turned eighteen, we'd get our motorcycle licenses and buy sport bikes. Ride them together." He pulls out his phone again and shows me another picture, this time of a sleek blue-and-black bike. "I'll be eighteen in December. This is the one I want."

"That's pretty hot," I say, and a surge of warmth creeps up my neck. I have to resist the urge to fan my cheeks. Picturing Liam on that bike is even hotter.

From the way he's eyeing me, I'm sure he knows what I'm thinking.

"Do you"—my voice squeaks, and I clear my throat—"have a girlfriend?" Did that really just pop out of my mouth? Panic flares in my chest, and I jab a finger at the picture. "Because I'm sure she'll want a ride."

His lips quiver, like he's trying to keep from laughing at me. Probably staring at his lips right now isn't the right call, so I jerk my gaze to the nearly empty glass in my hands.

"No, I don't. I was dating this girl last year, but after basketball, and then what happened with James, we broke up." He presses his fingers to his forehead, then shakes his head. "And now, with this scholarship, I kind of took a break. From dating."

"Ah." When I glance back at him, I'm a little surprised to see a faint tint to his cheeks. "I'm not with anybody either," I say. As if that shouldn't be completely obvious after what happened. "Especially Dylan."

"Good, because he doesn't deserve you." He delivers the words matter-of-factly, as if there's no room to argue. Guilt eats at me. This would be another prime opportunity to tell the whole truth, but I can't. Not when we just became friends again.

"You're sweet," I say, both because it's true, and it's safe.

He holds my gaze, making my insides flutter. We may be halfway through this flight, but we'll still have at least a few days together in Paris—enough time for something more to happen if he's ready to move on. After all those wasted years pining over Dylan . . . maybe this is my chance to get it right. To do something for myself that doesn't involve Nikki *or* fixing my parents' issues.

As much as I'd love to spend the rest of the night peering into his blue eyes, I know the others will come looking for us any minute. Finally, I break the mood and say, "I guess we should head back downstairs."

"Yeah, I guess so."

I stand, and he follows me out of the lounge. My hand slides along the smooth railing, his just behind, sometimes only a hair's breadth from touching mine. For a few seconds, I forget about homelessness and cheating and the horrors of the day, and I dissolve into the simple pleasure of being a girl flirting with a cute boy.

Then we walk into the lounge and back into reality.

14

MISSING PIECES

9:50 p.m. CDT

Liam and I give the lavatory a wide berth as we enter the lounge. Somebody closed the door since the last time I was in here, and now there's a strip of blue tape stretched across it to seal it in place. The others sit in clusters around the room, even Taylor. Simon has reappeared too, poring over his book in a back corner.

I walk over to Taylor, Liam behind me. I still can't help wondering why she came in here for the bathroom earlier, instead of using the one in the nose. "Hey," I ask as we reach her, "feeling any better?"

"Yeah, I'm hanging in there." She gives me a weak smile.

"I'm surprised O'Connor let you out." It's only been about half an hour since they made her go back up front.

"I haven't seen her for a while. Not since . . ." She glances at the sealed lavatory door.

A shudder ripples down my spine. Where did they take Paige's body? Upstairs, to some hidden staff room behind the lounge?

Now would be a good time to ask Taylor about her lavatory choices, but before I can come up with a casual way to bring it up, she offers the information herself.

"I'm sick of being alone. That's why I came in here to use the restroom in the first place—I needed to be around other people before I went crazy. They didn't let me stay for the video. What's going on, anyway? What are we supposed to be doing?"

"Hamlin basically told us to take it easy for a few hours," I say, "and then we're supposed to have breakfast and another game before we land."

She frowns, probably thinking about the idea of another meal on this plane.

I point toward the entryway. "There are prepackaged snacks up there, like pretzels and chips. I can grab you something if you get hungry."

At the smile that lights up her face, my insides grow warm. It feels good to think about someone else, rather than my own messy problems.

"I'm good for now," she says, "but thanks."

I nod toward Liam and the others. "We're going to swap puzzle pieces so we can at least finish the puzzles. Who knows if the committee will care, but it seems like we might as well complete the task, you know?"

She nods. "Sure. Just let me know how I can help."

"Hey," Lily says as she and Ann join us. "Did you find Dylan or Evan?"

"Why? Are they missing?" I scan the room. Sure enough, neither of them is here. For a second, I'm caught off guard by the fact I hadn't even noticed Dylan's absence. He's usually the first person I spot in any room. Maybe the spell that's had a hold on me for so many years has finally broken. "Dylan said he was going to watch a movie."

"We checked the seating area." Lily throws a thumb over her shoulder in the general direction and offers me a sympathetic frown. "Simon was there, but no Dylan."

"Huh." I suck on my lip. "Wait, does Olivia know? I thought maybe she was with him."

"I'll ask her," Ann says.

Olivia's sitting on one of the benches near the windows, talking to Blake. Simon hovers close by, scowling but not engaging with them. What was he doing the whole time since we dispersed?

Ann weaves through the chairs to Olivia, then bends low. I can't hear the response, but the shake of her head and blond hair is unmistakable. Ann confirms when she comes back. "She hasn't seen him for a while. Apparently, they were going to watch a movie together but then Dylan changed his mind."

"Wait, if it's Dylan *and* Evan," I say, "maybe they went to work on their puzzle." That *is* the most reasonable explanation, right? Not that they've vanished or are busy planting peanut wrappers in people's luggage. Besides, I've already ruled the two of them out as suspects.

"That's probably where they went," Liam says from behind me. Amir stands next to him, and I make room to let them into the circle around Taylor. "Emily and I can go check."

It feels eerily silent above the ever-present vibration of the engines as Liam and I make our way toward the tail of the plane. Almost like we're entering a tomb built next to a generator. Weren't the flight attendants supposed to stay with us?

The dining room is empty, the Spades' puzzle nearly finished except for the handful of missing pieces. As stupid as it is, I glance beneath the table as we pass, like I'm going to find a body under there, or maybe just Dylan and Evan hiding and laughing at the rest of us.

Nobody is in the workstation compartment or our office either. That leaves the bedroom suite. We walk in through the doorway between the two closets. The bedroom is still, but a low rustling comes from the bathroom.

We peek in through the door, and the tension in my chest deflates instantly. Dylan is there, sitting on the cold tile, mounding up puzzle pieces and dropping them into his team's sack. He glances at us when we enter.

"Hey, what's going on?"

"Hey, man," Liam says—and I'm rather awed by how friendly he keeps his tone. "We're gathering back in the lounge to swap puzzle pieces."

I crouch next to Dylan. "Lily and her teammates tried to tell everyone earlier, but they couldn't find you."

"Did they check back here?" He scratches the top of his head. "I did use that lavatory in the nose. Maybe they missed me somehow."

"We're also looking for Evan," Liam adds, glancing around the bathroom. Not very many places to conceal another person in here, besides the shower, and somehow I doubt he's hiding out in there. "Have you seen him?"

Dylan shakes his head. "Not since earlier, when we were watching that foundation video." He slides the last pile into his bag.

"Why did you break it apart?" My eyebrows pull together as I point at the now-empty floor. "You guys had a lot left, but still . . ."

He shakes his head. "Blake busted it up when he came back here to argue about Paige." His eyes meet mine. When he sees me stiffen, he shrugs. "I think it was an accident. He was pretty upset."

"We heard him. But we're planning on swapping missing pieces to get the task finished." I eye the bag. "We kind of need to get yours done."

His shoulders slump, and he unties the string. He's about to dump the contents again when Liam stops him.

"Can we take it back to the front?"

"Or the upstairs lounge," I say, climbing to my feet. "It's way more comfortable. Plus maybe Taylor will want to help."

And there are snacks and drinks. I don't say it aloud, because here I am, thinking with my stomach again. It can't be normal for a teenage girl to be this obsessed with free food, can it?

"Good call." Dylan scrambles to his feet, and we all head out of the bathroom. "Should we keep searching for Evan?"

Liam shrugs. "I guess I could check the forward compartment."

When we reach the entertainment salon, Evan still isn't there. He's probably out cold somewhere, sleeping off this terrible flight. Liam heads for the compartment in the plane's nose.

Dylan holds up the bag to show the others. It's hard to tell in the dim lighting, but his cheeks look like they're tinted pink as he says, "We're not done."

Taylor groans. "What happened? I thought you guys started it."

"I'm sorry. It was my fault." Blake has the decency to look chagrined. "I accidentally stepped on it. They were building it on the floor. But I can help fix it."

"Let's take it upstairs," I say, pointing toward the entryway. "Anyone who wants to can help."

"I'm game." Taylor rises to her feet. When she wobbles slightly, Amir catches her arm.

"You sure?" he asks.

Taylor nods. "I need some food in me. Something safe. Emily said there are snacks up there."

"I'll come with you," I volunteer. Because while I may not be the class valedictorian or a top athlete or a brilliant anything else, turns out I *can* assemble a puzzle.

A small group of us head upstairs—me, Blake, Dylan, and Taylor, leaning on Amir's arm. For only being fifteen, he's admirably solicitous about his classmate's health.

When we reach the center bar, Amir and Taylor stop to get a snack while the rest of us head to one of the small tables. I perch on a seat as Dylan dumps the pieces out.

Still standing, Blake watches Amir and Taylor, then glances over his shoulder in the other direction. Does he expect someone else up here? Or is he just distracted?

"Want to lend a hand?" I say to him, managing to keep the sarcasm out of my tone. After all, he did just lose his girlfriend under horrible circumstances. Maybe this will help keep his mind busy.

Finally, he plops into a chair opposite Dylan. "Sure."

"Great. Find the edge pieces."

We work in silence for a few minutes until Taylor and Amir come back. She's holding a bag of pretzels and a can of Sprite, and as she takes a sip, her posture relaxes. She already looks less wobbly.

She smiles at me. "So much better. I think my blood sugar was getting too low. That epinephrine makes a person jittery."

As she takes the chair opposite me, Blake stands and offers his seat to Amir. "You can sit. I'm going to grab a drink."

As we work, I glance between Amir and Taylor. I hardly know anything about them beyond what the messages said earlier, and I'm going to give them the benefit of the doubt that none of it was true.

"Your school is in Boston, right?" I ask.

Amir nods without looking up. "Cambridge area, not far from MIT."

"Actually, it's closer to Harvard," Taylor says. "The area is very historic, beautiful old buildings, brick side streets, lots of green space." She pulls a pretzel out of her bag and turns to me. "Have you been to Boston?"

I exchange a look with Dylan and catch the grin playing on his lips. "In eighth grade, they took us up for a field trip to see the USS *Constitution* and Paul Revere's house. We had lunch at Faneuil Hall." I leave out the part where Nikki and I decided to explore the markets without telling anyone and would've missed the bus if Dylan and Braden hadn't found us. Ah, those were the good old days.

"So I gotta ask, Amir," Dylan says as he shifts pieces around, "did you really cut the power for three days?"

"Dylan." I subtly kick his ankle next to me. He can't just ask something like that, not unless we're all going to start talking about what the messages said about us.

But Amir flashes us one of his wide grins, and laughter crinkles around his eyes. "I'm going to plead the Fifth on that one. If whoever did it gets caught, they'd get in a crap ton of trouble. But it must've been some pretty admirable hacking." The underlying hint of pride in his tone is obvious.

"Must've made some people pretty upset," I say, hoping to pry a little deeper.

"Yeah"—he laughs—"the power company and city officials who had to figure out why their system wasn't secure."

Dylan laughs along with Amir, but I can't shake the irritation prickling my insides. After having lived with only a car battery and a cooler for two weeks, I can testify to the usefulness of appliances. Sometimes guys can be so immature.

"It'd be really annoying to lose power for that long," I say.

Amir shrugs. "It was only a couple of days. Besides, the weather was nice."

"It sucked." Taylor frowns. "I have an aunt who lives in South

Boston and had to pack her meds on ice to keep them from going bad."

The smile fades from Amir's face. "Whoever did it must not have thought about that kind of stuff." He casts his eyes back down to the puzzle.

Between his smile and his sense of humor, nothing about him shouts "evil mastermind." He genuinely seems like he wasn't trying to hurt anyone. A prank gone wrong? Most of us know a thing or two about that.

Taylor clears her throat. "What do you think this is a picture of?"

"Our puzzle is the Eiffel Tower," I offer. "You guys have the Arc de Triomphe, right, Amir?"

"Yeah," he says.

"So maybe another tourist attraction." Taylor tilts her head, scanning the pieces. "Any ideas?"

Several of the pieces are blue—sky, no doubt—along with some puffy white clouds. The majority, though, are shades of gray and black. Like the stonework of the Arc de Triomphe but darker.

"It must be a building," Dylan says after a moment. "Or a street, like the Champs-Élysées."

I squint, then pick up one of the pieces. A tiny pair of black eyes stares back at me. *Oh, that's creepy.* "Is this part of a face?"

"A gargoyle." Dylan's eyes light up. "Notre-Dame."

Of course. Why didn't I think of that? "Looks right to me." I snap the little face into place along a stretch of roof. "I wish we could've seen it before the fire there."

"Me too," Taylor says.

Blake drifts over to us, a Red Bull in one hand and a granola bar in the other. So much for helping. "How's it going?"

"Almost done," Amir says. "Now we're just looking for the extras."

Like the ones with the lighter-gray stonework . . . I hold one up triumphantly. "I think you've got part of the Spades' Arc de Triomphe."

Amir's big smile returns. "Now we just need all six of them."

Blake sets aside his drink and crouches between Dylan and Amir to help sort through the remaining pieces. But before we're finished, thumping sounds on the stairs.

"You guys almost ready?" Lily calls.

"Five minutes," I say.

"Okay." She vanishes back down the stairs.

"I wonder if they found Evan," I mutter.

"Yeah, it's weird." Dylan's brow furrows. "He would want to help if he knew we were working on this."

With a soft curse, Blake accidentally knocks some pieces off the table and bends over to pick them up. Is it my imagination, or is his face paler than it was a moment ago? Does he know something he's not telling?

As much as I'd like to believe we're all trustworthy, *somebody* aired those messages about us. And left Paige a razor blade. And stuffed an empty peanut wrapper into the overhead bin. Maybe even put the peanuts in Taylor's food. And while Simon seems like the most likely culprit so far, is it possible I'm wrong?

Could Blake have had something to do with it? But why?

Does he need to win so badly he'd put his own girlfriend in jeopardy?

It hardly seems possible. But if the recording was right about him, maybe between his grades and steroid use, he's in danger of being kicked off the football team. That would rule out his chances at a college athletic scholarship and a future in the NFL, which could make this competition a lifeline.

And what about Simon? With his brains, can't he get into any Ivy League school he wants? I suck on the inside of my cheek. There must be something I'm overlooking, some clue that will snap everything into place and complete the picture, like the missing puzzle pieces.

In a few more minutes, we've found all six of the extra pieces, which I hold out in my hand. "Here are the extras. Should we go down now?"

Dylan stands and stretches. A yawn slips out as he says, "Yeah, I think we're good here."

The others stand too—except for Blake, whose gaze flits between the pile in my hand and my face, almost like his thoughts are focused somewhere else entirely. Finally, he says, "You all take them. I'll stay here to finish."

"Are you sure?" Taylor asks. "We can all stay. There isn't much left."

"No, it'll only take me a minute or two."

We glance at each other. Taylor shrugs, I say, "Okay," and Dylan leads the way to the stairs. I look back at Blake as I head out of sight around the bar. He's taken Amir's seat and is staring at some point on the wall above the closed window shades, lost in thought.

After what he's been through today, wanting time alone is perfectly understandable. Right?

As we enter the downstairs entertainment salon, the others look up expectantly.

"Is Evan back?" Dylan asks them.

Liam shakes his head. "No one has seen him. He wasn't up front."

Where did Evan go? It's not like there are a lot of options. We're on an airplane, forty-two thousand feet in the air. Uneasiness pulls at my stomach. Maybe we should've checked the lavatories upstairs.

The others seem to sense the change in mood too. They shift in their seats, talking in low voices. Olivia keeps scanning the room like she expects Evan's dead body to appear out of thin air any second. I'd like to keep imagining he's just taking a nap somewhere, but after what happened to Taylor, and then Paige, not to mention those humiliating messages . . .

Lily and Ann have already laid a pile of their extra pieces on the coffee table in the center of the sitting space. Even from here, the metal bars of the Eiffel Tower are obvious. I drop the ones from upstairs in a different corner, and Liam adds our extras. It only takes a moment to claim the correct piles. Liam grabs ours, Amir collects the Spades', and I gather the last one. Another gargoyle head stares at me. "I'll run these back up to Blake."

Without waiting for a response, I take the stairs to the second floor. But when I round the edge of the center bar and the Notre-Dame puzzle comes into view, Blake is gone.

A few of his puzzle pieces lie scattered on the floor. *Weird.*

Despite the fact there's probably some perfectly reasonable explanation, my breath freezes in my lungs. I check around the back of the bar, with its ceiling-height refrigerator case, but he isn't there.

My chest tightens, and I force myself to set the handful of pieces down on the table. I pick up the ones on the floor and add them to the pile, as if that will set the world straight. It's ridiculous to react this way.

The puzzle is nearly done. Maybe Blake went to the bathroom. Despite the way my hand is trembling—low blood sugar like Taylor?—I push the remaining pieces into place. The last one snaps into the sky with a soft, satisfying click. The fact that it's not my team's puzzle doesn't diminish my sense of accomplishment.

If only the rest of my life worked this way—scattered pieces that I could gather and fit into place, creating a beautiful picture. But I'm afraid my life is far more like the bags we were given originally: some pieces missing, some belonging to someone else's puzzle. I'll never make a whole picture. I'll never be in control.

I'll always be someone who has to cheat to get a chance at a top college, because she's not good enough to earn a scholarship fair and square. Not with my life upside down and a bad GPA I can't repair in time and a gorgeous best friend everyone loves, thanks to whom I gave up my shot at an athletic scholarship for softball too.

Maybe it's not that I'm missing pieces. Maybe I don't even have my own puzzle. Maybe I'm just a piece in Nikki's.

And not just hers—my mom's, my other friends', Dylan's. All the people I'm always trying to please, instead of taking responsibility for my own life. The thought knocks the air out of my lungs. How did I let things get to this place?

Then I shake my head and force my tired feet back around the bar toward the top of the stairs.

I'm halfway across the room when the lights go out.

15

THE THIRD GAME

10:19 p.m. CDT

The room plunges into darkness. Down below, somebody screams, high-pitched and frantic, launching my pounding heart into my throat.

The absolute we're-going-to-crash-and-die blackness lasts for a microsecond before I realize emergency strips are glowing in blue tracks running along the edges of the floor and in a path leading to the stairs. Probably meant to guide passengers to the nearest exit.

At the same time, the captain makes an announcement over the intercom. "Sorry, folks, looks like we're having an issue with the cabin lighting. Hang tight for a minute while we get it squared away."

His calm tone settles some of my nerves, and I'm cautiously continuing toward the stairs when I hear thumping coming from the back of the lounge. And more yelling, but this time it's on this level of the plane.

After flipping on my phone's flashlight, I spin around and inch toward the noise, running a hand along the edge of the bar counter to orient myself. A voice in my head wisely insists I go away from the sound instead of *toward* it, but somebody needs help—I can't just run. Past the bar, a white-and-red EXIT sign glows above the door leading to the staff quarters. There must be an emergency exit back there.

The thumping, though, is coming from behind a bulkhead.

"Hey," a muffled voice calls from one of the lavatories. *Blake?* "Who shut off the lights?"

I stop outside the door on the left. "Blake, is that you?"

"Yeah," he says. Some of the worry in my chest deflates like a balloon. At least now I know where he's been. "Can you get me out of here? The latch is stuck."

The OCCUPIED sign casts a soft orange glow near the door's handle. It's the kind of door that folds inward, like you'd find on a typical commercial airline. I push on it, but it doesn't budge.

"Can't you just slide it open?" I ask.

"No, it won't move."

I shake the handle, which only succeeds in rattling the flimsy door. The flight attendants had some way to unlock the lavatory downstairs. Maybe they can open this one too. "I'll have to get help. There's nothing I can do from out here."

"Okay. Just hurry," he says. "I'm getting claustrophobic."

Ugh, I can't blame him. Being locked in an airplane lavatory nearly ranks up there with being trapped in a porta-potty on my list of worst-case scenarios. And after the way we found Paige, this situation must be extra traumatic for him.

I try the staff door first, but as I expected, it's locked. Besides, the flight attendants were supposed to stay with us. Though now that I think about it, I haven't seen any of them for a while.

The lights are still out by the time I make it back to the entertainment salon. At least no creepy messages have been broadcast over the intercom. And no one has died.

Both big pluses after the flight we've had so far. It's hard to imagine we'll still have to compete for a scholarship once this nightmare is over.

Dark, still shapes fill the compartment like a nighttime game of

Statues in the Garden. Phone screens flicker in bursts of flashing blue light. Nobody is screaming anymore, but their soft murmuring whispers create a low buzz that harmonizes with the engines.

I step into the room and walk to the nearest person—a girl with long hair, probably Olivia—and touch her gently on the arm. "Hey, have you seen—"

She lets out a little shriek, jumping a good six inches and pressing a hand to her heart while offering a few choice words. Definitely Olivia.

"It's me. Emily," I say. "Chill out."

"Are you the one who turned off the lights?"

"*No*, of course not." Don't tell me they're going to blame *me* again. "Blake's stuck in a lavatory upstairs. Where are the flight attendants?"

"I don't know. We haven't seen them," she says.

Another shape looms next to her—tall enough it's got to be one of the guys—and the whiff of ocean scent tells me it's Dylan. He steps around Olivia and wraps his hands around my shoulders, pulling me into him. "You're okay," he says, relief gushing out of his voice.

It's sweet he was worried about me, but I place my hands on his chest and wriggle free.

"Yeah, I'm fine," I say casually. If our last conversation wasn't enough for him to take the hint, I'll just have to keep making it clear I'm not interested. Because I'm not. "Is everyone else here?"

It's impossible to tell in the darkness. The phone lights randomly illuminating bright patches only make things more disorienting. We're still whispering too, which doesn't make sense. Why do we need to whisper just because the lights are out?

I take a few steps deeper into the room. "Hey, has anybody seen the flight attendants?" The words feel painfully loud in the dark room, like I'm violating some ancient Egyptian crypt.

There's a general and unhelpful chorus of nos in response, and one of the taller statues moves over to my side.

"Em, is that you?" Liam's voice instantly calms some of my nerves, like a hot bath at the end of a long day. His phone light sweeps across my face, then drops to my feet. The heat emanating from him makes me want to slide closer.

I tell him about Blake, trapped upstairs.

"Huh," he says. I can't see his face in the dark, but I can imagine his blue eyes lost in thought. "I'm kind of surprised one of the flight attendants isn't in here with a flashlight."

"Yeah, me too." I press my lips together as uneasiness burns a hole through my chest. The lights go out, there's a kid trapped in the lavatory, and now the flight attendants are conspicuously absent. What's more, nobody's seen Evan in far too long. And where is Simon? Is he here, or did he conveniently vanish again? "Is anybody else missing?"

Liam shines his phone flashlight around the room, catching more than one person blinking and covering their face in the bright beam. Ah, there's Simon, just stepping into the room from the seating compartment. Where has *he* been?

"Only Blake and Evan," Liam says. He turns to Simon. "Did you see the attendants back there?"

Simon shakes his head. "No, but I wasn't paying attention." He must have been finishing our puzzle. Is it possible he tampered with the lights? Somehow, it feels like too big of a stretch. He wasn't gone *that* long, was he? Just the amount of time I was upstairs finishing Dylan's puzzle.

"Maybe the attendants are trying to get the power back on,"

I offer, though that's a feeble excuse. All three of them?

"Maybe." Liam sounds like he's only saying it for my sake.

The floor shifts as the plane bounces through a pocket of rough air, knocking me off-balance. When I accidentally bump into Liam, he slips an arm around me and pulls me close, his hand resting on the small of my back. A light, fresh scent of cotton and citrus wraps around my senses.

"Steady?"

"Yeah." I breathe the word out in a mere whisper, because how can I think straight cocooned against him like this? Even if he *is* only doing it to make sure I don't fall.

A moment later, he raps on the nearest table. "Hey, guys, listen up!" His voice carries this calm, confident air of authority that makes everybody get quiet. Maybe he's taken my words to heart. "Blake's trapped in the bathroom upstairs, and we've got to find the attendants to unlock it for him."

"In the dark?" Olivia squeaks.

"You have a flashlight on your phone." Liam doesn't bother checking his derisive tone. "Find a partner if it makes you feel better," he says to Olivia. Then to everyone, "Meet back here in ten minutes."

Liam tugs my hand in the dark. "Come on."

Heat pulses through my veins as I wrap my hand around his, making me suddenly giddy despite the circumstances. Of course he's just keeping us together to search—it's not like we're *holding hands* holding hands. But of all these people, he chose me.

"This is kind of ridiculous," I say, just to get my mind to focus on anything besides how good his hand feels around mine. "Is the scholarship committee messing with us? Like, the third game is Find the Flight Attendants in the Dark?"

"I hope not. Otherwise, I made a serious mistake signing up for this competition." He leads the way aft, guided by the emergency strips and his bright phone light. The others head in different directions.

We pause in the seating compartment, scanning the seats and aisles, but there's no sign of Evan or any flight attendants, so we keep going.

Lily, Ann, and Amir are in the dining compartment, checking beneath the table when we enter. I let go of Liam's hand before any of them notice.

"You guys want to double-check the kitchen and storage too?" Liam asks.

"Sure," Amir says.

We continue past them, through the hallway with the doors for the staff spaces, and on into the room with the workstations. There's no one here. It's like the flight attendants have vanished, the same as Evan.

"The door to the staff area upstairs was locked," I say. "Maybe they're up there."

"Fixing the lights?" Liam asks. "Surely one of them would've come down, like they did when the intercom failed."

Unless . . . they *can't* come check on us. I banish the awful thought.

Our puzzle still lies on the desk in the office suite, only now it's finished. I pause, shining my light on it, and admire the completed Eiffel Tower.

"You'll get to see it soon," Liam says softly.

A little thrill zips through my body. I've seen the world's famous landmarks so many times in pictures, but never in person. "You're telling me this flight is going to be worth it?"

"Absolutely. And I speak from experience."

"You've been to Paris?"

"I've been all over Europe. Hong Kong and Japan too. My father is a management consultant and travels a lot for work. When I was younger, my mom would take my sister and me along. To see part of the world, they said."

Sadness tinges my heart at his words. Dad and I had some fun on our trips during my middle school years, seeing the country. He'd take me with him when he had work conferences, back before Mom made him so angry with her insistence on dumping cash into that home-based "business" that he quit paying child support. And quit coming to see me. But somehow, even though my dad is long gone, traveling makes me feel a little closer to him, a little more like the way things used to be.

"Is that what you want to do when you grow up?" I smile at the last few words. We're entering our senior year in high school—we're practically grown up already. "Go into consulting?"

In the darkness, I can hear him scratching his head. "My dad wants me to, but I'm not sure about it." His words remind me of what the message said about him, about his father never showing up to his games. Maybe his family isn't Facebook-perfect either.

"Does that bother him?" I ask.

He's silent, and I bite the inside of my cheek. *Note to self—learn to keep mouth shut.* But in all honesty, it feels pretty darn good to have a real conversation with somebody for a change. When did my relationships get so surfacy and shallow?

"Yeah," he says finally. "I think so. He's not into sports the way I am. Doesn't understand how I could want to be a broadcast sports journalist. I guess . . . it's hard to live up to family expectations."

At least his family *has* expectations. Mine is just trying to stay afloat.

"What about you?" he asks.

My mouth goes dry, and I swallow. "I . . ." I can't even think of a decent lie, so I throw caution to the wind. "I have no clue. My life is kind of messy right now."

"You don't say." His voice quivers, like he thinks I'm referring only to the chaos here on the plane, and the irony of what I've just said hits me full force. Laughter bubbles up inside me, and I can't keep it in. He laughs too.

I've been pretending to have it together for so long it feels blessedly comfortable to tell him even a bit of the truth. Part of me wants to just blurt out everything—about my parents, and living in my mom's car, and needing this scholarship so badly I cheated. But how much can I dump on him before he walks away? The way my dad left my mom. If she deserved it, I certainly do.

He saves me from saying anything I'll regret. "So that lawyer thing you said during the introduction . . . ?"

I shrug. "It sounded good, didn't it?"

"Yeah, it did." In the edge of my phone's flashlight, he's looking at me with that you're-adorable smile that makes my insides melt. Except this time, it isn't coming from Dylan, and it's true and real and meant only for me.

"I'll figure it out eventually." My voice squeaks, but thankfully he doesn't seem to notice.

Every nerve in my body fires as I realize how close we're standing, like we've unconsciously gravitated toward each other in the last few minutes. His soft scent wraps around me like a warm blanket, drawing me toward him. Does he realize the effect he has on me?

Does he feel the same way?

"I suspect you'll be great at whatever you choose," he says.

"Just as long as you stop underestimating yourself."

"Thanks." Heat floods my cheeks at the undeserved praise, but the darkness covers my embarrassment. I tuck a strand of hair behind my ear.

My heart skips as Liam's hand follows mine, his fingers slowly tracing the length of hair like it's the finest of silk. He clears his throat as he lets go. "Sorry, I've been wanting to do that since I met you."

"I don't mind." My voice comes out all breathy, and I clamp my lips shut before something stupid pops out. Like *Please kiss me.*

Unless he's thinking the same thing.

I don't breathe as time stills. The air between us crackles.

But before either of us moves, light flickers outside the doorway to the office. The others have caught up.

Liam clears his throat. Rubs a hand on the back of his neck.

"Guess we should keep looking." My voice comes out an octave too high.

"Hey," Amir says as he enters. "You guys check the bedroom suite yet?" He points his phone at the door, and for the first time, I realize someone has pulled it shut.

"No, we were going there next," Liam answers.

I walk around the desk. My hand hovers over the inset metal handle. "Who closed the door?" I ask Liam. "Was it like this earlier when you all finished the puzzle?"

He shrugs. "I don't know. Simon was the only one who came back here."

The skin on my arms prickles as I slide the door into its recessed slot. It's dark in here, even darker than the rest of the plane. There's no lighting on the floor, but there are a couple of emergency lights tucked into the ceiling.

The bedroom is empty.

Through the open bathroom doorway, the beam of light from my phone tracks across gleaming white tile and stops on something dark on the floor. The edge is . . . fluid. Like a puddle. Goose bumps pop on my arms as a chill tracks its way up my spine. That wasn't there before.

The air doesn't smell the same either. Before, it had that recirculated-air scent mixed with some sort of light, fresh fragrance, like bathroom soap. Now, though, something metallic bites at my nose as I slowly cross the bedroom.

"Emily . . ." Liam's voice is low, his tone nervous—like he, too, senses something is very wrong.

The narrow beam of my phone light stays locked on the dark puddle as I reach the doorway, and the sharp tang fills my senses. Blood.

It's blood.

That image of Paige—her arms dangling, head lolling back as the flight attendant carried her lifeless body away—flashes so forcefully into my mind my legs tremble. More beams of light hit my back, casting a giant shadow version of myself onto the glass shower door at the far end of the tile. The others press behind me.

"What happened?"

"Who is it?"

I hear the words, but the questions don't fully register as I reach the doorway and sweep my light across the space. This isn't a *puddle* of blood; it's a *lake*. And the island in the center is Evan Randall.

Bile burns my throat. I clutch the doorway, swaying slightly, and tighten my grip on my phone. When my knees start to give way, Liam catches me and keeps me from falling. My breath comes shallow and fast, and it takes serious effort to force myself to breathe deep enough to avoid hyperventilating. I lean into Liam's chest, but I can't stop myself from looking back.

Evan lies at an awkward angle, his feet toward the door, arms splayed at his sides, upper body slumped against the big Jacuzzi tub next to the shower. His hands are ashy gray, the fingers curled in like he was clinging to life until the last possible second.

Even before I see his face, I know there won't be anything we can do to help.

My beam of light trembles as I let go of Liam and force my hand upward, stalling out on the ragged gash across Evan's neck. That explains the blood.

He stares at me with glass-marble eyes, like he could be a figure in a wax museum. Not a boy I saw alive an hour ago. A boy who wanted to play baseball and win a college scholarship and make his family proud. Even if he was failing school and concealing an injury, he didn't deserve *this*.

"Oh my—" Ann shrieks beside me, then mutes herself as she presses her hands to her mouth. Lily and Amir try to peek in around our shoulders.

Each second feels unnaturally long as we stare at the empty shell that used to be Evan. Liam places a hand on my shoulder and squeezes between me and Ann to enter the bathroom. He steps gingerly around Evan's feet, keeping his flashlight beam on the ruby-hued liquid marring the white marble tile. The rest of us stay locked in place, watching wide-eyed.

Liam crouches down on the far side of Evan's body, keeping his distance from the edge of the blood, and aims his light at the sliced skin of his neck. The phone's radiance illuminates the shadowy darkness, revealing the grisly truth. Beside me, Lily turns away and lets out a muffled scream, like she's pressing her face into her elbow.

The cut is deep—deep enough to expose and sever the delicate arteries and veins of Evan's neck, which stick out like fading red and blue straws.

"He did not do this to himself." In our phone beams, Liam's face is so pale it's almost green. "The cut is way too deep. Nobody could force themselves to do *that*."

"What if . . . he fell on something?" Ann asks. "Like set up a blade and . . ."

I sweep my phone across the bathroom. Nothing appears out of place.

"Besides"—I shake my head—"we were just back here with Dylan like thirty minutes ago. There was definitely no dead body."

Liam glances at me, a question written across his features. Does he think Dylan did it? That maybe he locked Evan up in the closet, or even in that big tub, and then snuck back here to kill him after we left?

I keep shaking my head. "Dylan didn't do this." He wouldn't. Every cell in my body refuses to accept that idea, even though just six hours ago I would've claimed he'd never cheat on Nikki either. "It had to be someone else."

My thoughts immediately flit to Simon, who was absent earlier, when Evan went missing. The others found him in the seating compartment, but no one found Evan until now. Could Simon have done this after he finished the puzzle?

Threatening the competition is one thing, but killing us off . . . ? The idea is horrifying.

"Wait, is he holding something?" Lily shines her light on Evan's left hand. Unlike the other hand, which lies palm-up and empty, his left fingers are curled around something white and crumpled.

"Keep the light on it for me." Liam sets his phone down on the floor and pries open the fingers, extracting a piece of paper. He retrieves his phone and gingerly tiptoes back around the body, careful not to disturb it.

"Should we close his eyes?" Amir asks. "It's what they do in movies."

We stare once again at the lifeless face. There's enough blood that it would be hard to reach his eyelids without stepping in it. And touching that waxy, gray skin . . .

"Maybe just close the door for now," I suggest. "We've still got to find the flight attendants. Either way, we probably shouldn't disturb the scene."

"What about when we land, though?" Ann asks, her voice weak.

The same thought occurs to all of us: the jostling, bouncing plane touching down and slamming on the brakes with a dead body loose in the bathroom in a lake of congealed blood. Lily's nose crinkles, and Ann frowns. Maybe it's hysteria caused by trauma, but for one mad second I feel like laughing. Like we're in some modern version of *Monty Python and the Holy Grail* and Evan's not really dead. Just an actor surrounded by ketchup.

"The flight attendants can decide what's best," Amir says, saving me from the mortification of giving in to what would've been entirely inappropriate.

"We'd better go tell the others." Ann heads for the office.

"What does the paper say?" Lily asks.

I'd nearly forgotten it. Now we all stop and watch as Liam unfurls the crumpled ball. The paper crackles as he holds it out.

My heart lurches. Four words, in the same handwriting I've seen far too often on this flight.

New game. Who's next?

16

STRANDED

10:40 p.m. CDT

The five of us stick close together as we work our way back through the plane, the words on that paper hovering like an invisible sword of Damocles over our heads. Lights flicker in our faces when we reach the dining compartment, and Amir, who is in the lead, throws his arms up to shield his eyes.

"Hey, we can't see," he says.

"Sorry." Dylan drops his light, and the glimpse of curly dark hair and blue blazer behind him must be Taylor.

"Did anybody find the flight staff?" Ann asks. Her voice floats at the end of the question with a hint of hopefulness.

Silence.

"Something must have happened to them." I hate to be the one to say it, but after what happened to Evan, it's the only logical conclusion. It's hard to keep my voice steady.

"Why?" Taylor asks. "What did you guys find?"

Dylan walks around her, stopping a few paces from me. He scans me with his light, and I blink furiously in the blinding beam before he drops it again. "You okay?"

No, not really. But since I'm trying to act like I've got things together, all I say is, "We found Evan. In the bathroom." I jerk my thumb over my shoulder, though no one can see in the dark.

"The bathroom?" Dylan repeats, like the words don't make sense.

"He's dead." Liam's words ring in the silence.

Taylor gasps, swaying like she might go down, until Amir offers her an arm.

"What . . . what happened?" she stammers.

"We don't know," Lily says. "His throat was . . . slit."

Next to me, Dylan places both hands on the top of his head, his flashlight beam illuminating his hair like a golden halo. He lets out several quick, short breaths in succession.

"What are we gonna do?"

"We need to gather the others," Liam says, his voice steady and sure.

Like stray cats. We've spent half this flight trying to "gather the others." Is that when the killer makes his or her moves? Because there *is* a killer on board. If what happened with Taylor and Paige wasn't enough to prove it, Evan's death has removed all doubt.

"And we really need to find an adult," Ann adds.

I'm caught off guard by the sudden, intense longing for everything to be okay. A need for security. How long has it been since I truly felt safe? Like someone capable was taking care of me? Maybe not since Dad left and me and Mom were on our own. Even my friendship with Nikki, my cornerstone for years, has decayed without me knowing it. I've become a piece of driftwood tossing on the churning ocean waves.

"The pilots." Dylan's words snap me out of my uncomfortable thoughts. He pushes past me, like he's going to bust open the cockpit door this second.

"Hold up, man," Liam says, grabbing his arm. "We need to make a plan. Together. Without freaking out."

"I'm not freaking out." Dylan shakes him off, but then I catch his blazer sleeve.

"Dylan, wait. We can't just barge in there. They can't come out, legally. I mean, maybe the copilot could, but if something happened to him . . . What if that's the killer's end goal? To get into the cockpit?" All we need is a plane crash to top off this lovely experience.

"If we told them," Amir says, "maybe they could get us to a nearer airport at least."

"We're halfway across the Atlantic right now," Lily says. "Where can they possibly go?"

Dylan slumps back, leaning against one of the dining room chairs. "Bermuda?" He says it wearily, no trace of humor, but I almost laugh. Where else should we end up but the Bermuda Triangle? Hysteria must be unraveling the edges of my sanity, already frayed by so many hours of unshakable anxiety.

"Preferably somewhere with a hospital and a police force," Taylor says.

"Let's just find Simon and Olivia, okay?" Lily says. "Then we can try to find a way to communicate with the pilots."

As we head through the seating compartment toward the salon, out of nowhere the lights flicker, then turn on. Not full strength, but dimmed for night, the way they were before they went out. We breathe a collective sigh of relief.

A hopeful smile flutters across Ann's face. "Maybe the flight attendants did this. Maybe they're fine."

Up above, the captain's voice issues from the speakers. "Thanks for your patience, folks. Looks like we're back up and running with normal lighting. Please relax and enjoy the flight."

I snort. As if we're going to do any relaxing with a growing body count. "If we can't find the flight attendants, we've *got* to tell the pilots. They need to know what's going on out here."

Liam keeps close as we follow the aisle toward the entertainment salon. "It's a good idea, but let's tell the others first. And see if the flight staff shows up now that the lights are on again."

His presence and his words are reassuring, reminding me I'm not alone in this mess. The thought is like a balm to my tattered soul, and I edge a little closer to him.

The entertainment compartment is starting to feel like home, despite my growing collection of bad memories. The comfy, cream-colored leather furniture invites us in, and we wearily collapse onto it.

"Oh, look what we found in my seat." Taylor nods toward Dylan, who pulls a tiny gold box tied with a red ribbon out of his blazer pocket. He opens it, keeping it away from Taylor. Brown bits sit nestled inside. "Chopped peanuts."

Probably straight out of that package someone left near my bag. My throat tightens. Someone *did* try to kill Taylor, and now they want us to know it.

Then Paige, then Evan.

This. Is. A. Nightmare.

Blake enters a few seconds later. There's a spring to his step that was missing before, like that Red Bull he drank gave him a second wind. When I catch his gaze, my eyebrows shooting up in question, he lifts a hand. "I finally got the stupid thing open. Had to brace my foot against the sink and yank." He pauses, glancing around at our pale faces. "What happened?"

Nobody bothers answering. Not yet.

Finally, Simon and Olivia walk in through the entryway, Olivia in front, Simon two steps behind. Despite being alone with him, she looks unharmed, except for the scowl etched on her face. And Simon . . . He almost looks like he's *smiling*. Like his entire endgame is tormenting Olivia. My brows pinch together. Is it possible I'm wrong about him?

Liam rises once everyone is assembled. Runs a hand through his hair, paces back and forth. Then he pauses and surveys our faces. "We found Evan."

"Dead," Ann adds. Her jaw clenches. "In the tail bathroom."

The three of them take the news about as well as we did. Olivia's face pales, and she wraps her arms across her stomach. Dylan crosses over to her in a second, tugging her against his side into a short embrace. Blake runs both hands through his hair, and his chest rises and falls in rapid breaths. Even Simon looks rattled.

Liam gives them a chance to absorb the news, then asks, "Simon, was the bedroom door shut when you finished the puzzle?"

Simon's face scrunches into a frown, then he slowly shakes his head. "Maybe? I didn't look."

Liam nods. "Anyone see the flight attendants?"

Nine heads shake in response, mine included, though he already knows what *I* found.

Amir drops into a seat, clutching his head with his hands. "This can't be happening," he mutters. Then he straightens. "They've got to be upstairs," he says, hope making his eyes grow wide again.

"Or below." Simon huffs out another big you-guys-are-hopelessly-dense sigh to accompany his eye roll. Like this should be totally obvious. "A plane this size has another full level down there for cargo and mechanicals." I'm kind of surprised he could dig his nose out of his calculus book long enough to bother sharing this tidbit of knowledge.

Liam stares past us. "Yeah, you're right. I hadn't thought about that. Access must be from the staff quarters."

"It is." All eyes turn to Simon, and he holds up his hands as if to fend us off. His cell phone glows white in one palm. "I don't know from *experience*. But it's hardly rocket science to google 'A380 floor plan.' Three levels are standard, with the lowest accessible from the exterior and from an interior elevator shaft."

More than one of us start tapping on our phones, our faces glowing in the light of the screens.

"Don't bother." Simon's voice is matter-of-fact. "They shut off the Wi-Fi before dinner, remember? I downloaded this earlier."

Sure enough, I get a dinosaur instead of a Google search tab when I open Chrome. A sinking feeling develops in the pit of my stomach. Or maybe it's just deepening, because it's been there all along. The flight attendants are gone, Evan and Paige are dead, and we have no connection with the outside world. Not that anyone could help us, so many miles above the frigid Atlantic.

We're stranded.

What's even scarier, though, is that the killer must be right here in this room. One of these agitated, frightened-looking teenagers who wants to win so badly they're willing to literally eliminate the competition. Someone here is an excellent actor.

"Who did it?" Olivia squeaks, her words reflecting the dark direction of my own thoughts.

Taylor, who's sitting next to her, has her arms wrapped across her chest as her gaze flits around the room. "Surely not one of us?"

I feel her question viscerally, like it grates against every fiber of my being to believe one of us could be so evil. But what other answer is there?

"Okay, hold on," Liam says. He starts pacing back and forth again. "There's no reason to assume that. Maybe the foundation is messing with us. Not Evan and Paige . . . but the other stuff that happened. The messages. The lights."

"Because *that* would be totally legal . . ." Simon's sneer fades away at Liam's sharp look.

"What motive would they have?" Ann asks. "They already have the competition set up to pick one of us for the scholarship. There's no point."

"It could be a personal attack, from one of the committee members."

"Like Hamlin himself? Out to get all of us?" Dylan says. The inflection in his voice tells me he's being sarcastic, taking a jab at Liam, but Liam shakes his head.

"We can't rule out the possibility," he insists, "not yet. Is there something we all have in common? Something linking us together?"

We glance at each other, a few people shrugging, a few eyebrows rising.

Blake scratches his head. "We all go to boarding schools?"

Huh. On the surface, that's the obvious answer. Like, so obvious, why even say it? But—

"That's a good point," Ann speaks up. "If the foundation was searching out the top twelve candidates all over the country, why only our schools? Why not private day schools, or even students from public schools?"

"Hasn't this competition always been among boarding schools?" Amir points out.

Liam is still pacing like he's going to wear a hole in the carpet. "Then is it our specific schools?"

But why? I suck my lip. "Or is it us? Are we connected to each other in some way that's making us targets?"

I glance around the room as if the answer is written across our foreheads, but we're such a mishmash of people. Athletes, class presidents, math geniuses, popular kids, ordinary ones. What *do* we have in common?

"Does it matter?" Olivia throws up her hands. "We're just tossing out random guesses. We don't even know if it *is* the foundation. Besides, what about Evan? They definitely, one hundred percent, would *not* kill one of us."

"Maybe it was suicide," Blake offers hopefully, but those of us who saw Evan's body shake our heads.

"Somebody else killed him," Lily confirms.

But who? None of us *look* like cold-blooded killers. Could it be the mental strain? Did somebody just snap? But then what about Taylor and the peanuts? Or the notes? There's no question the notes were intentional.

Blake drops onto an armrest and presses both hands to his mouth. His breath whistles through his fingers. "If there's a killer on board . . . then Paige's death wasn't a suicide."

And someone is picking us off, one by one.

Liam stops pacing, his eyes bright. "We need to find those attendants. Figure out if they're involved in some way."

Could it be one of them? Or someone else hidden on the plane?

As horrible as that thought is, I latch on to it with ferocious hope. The last thing I want to believe is that one of us is a killer. Even socially inept Simon.

In the far corner, Blake rises and cracks his knuckles. His eyes aren't puffy anymore, but now he's got a spacey, shell-shocked sort of look. Like he's desperate to *do* something, not just stand here talking. "Want me to bust through that door upstairs?"

"Dude," Dylan says, also standing. "I'm sure there's a way to open it without resorting to brute force."

The rest of us follow as Dylan, Blake, and Liam lead the way to the second floor. *Could* someone at the foundation be doing this to us? They'd have access to all our personal information, and the resources to dig up our secrets. But why? Surely Simon's right—a respectable nonprofit organization would never risk the media backlash from torturing teens on an overseas flight, even if none of us were supposed to die. They'd be arrested. And the entire foundation canceled.

One thing's for sure, regardless of who orchestrated the messages and the lights going out, Evan's death wasn't an accident. So why was he targeted?

And *someone* attempted to frame me with that peanut bag. Will they try to pin Evan's death on me too? Goose bumps pop up on my arms.

As we pass through the upstairs lounge, another possibility strikes me. Here I've been suspecting Simon, but what about Evan? I touch Lily's elbow. "Hey, I just had a thought. You know how that note in Evan's hand was the same handwriting as the Two Truths papers we got earlier?"

"Yeah?" Her thick eyebrows lift, reminding me of two fuzzy red caterpillars.

"What if he was the one who wrote all the notes? Somebody figured it out, and that's why they killed him." This explanation helps soothe the nerves flaring in my system, because at least his death would've had a purpose. Maybe that could be the end of it all. I dig out the note from the forward lavatory. "This one was with Paige, underneath the razor blade. I showed it to Blake earlier. What if he figured out Evan was the one who intimidated Paige into killing herself?"

But when could he have killed Evan? While we were working

on the puzzle and I thought he was getting a drink? Was he gone *that* long?

"Did you show that to anyone else?"

I shake my head. "I didn't want whoever planted it to know I'd found it."

She rubs her freckled nose. "But why would Evan have written the one he was holding? *New game. Who's next?*"

I shrug. "Maybe he was going to plant it somewhere. Or maybe it wasn't about murder, but about who he'd target next."

"Like with more messages?"

Even as we discuss it, I know I'm grasping at straws. "I don't know—maybe it doesn't work. I just can't imagine one of us . . ."

"There are some people here who want to win pretty desperately." Lily's voice has dropped to a whisper so low I can scarcely hear it. "Evan was one of them."

Does she know more than she's been able to share about some of our competitors? I want to ask, but we have to end the conversation for now, because the others have reached the door to the staff quarters.

It's a sliding door, like the ones below, held shut by some sort of latching mechanism. Blake pushes the center panel of the door, and even from here I can see the way the whole thing vibrates.

"It'd be easy enough to break," he says.

Dylan stoops closer to examine the edge of the door, running his fingers along the seam where it fits against the wall to the left. "There must be a sliding bolt on the other side, but how do we unlock it from here?"

Lily and I are far enough away that there isn't much we can do to contribute, and we're not the only ones losing interest in the proceedings. The others are moving apart, whispering, glancing at each other when they think no one's looking.

"So do you know something else?" I ask Lily. "Anything that might clue us in on who it is?"

"Evan definitely had a shoulder injury," she whispers. "He missed some school and wore a sling for a while near the start of last season, but I don't know about his grades or whether he faked his doctor's approval."

Right, I keep forgetting she and Evan go—or *went*—to the same school. "So maybe there was some truth to the messages," I say. "But why would he tell us that stuff about himself?"

"To avoid suspicion?"

"Wouldn't it be too risky?" I press. "What if the committee or someone else reported back to your school?" I'm not sure why I'm arguing—this was my idea after all. But now that I'm talking it out, it sounds less believable.

Lily's mouth crinkles to one side as she shrugs. "I have no idea. We heard awful things about everyone, so whoever did it must be hoping it'll rattle the competition without leading back to them."

Everyone except me. I swallow, debating whether to point this fact out to Lily. She trusts me right now, and I'd like to keep it that way. "It cut off before it got to me," I whisper, tugging the ends of my blazer sleeves to keep my hands occupied. "But I didn't have anything to do with it," I add. Just in case.

"Of course not," Lily says.

Some of the tension deflates from my chest. I need her on my side.

She's quiet again for a minute as we watch Dylan and Blake

work on the door, then she leans in closer. "It was self-defense, in case you were curious."

My nose crinkles. "What?"

"My stepfather—well, my first one. He was an alcoholic, and he'd get aggressive sometimes, shouting and stuff. One day while my mom was gone, he just . . . snapped. He started hitting my little brother, who was only two." Her eyes drop, and her voice grows so quiet that I have to lean in to hear. "I was eight. I didn't know what to do. So I grabbed one of the big kitchen knives from the knife block."

When she looks up again, her brown eyes glisten. So awful. I wish I could throw my arms around her and hug her, but that might be awkward since we just met, so I settle for lightly touching her elbow. "Oh, Lily, I'm so sorry."

She blinks rapidly, then laughs. "I'm not normally the stabby kind."

"Of course you're not."

I want to ask her more—what happened afterward, who called the police, how her mom reacted—but this isn't the place or time. She already admitted to more than she probably should've, given the circumstances. So I change the subject.

"I'm pretty sure he really did hack into the city's power grid," I say, tipping my head toward Amir, where he stands with Ann.

She nods. "I think so too. And Ann told us she never wanted to go to boarding school, but her parents made her because she wasn't a good enough student."

"So she's trying to prove them wrong or something?" Would the fear of failure be enough to drive someone to kill? On the surface, no . . . but when I think about my own deep-seated need for security, Ann's possible desperation becomes a little more real.

Still, I've already written almost all these people off my suspect list.

Everyone except Simon. And possibly Blake.

Lily shrugs. "It isn't much to go on."

"Blake would have the motive, if he's really in danger of losing his chance to play football." I glance at him, working on the door with the other two. "But he'd never hurt Paige."

She frowns. "It doesn't seem like it."

"What about Simon?" I whisper. "He's got the brains to pull off the tech stuff. But I can't figure out a motive."

"Huh." She chews her lip. "If it *was* him, then he could've made up whatever he wanted for the recording. We wouldn't know his real motive."

An excellent point. Especially since the things said about him weren't *that* awful.

"To be fair, though," she adds, "I'm sure we all have a motive."

The knot in my stomach tightens ever so slightly. If she and the others ever find out I cheated to get here, what else will they think I'm capable of? Suddenly, I wish I'd confessed to Liam when I had the chance. I can't say anything *now*.

"So what's yours?" I lean in, like she's about to tell me a juicy secret.

"Pay for college. Why else?" Laughter dances in her eyes. "I want to major in English, become a teacher, and write the next great American novel while working on my MFA at night."

I blink, hardly sure what to say. Her plan is so . . . *normal*. And so detailed. I envy her confidence. "That's cool you have it figured out. So winning would mean . . . ?"

"Better choices in colleges. And no debt from student loans." She looks at her hands, scratching absently at her knuckles. "My mom and stepdad will help out with a state school, but with my brother's treatment, they don't have much extra."

"Treatment?"

She looks at me, a slight frown tugging at her lips. "He was born with cerebral palsy. Needs a lot of specialized care, and medical insurance doesn't cover everything."

"Is that a lifelong condition?"

"Yeah." She draws a deep breath. "His is moderate, bordering on severe, but he's eleven now and doing fairly well. They're really optimistic he'll make it into adulthood."

Moisture creeps its way into my eyes, and I blink it away. How hard, to have that threat of death lingering constantly over your family. And here I thought I was the only one who needed this scholarship. My stomach tightens. Could I have been more near-sighted? More *selfish*?

"I hope you win," I manage to squeak out.

Lily bats away the words with a casual flick of her hand. "Win or lose, it'll work out. Plenty of people here deserve it."

Our conversation cuts off abruptly when the door slides open with a loud crash. Dylan and Blake give each other a high five, and Liam pumps his fist.

We're in.

The staff quarters on the other side are subdued compared to the luxury of the rest of the plane. The large compartment resembles a combination of the workstation and seating cabins below, with clusters of chairs grouped around tables and rows of seats toward the back. Another door stands open at the rear of the compartment, leading into a narrow passageway that mirrors the one below.

We trickle past the empty seats and into the hallway. My internal navigation isn't always the greatest, but I'd guess we're above the dining room right now. Or maybe the kitchen. This passage is a lot longer than the one beneath us, containing a lavatory, storage closets, and an unmarked door that might just be an elevator shaft to the lowest level.

The plane narrows as we head aft, and the ceiling grows noticeably more rounded. Like the forward compartment downstairs, the last room is filled with private first-class-style alcoves. There are six in total—four open, two with the frosted glass doors pulled shut.

Wordlessly, we separate and drift through the space, checking inside the open doors. Each alcove is immaculately clean.

I clench my teeth as Liam and Dylan pull open one of the closed doors. Surely Paige's body is up here, stretched out on one of the pull-out beds.

The bed *is* pulled out, but there's no body. Air whistles out of my teeth as I exhale. From the rust-colored droplets spattering the carpet, it looks like they carried her here. Maybe after they bagged her body, they transferred it to the hold on the lowest level.

Blake runs a hand over his chin as the others pull open the last door.

"Great." Dylan's tone is pure sarcasm. The rest of us press closer, straining to see.

The three flight attendants are propped up in seats, buckled into place, but their heads and shoulders slump forward as if they're completely out.

Or dead.

17

CROSS-CHECK AND REPORT

10:48 p.m. CDT

Behind me, Taylor starts hyperventilating, her sharp inhalations matching the jackhammer thrum of my own heart. My hands drift up to cover my ears just in case. But she's not the one who screams—it's Olivia.

"Are they . . . dead?" Blake asks.

The full impact of our situation crushes the air out of my lungs like a concrete block sitting on my chest. There's no adult to help us. We're on our own.

The space isn't large enough for more than an extra person or two to squeeze in and check their pulses. Liam doesn't hesitate, but Dylan and Blake hang back, allowing Ann in instead. After the way she wielded the EpiPen to save Taylor, she seems like the most qualified person in the group.

Liam presses his fingers to Kumar's wrist. "She's alive."

Ann confirms the same for O'Connor, who sits next to her, and for Allard, opposite.

The palpable tension around me relaxes ever so slightly.

"Can you wake any of them?" Amir asks.

After a few moments of gentle shaking, Ann and Liam give up. "No, they're out cold," Liam says. "Like *drugged* out."

"But how?" Olivia asks, her voice petulant. "The door was bolted."

"The elevator shaft?" Simon stabs his textbook—which he's

still hauling around like a security blanket—in the direction of the hallway with the unmarked door.

"Or the attendants bolted the door themselves," Taylor suggests. "If someone slipped something into their drinks, they might not have known right away. An overdose of sleep aids could do it, but not instantly."

I shift my weight from one leg to the other. Something is bothering me about this, like I'm forgetting a relevant piece of information. "But they were supposed to be downstairs with us."

Taylor shrugs. "Maybe they were taking a break?"

"Do they have drinking glasses in there?" I squeeze past the others to peer in through the door, but there's nothing except the three attendants. Did they buckle themselves, or did someone else do it? They're not large women, but still, it would be awkward to haul their bodies back here and strap them into place.

"I guess we know it's not the foundation after us," Ann mutters. My stomach sinks. I hadn't realized just how strongly I'd latched on to that possibility. "The pilots didn't drug them. It had to be one of us."

"Unless there's someone else hidden on the plane," Olivia offers hopefully.

"Or"—Liam holds up a hand, his gaze drifting toward the ceiling like he's deep in thought—"what if the attendants drugged themselves on the foundation's orders?"

I want to believe it wasn't one of us as badly as the rest of them, but . . . "What about Evan, though?" I say. "Torturing us through crazy psychological tests is one thing, but murder?"

Amir shakes his head. "There's no way they could get away with it."

Dylan's face goes slack. "We have to look for evidence. Find their drinks, search the trash cans, that kind of thing. Maybe we can figure out how it happened."

"Is that a good idea with a killer on the loose?" Taylor asks. "Evan's death might only be the first."

"Don't you mean the second?" Blake counters. "What about Paige?"

"You mean there might be more?" Olivia's voice reaches a whole new octave.

Liam clears his throat, then digs the crumpled paper out of his pocket. "We found this in Evan's hand. He didn't kill himself." He holds it up for everyone to read. Olivia clutches on to Dylan's arm, and Ann slumps against the bulkhead, her face unnaturally pale. Her hands make jerky movements next to her sides, and she stuffs them under her arms across her chest.

I weave past a few of the others to stand next to her near the room's entrance. For someone who normally looks so controlled, she seems like she's on the brink of losing it. The last thing we need is for her to panic and throw open an emergency exit. Stress does funny things to people.

"Hey," I say, letting my hand hover just above one of her arms, "are you okay?"

She sucks in several deep breaths and nods, but her gaze never leaves the open door to the attendants' alcove. "Yeah, sorry. I get panic attacks sometimes when I'm super stressed. It'll pass." She offers a weak smile.

I squeeze her arm and smile back. "I know all about anxiety. This is definitely a stressful situation."

"You seem pretty calm," she says, rubbing her hands briskly up and down her arms.

Her tone doesn't sound accusatory, but I feel like I'm on thin ice after the attempts to frame me. I force a laugh. "I think I'm still living in denial."

The others drift toward us, and Liam motions to the doorway next to Ann. "There isn't anything we can do for the attendants right now. We should all go back down. Figure out what to do next."

I fall in step behind him, but then linger when I notice Lily at the tail end of the group again. Liam glances back, his gaze catching on me. He lets the others pass and joins the two of us.

"I was taking a closer look at the attendants," Lily says softly.

"Did you find anything? Any sign of violence?"

She shakes her head. "No, but that's to be expected if they drank whatever drugged them."

"Or it could have been an injection," Liam says.

"Right. That wouldn't show up either," Lily agrees.

"An injection?" I say. My mind scrambles to figure out how someone could've managed to stick each attendant with a needle. "Do you think they've got needles in the medical kits?"

Lily's mouth goes round like her eyes. "What if Taylor smuggled a couple of extra EpiPens full of some anesthesia?"

Liam frowns. "But then when Ann gave her the injection earlier, what if she'd used the wrong one?"

"Doesn't seem likely," I say. "They'd have to be buried deep in her bag. Plus, she'd have to get each attendant alone."

"Then haul them up here to buckle them in," Liam adds. "Would she return the used needles to her bag? Or throw them away somewhere on the plane?"

"I don't know," I reply. "It'd be risky either way."

But isn't killing people risky no matter how one goes about it?

"What if she faked her allergic reaction too?" Lily says. "Maybe that EpiPen was a placebo, just to make sure we'd never suspect her. Then she planted that box of nuts in her own seat as an extra way to throw us off the trail."

The thought has crossed my mind—she *is* an actor, after all. But nothing about that near-death experience looked fake. And why would Taylor do it? "Does she need to win that badly, though?"

"It's hard to know what's going on in someone's head," Liam says.

"Amir mentioned he's seen her onstage and she's really good," Lily adds. "But I know how competitive theater is, especially to get those top roles on Broadway. It's almost as hard as writing a *New York Times* bestseller." Her mouth quirks.

That's right—Lily wants to be an author. I nudge her shoulder. "Don't worry. You'll make it."

By now, we've passed through the staff quarters and are walking through the upstairs lounge, next to the bar. The refrigerator catches my eye, and I grab another Diet Coke, suddenly desperate for more caffeine. The way this night is going, I might have to resort to a Red Bull eventually.

Liam shakes his head as I pop the top open. "You know that stuff has enough chemicals to preserve your insides, don't you?"

"Like a mummy? After this trip, I might need it." I wink, then feel heat creeping into my cheeks. When have I ever winked at a guy before? Nikki's not going to recognize me by the time I get home. Still, there's no denying how good this surge of confidence feels, especially when Liam's smile lingers.

"We should find a way to search her stuff," he whispers to Lily and me when we reach the top of the stairs.

"Simon's too," I add. "I'm not sure Taylor has the tech skills to pull off the messages, but *he* definitely does. Plus there was a stretch of time earlier where he wasn't around the rest of us, right after those videos played."

"Do you think it was long enough he could've drugged them and moved them upstairs?" Lily whispers.

"Maybe," I say. But is he even strong enough to move them?

Everyone else is flopped on chairs or pacing restlessly up the aisles as we enter. Blake points at my can of Diet Coke. "I need one of those." His voice cracks, like it's grown rusty from grief. "Where'd you get it? Upstairs?"

He heads for the stairway, but Liam cuts him off. "Hold up, man. We've got to talk first."

The football player scowls, his blue eyes clouding beneath the thick ridge of his brow. "After everything that's happened, the least you can do is let me grab a drink."

The comment falls like a shroud over the soft conversation in the room, and we all grow silent. An image of Paige being carried out of the lavatory fills my vision. Sometimes, I can almost pretend she's not *gone* gone. Just taking a nap in a seat somewhere. Near Evan.

Liam casts a helpless glance over Blake's shoulder to the rest of us. Amir, who's on Blake's team, stands. "I'll go with him. Anybody else want something?"

A few people shout requests, and then the two of them tromp up the stairs loudly enough we could probably hear them from the aft bedroom suite. As we wait, that nagging feeling I'm missing something pricks at the back of my mind.

When Amir and Blake return, arms full of soda cans, it hits me—Blake was upstairs, supposedly locked in the lavatory, that entire time we were down here searching. As long as he could get that door to the staff quarters open, he would've had unmonitored access to the back to drug the flight attendants. *And* he's strong enough to move them. Paige was supposedly addicted to painkillers. Could Blake have accessed her supply and used an opioid to knock the attendants out? I don't know much about codeine—would that even work?

But if he killed Evan as an act of revenge for Paige, mistakenly believing Evan played the messages, why would he also have drugged the flight attendants?

Blake downs several gulps of his drink, then stares at a random patch of carpet. Liam and Lily need to hear my suspicions, but I can't exactly blurt them out in front of everyone. So I slide a step closer to Lily and plop on the armrest of the love seat where she's sitting. It takes me a moment to notice Dylan has gotten awfully cozy with Olivia on another one of the love seats. He doesn't even glance my way.

Not gonna lie—his indifference stings. Is it because I put space between us? But then I douse the unwelcome feeling and straighten my spine. After so many years of fruitless pining and all the ways I've hurt Nikki, it feels good to move on.

Simon stands a short distance behind Olivia, alone, thumping his textbook against the back of a chair in an arrhythmic pattern—like he's *trying* to be annoying.

All eyes focus on Liam as he stands in front of the flat-screen TV on the bulkhead, where he slides perfectly into the role of leader. Nobody objects.

"Guys, I think we need to stick together." He paces as he talks, one hand rubbing the back of his head. "In groups of three or more. Because"—he pauses, and his bright-blue eyes rove across our faces—"until we find evidence there's someone else hiding on this plane, we have to assume one of us is a killer."

"Does anyone even want to be in a group of three with a murderer?" Olivia waves her hand. "I don't. What if we figure out who it is and lock them up until we land? There are, what—three hours left?"

Taylor glances at her wristwatch. "More like two and a half. We're supposed to land at one fifteen a.m. Chicago time."

Two and a half hours. That's how long the rest of us have to stay alive before we can get off this airplane ride of terror.

Dylan pulls away from Olivia, leaning forward on his elbows as he looks at her. "How are we going to do that? Hold a vote? This isn't a reality TV show. It's life, and people are dying."

I raise my hand, like we're back in school. Time to see how the others react.

Liam points at me, his eyes locking on mine. "Emily, you have an idea?"

"What about searching for evidence, like Dylan suggested earlier? Whoever drugged the attendants must've left trash *somewhere*. We're on a plane, after all. There's no way to completely hide the evidence."

No one flinches or objects. Whoever did it must feel confident we're not going to find anything.

"And there's the body." Lily grimaces. "We can't just leave it back there, can we?"

Amir frowns. "It's a crime scene. We shouldn't disturb it, should we?"

"But when we land, won't everything shift around?" she asks.

We all know what she means by "everything." I'd suggest documenting the scene first, but the idea of having pictures of a bloody murder on my phone reaches a whole new level of no.

"If we tell the police exactly what we did," I offer, "won't they be able to sort it out?"

"What's wrong with just sitting here? All of us together." Taylor holds out her hands. "That way no one can kill anybody, and we'll all make it to Paris. The police can deal with the situation in the bathroom."

Or the killer can pick us off one at a time. My throat squeezes, but I force in a breath, because that's ridiculous. Nobody would attempt something like that if we're together.

Would they?

But what if the lights go out again, and having us all in one place is part of someone's plan?

Dylan shakes his head. "We at least have to notify the pilots. If you want to all go together, fine." He points toward the onboard radio system near the lavatory. "There's got to be some way to call them."

Liam nods, then stares at the floor. "Here's what I think. We split up into two groups. One group will move Evan's body upstairs and secure it in one of those alcoves in the staff quarters, then search for evidence up there. The rest will contact the pilots and search down here."

Everyone else looks at each other as Liam waits.

"I'm in." Blake raises his hand. "But we need guys to move the body. You"—he points at Liam—"me, Dylan. Amir or Simon, one of you could help too."

Amir glances at Simon, who is suddenly absorbed again in his book. With a shrug, Amir says, "I'll do it."

Nobody objects as Blake heads aft. Dylan glances at me on his way out but keeps going when Liam stops next to me.

He squeezes my arm lightly. "You good with this?"

I nod, though for a brief second I want to dive into his solid arms and hide from everyone else. I only met him today—or is it yesterday by now?—and yet somehow he's become my safe place.

His gaze lingers on me. Then he vanishes with the others, leaving me to wonder if he feels this same giddiness about me.

Once the four of them are gone, the rest of us stand in silence, waiting for someone to step up and take charge. Finally, Lily clears her throat. She's far more assertive than I gave her credit for when I first met her.

"Should we split up again? Maybe Ann, Olivia, and Taylor could try the pilots, while the rest of us start checking everyone's bags." She waves a thumb toward the seating compartment. "We're looking for some kind of sedative or anything else that might have been used against the flight attendants."

"Sure." Taylor stands. "Remember, I've got an EpiPen." Her tone remains even, and she doesn't fidget or glance around as she talks. Like she's got nothing to hide. "Anybody else carrying anything that might be suspicious?"

"If the messages about Paige were true, her bag might have painkillers," I point out. Unless Blake already pocketed them. And what about those steroids he's supposedly using?

Lily's gaze meets mine, her eyebrows raising slightly, like she's just had the same thought I did earlier. But all she says is, "We'll keep an eye out for them."

When no one else adds anything, we part ways, and I follow Lily and Simon to the seating compartment. Simon heads to the bin over his seat and tugs out his bag, a black duffel that looks like the kind snipers use in movies to carry their disassembled rifles. He drops it unceremoniously on the ground and heads back for the next bag. Lily and I start clearing out the other overhead bins. Green, blue, and brown blur together as we line the bags up against the forward bulkhead, where a wider row creates a little extra room.

"You realize this is a pointless waste of time, don't you?" Simon asks.

Love the optimism. Or is he trying to get us to quit before we find anything that might incriminate him? I clear my throat. "Why do you think that?"

"Because nobody would be stupid enough to leave the evidence in their own bag. At the very least, they'd stuff it into someone else's."

"Sounds like you've given it a lot of thought," I say pointedly, but Simon merely shrugs.

"It's simple logic." Gotta give him credit, he hides quite efficiently behind reason.

"Unless"—Lily points at him—"whoever did it knows we'll all reach that conclusion, so they left it in their own bag to appear like they were framed."

It's like that scene in *The Princess Bride*, where the guy hired to kidnap Buttercup has to decide which cup Westley dumped the poison into. Yeah, that didn't work out so well.

"It won't matter anyway unless we find something." I retrieve my messenger bag from the overhead bin, relieved when no more peanut wrappers fall out. My fingers rub against the supple leather strap, a little glimpse of the familiar in the chaos. The bag was the last gift my dad gave me, the year I started ninth grade, because, he said, "High school is a big deal." At the time, of course, he and my mom were still talking. He probably wasn't planning on completely abandoning us. Or that high school would suddenly sink to the bottom of my priority list as everything else dissolved away.

After setting it in line with the others, I help check the rest of the seats and gather the bags of the guys who are moving the body. I don't envy them that task.

We've barely got all of them lined up when the other three appear in the doorway. I glance at Ann, who shakes her head.

"What happened?" I ask.

Taylor blows out a long breath through pursed lips. "The intercom was dead. Both the one in the entertainment salon and the one upstairs outside the flight deck. We tried banging on the door, but nobody answered."

Lily's brow furrows. "But didn't the pilots make an announcement?"

"It could be a separate system," Ann says.

"It is." Simon unzips his bag, not even bothering to look up. "They both wire into the same set of speakers, but they operate on separate circuits. It wouldn't be hard to cut one and not the other. Otherwise, the pilots would realize something was wrong. And even though the access is upstairs, the actual flight deck is on this level. That's why they can't hear you."

"It's remarkable how much you know about this plane, Simon." Olivia toes his bag with one of her leather Mary Janes.

He scowls at her. "Not really. What's remarkable is how clueless the rest of you are."

Olivia bristles, opening her mouth like she's gearing up for a nasty retort, but Lily clears her throat.

"Thanks for trying," she says. "Maybe we'll think of something else. Should we start with our own bags?" She sits on the ground and reaches for a scuffed green backpack with L.L.BEAN embroidered across the top, near the zipper. Like her, the bag is . . . ordinary. A million other kids must carry the same backpack to school. Yet she doesn't appear bothered as she pulls it out from between a Vera Wang duffel and a Kate Spade satchel. Once again, I find myself envying her confidence. She knows who she is, and she doesn't expect herself to be someone else.

Maybe it hits me so hard because that's exactly what I've been doing for as long as I can remember. I'm not Emily—I'm Nikki's friend, the girl who follows Nikki around like a shadow. The girl who gives everything up without a fight because Nikki wants her to and then steals what Nikki has without trying to earn it herself.

My life has gotten so wrapped up in hers I'm not even sure who I am anymore. All at once, I feel cold and numb.

A lump forms in my throat. How have I let myself slip away so completely?

Is that the real reason I stole her place on this trip? To get away from her? I've lived in her shadow for so long I've become a plant withering in the darkness. Did some desperate part of me realize I had to *do* something to get into the sunlight?

And it's not just her. What about Mom? She's too proud to reach out to relatives, so to keep her happy I haven't said anything either. How long will I quietly live in a car, letting someone else make all the decisions for me?

The worst of it is, it's not entirely their fault. It's *my* fault too. I'm the one who let things reach this point. I'm the one who chose not to do anything, and when I finally did, it was on impulse. Cheating Nikki out of her chance for this scholarship wasn't right. And neither was making out with her boyfriend, no matter how willing he was.

That person isn't me. Not the me I want to be.

As I kneel beside Lily and wrestle with the buckles on my bag, the empty feeling inside gives way to something stronger, firmer. And though it's tiny at first, it grows until I can't help but sit a little straighter. I don't *have* to be this way—a cheating liar. Nor do I have to be a shadow.

I can be the girl who Liam wants to be around, the one Lily wants to be friends with, the one who accomplishes things and helps protect the people around her—my eye catches on Olivia—even if they don't deserve it. And it's not because I need some major personality overhaul. It can happen one small decision at a time.

I'm going to reach out to our family when we land. Maybe I'll start with Mom's sister, Aunt Kacie. We need help.

And I'm going to make things right with Nikki. Yes, things are a mess right now, but deep in my soul, I know our friendship is worth saving. On that awful day in fifth grade when my mom called to tell me Dad had moved out, Nikki was the one who let me ugly cry all over Creamy, her favorite kitty Squishmallow. And in ninth grade, when Dad changed his cell number and stopped writing? She threw me a surprise party for my birthday with our friends. Then there was that time when we were twelve and she had the flu, and I read an entire *Wings of Fire* book out loud to her while she lay in bed. We've been each other's rock for years.

And I know we can have that friendship back again if we work for it.

A sense of purpose, of resolve, settles like a comfortable weight beneath my ribs, chasing away some of the anxiety that's plagued me for the last day. No, for the last several days. Suddenly, the future—despite its unknowns—seems bearable.

A smile flits across my lips as I finally get the buckles unlatched and reach inside my bag. Around me, the others are spreading out their stuff like some sort of weird in-flight garage sale. Quart-size baggies filled with liquids, notebooks and pens, laptops, earbuds, e-readers. Lily's toting around copies of *The Importance of Being Earnest* and *The Count of Monte Cristo*, which looks thick enough to use for weightlifting. The color rises in her cheeks when I point at the books, but then she shrugs. I guess she *does* want to be an English major.

Time to lay out my collection, which mainly consists of a few toiletries, a hairbrush and scrunchies, a lone sketchbook, and my earbuds. I'd pretty much banked on using my phone for entertainment.

My fingertips trace across an unfamiliar shape, something smooth and round but too wide to be the barrel of my brush. I close my fingers around a hard plastic container, freezing when it rattles. The comforting sense of purpose in my chest melts away like ice in the desert as I slowly lift a bottle out of the dark recesses of the bag.

It's an orange prescription pill container, something I did *not* pack.

I rotate it to check the white label wrapped around the other side, fully expecting it to be codeine or whatever Paige supposedly takes. Blake must have stashed it in my bag, trying to frame me, unless someone else knew where she kept her supply.

No surprise, the person's name has been ripped off. But the medication name is clear, and it's *not* codeine. I stare at the words in front of me, chest tightening, trying to make sense of what I see.

Ambien. For treating insomnia.

18

HEAVY ARTICLES MAY HAVE SHIFTED

11:07 p.m. CDT

My throat sticks shut like I've swallowed a pound of saltwater taffy. There's no question anymore—someone is trying to frame me. But who? *Who hid this in my bag?*

I glance around the space, doing my best to act casual, to see if anyone is watching. Waiting for me to find what they've planted.

No one appears to be paying attention. The worst thing to do right now is act guilty, despite the fact it's almost an automatic reflex to jerk my gaze back to my bag. Slowly, so as not to let those pills rattle, I lower the bottle into the bag and start pulling out my actual stuff instead.

There's got to be some way out of this mess, but what? If I whip out that bottle, they'll all think *I* drugged the flight attendants. They might even think I killed Evan. Black spots flicker at the edges of my vision, and I brace myself with one arm against the floor.

I may be a cheat and a liar, but I'm *not* a killer.

"Emily, you okay?" Lily's look of concern cuts me like a knife. I want so desperately to show her the bottle, to get her help, but what if she blames me too? She only met me a few hours ago. What reason does she have to trust me?

I nod as I pull out my notebook. "Yeah, I think I'm just exhausted. What time is it anyway? Like almost midnight?"

Olivia, who is literally surrounded by the largest pile of clothing and makeup I've ever seen—how did she fit that into a carry-on?—

checks the time on her phone. "Eleven oh eight, but that's Chicago time." She yawns loudly for effect, but unlike me, she doesn't look much worse off than when we boarded.

"Isn't that early for you?" Simon snickers. He's sitting just beyond Olivia's reach, so when she swats him with a copy of *Elle*, it falls short.

"It's not my fault I have an actual social life," she huffs, but the words lack their usual venom.

I rub my hands across my bleary eyes, no longer caring if I've just smeared the remains of my mascara across my cheeks. It's after midnight for those of us from the East Coast. Even Lily lets out a yawn behind the hand pressed to her mouth.

I've reached the bottom of my bag, where only one item still sits. There's no convenient secret compartment to hide it in, and I don't dare smuggle it out to stow in my blazer pocket. In an ideal world, I'd stash it in one of the compartments between the seats or put it in the kitchen. But I can hardly excuse myself from the group, and even getting up might look suspicious at this point. And if the pills shake . . .

What if I leave it in here and hope nobody notices? No, someone will surely double-check.

It'd be better to tell the truth for a change, wouldn't it?

Instead, I stall for time, watching as the others finish emptying their bags. Taylor, who's surrounded by a pile of notebooks, books, and gauzy scarves, pulls Amir's bag toward her. When she catches me watching her, she asks, "Emily, do you want to get Dylan's? Who's left?"

"I can get Liam's," Ann says, "and I think that black one near the end is Blake's."

"What about Paige and Evan?" I ask. "Did anyone empty their

bags?" Maybe I'm grasping at straws, but we need to know if Paige has a narcotic in there. I suppose it's too much to hope that Evan has self-incriminating evidence in his bag.

Lily points to the bright Vera Wang bag and shakes her head. "Paige's had nothing. Maybe she was clean."

"And Evan's was clear too," Taylor adds.

Regardless, there's still the problem of the bottle in *my* bag. I clear my throat, simultaneously hating myself and rejoicing at doing the right thing for once. "I don't think we need to search any further. Somebody stuffed this in my bag." Bracing for impact, I pull out the amber-hued bottle and shake the contents.

Lily glances between me and the bottle, then back to me again, her brow furrowing. The others stiffen, eyes narrowing. Simon frowns as he stares at my bag. Is he acting? Or legitimately surprised? Is it possible my hunches about him have been wrong and Blake is the true culprit? But then what about Paige?

Taylor, who's sitting next to Ann, draws closer to her, almost as if she's looking for protection. "Emily? Why do you have those?"

It's so silent you can hear my gaspy breaths, which I try desperately to control. *Hello, could I possibly look more guilty?* But it's not my fault adrenaline has made my heart rate shoot to the moon.

Ann frowns at me. "Didn't the messages cut off right before they got to your two truths and a lie? Very convenient."

"Hold up." Lily chews her lip. "Why would she leave the pills in her own bag? And then show them to us? Simon said it earlier—logically, nobody would do it."

"Because she didn't expect her bag to be searched," Taylor says, still clinging close to Ann. Imagine if she knew about the peanut wrapper. "Now she's hoping to pin the blame on someone else by acting like she's been framed."

Simon shrugs and looks at Lily. "That was your idea."

Finally, enough heat rises in my chest that an objection springs to my lips. I turn to Simon. "You're the one who didn't want us to search. Why? And you were alone *in the back of the plane* right before we found Evan."

He yawns. Literally a yawn. Like the whole thing is so boring to him. If this is what having a brother would've been like, I'm good as an only child. "Obviously, the five minutes I spent back there finishing the puzzle wasn't enough time to kill anybody. And why should we search the bags? I knew we wouldn't gain anything. Sure, we found a bottle of pills. So what? Maybe Emily did it. Maybe she was framed. Good luck figuring it out."

Huh. Never saw help coming from that quarter.

"That's *real* helpful, Simon." Olivia glares at him.

He shrugs and pulls another book from his bag, this time a big, floppy softcover about computer programming. Just imagining being that smart makes my brain hurt.

"Look," I say, "the police will easily be able to dust this bottle for fingerprints, and mine won't be the only ones on it." Unless the culprit wore gloves . . . But this isn't an episode of *CSI*. "Until then, if you want me to sit buckled in a seat under guard, fine. Just don't leave me alone with whoever killed Evan, because it wasn't me. There's no way I could overpower a guy like that."

"It wouldn't be that hard if you drugged him first." Simon glances up from his stuff, like he's offering a helpful fact I hadn't considered.

"Well, I didn't."

"Simon, as *if*! She obviously didn't hurt anybody." Olivia turns on him with an ugly scowl, and an unexpected little burst of warmth toward her fills my heart. She's actually standing up for me.

I give her a smile, just a small one as a peace offering, but she's already turned back to the pile of junk lying around her knees.

"Can I pack this all back up now?" she asks, her nose still crinkled, like the whole messy affair disgusts her.

"What about Emily?" The look of distrust in Taylor's eyes makes me feel like crawling underneath my bag. Even if all this blows over, have I lost my chance to become friends with these people? "What was the point of searching if we're just going to ignore the facts? Somebody drugged the flight attendants, and she's got a bottle of Ambien *in her bag*. Just because she's small and cute doesn't mean we should let her roam the plane killing people."

This time, I can't stop myself from standing up. "I didn't kill anyone!"

"Emily." Lily's voice carries a hint of warning as she reaches toward me.

Ann climbs to her feet and looks between me and Taylor. "Okay, you guys, chill." She scans the group as she talks. "For now, let's keep her with us, and when the others get back, we can decide what's best to do with her. Maybe vote."

"Let's throw her out the air lock," Simon says.

When the rest of us just stare at him, he starts laughing—first a snort, then a chuckle, then gales of laughter that shake his entire body.

Finally, he gets quiet enough for Ann to clear her throat. "Should we assign a couple of people to guard Emily?" she says. "To make sure she doesn't run when no one's looking?"

"It's an *airplane*," I point out. "Where am I going to go?"

Taylor shivers. "Somebody has managed to slip away and do a lot of damage on this flight."

"I'll do it," Lily says, and I breathe a sigh of relief.

"Good. Simon"—Ann points at him—"what about you?"

"Fine." A scowl creases his forehead. "But I'm repacking my belongings first."

"Did everybody get a chance to scan what was in the bags?" Lily asks. Ann, Taylor, and Olivia climb to their feet and wander through the messy compartment, which now resembles the average teenager's bedroom, strewn with clothing and books and electronics. I'd love to see too, but there's no point trying.

When I exchange a glance with Lily, she rises to her feet to scan the scattered piles on the floor. A moment later, she sits down next to me again, shaking her head. "Nothing I can see from here," she whispers. "Just Taylor's spare EpiPen, and it's unused."

Not surprising she wouldn't find anything, given someone planted the evidence in my bag. Did they leave it at the same time as the peanut wrapper? In fact, now that I think about it, my bag was open then, wasn't it?

When everyone's done checking, Lily gives the word, and we repack our stuff. Except for the orange prescription bottle. I hold it up. "Since you're all convinced this is mine, who wants to hold on to it?"

They glance at each other with expressions varying between disinterest and horror.

"We can't let her keep it," Ann insists.

Simon stands up with his bag and stuffs it back into an overhead bin. "What's she going to do, throw pills at you?"

"What if we leave it in a designated place?" Lily suggests. "Maybe in the kitchen somewhere."

Ann sucks on her lip. "Too risky. Give it to me. I'll hold on to it until the others come back and we decide what to do." When nobody objects, I pass the hated orange plastic bottle over to her, and she slips it into her blazer pocket.

In the ensuing disorganization, as everyone stows the rest of the bags, Lily stays close. "What's someone got against you?" she whispers.

"I have no idea. Maybe they picked a bag at random." Oh, how I wish this were true. But it's too much coincidence, the way the messages cut off right at my name, and the peanut wrapper planted near my bag. Still, can I risk saying that to Lily? How long before she turns on me too?

And though I'd like to believe someone is framing me just because my name happened to be last on the list and this is another handy way to knock out some of the competition, I can't help wondering if there's more to it. If it's personal in some way. But who here have I hurt? And how? I just met them, and there's no way someone could pull this off without a lot of planning.

"Good point," Lily says. "But who did it?"

I tuck a couple of long strands of hair behind my ear. "Somebody with a prescription for that stuff."

"It's a sleep aid," Lily muses, "and most of these people are overachieving, high-strung geniuses. It could be anyone."

Simon appears at my other side, a scowl on his face. I suddenly feel like one of those characters on death row in a movie, guards escorting me on either side. It's creepy.

"Here, I'll put your bag back," Olivia offers. Is that a tiny sympathetic smile curving her lips? My heart swells as I nod and hand my messenger bag over to her.

"Shall we check the galley now?" Lily asks.

Liam and the others aren't back yet. If I'm lucky, maybe they'll find something that proves I didn't do it. At least, like Lily, Liam will believe me.

Won't he?

I push away the doubts and walk between Simon and Lily as we follow the others to the compact stainless-steel galley. The space is too small to let in more than a few people, so Taylor, Ann, and Olivia slip inside. Simon and Lily hover by my elbows in the corridor.

Cabinet doors and drawers open and shut with soft clicks as the three of them dig through each possible storage location.

"Ha, so there *is* alcohol on this plane." Olivia smirks as she holds up a half-empty green glass bottle. The label reads JAMESON IRISH WHISKEY.

"Well, don't drink it. It's got to be laced with the Ambien," Ann says, pulling open a handle to reveal the world's narrowest dishwasher, not much wider than twelve inches, though the height looks about normal. Inside are a few plates along with four small tumblers. "The flight attendants must've helped themselves to a late-night drink."

I can picture it, the three stressed attendants sneaking in here and pouring themselves a quick shot of whiskey. In fact, I ran into O'Connor back here, didn't I? What time was that? "Then what?" I say. "They started to feel tired, so they went upstairs and buckled in?"

A few of them glare at me, and I press my lips together. *Right.* My thoughts probably aren't welcome at this point.

"It must be what they're trained to do if they're feeling incapacitated." Ann closes the dishwasher. "I mean, it makes sense, right? They wouldn't want to pass out somewhere without being buckled in. We're on an airplane, after all." She scans the wall of doors in front of her again. "Now where's the trash can?"

"Aha," Taylor barks as she opens a cabinet beneath the airplane's small sink. Inside the kitchen, Olivia shifts, blocking my view.

I glance up at Simon, who's taller than either me or Lily. "What is it? What did she find?"

He doesn't answer, but Olivia moves again, opening a narrow view for me to see. Taylor holds a folded stack of paper towels—the kind from the lavatory—between her index and forefingers. She lays them out on the silvery steel countertop, and my view vanishes as Olivia steps closer to look.

"Pink powder," Ann says. She pulls the prescription container from her pocket and opens it up to reveal a dozen or so small pink pills. "Looks the same to me. Whoever did it crushed the pills between these paper towels. Maybe using one of the water glasses from dinner."

"Whoever?" Taylor's pretty face contorts into a frown. "We *know* who did it."

"No, we don't," Lily says quietly, and even though I could hug her, I keep my arms pinned to my sides.

"I did see one of the attendants back here earlier," I say.

Behind us, an electric hum sings through the passage walls. We all spin around.

An unmarked door, next to the one labeled STORAGE, slides open as those of us out in the hall edge away. Dylan pokes his head out. "The elevator works."

He opens the door wider and steps out next to me, followed by Amir, Liam, and Blake, who pile into the corridor on his other side before he tugs the door shut.

"Does the elevator go down another level?" Lily asks.

"Yeah," Dylan says, "but it's locked. You have to know the code."

"You guys," Blake calls. His face is flushed, the most animated I've seen him since Paige's death. "We found a secret staircase in the bedroom suite."

"For real?" My face squinches. We spent so much time back there—how could we not have noticed?

Liam slides into view behind Blake, his eyes finding mine before he looks at anyone else. Warmth blooms in my chest. "Yeah," he says, "it's in the closet. One side is a staircase."

"Where does it lead? Upstairs?" Ann pokes her head out of the galley. She's got the same puzzled expression the rest of us have.

"The back of that room where we found the attendants. A door next to the lavatory."

Lily nods, her jaw set. "So whoever killed Evan had another escape route."

"Two, if we count the elevator." Dylan nods toward the panel.

"Where did you guys move him?" Ann asks.

Blake's face, so excited a moment before, goes pale. For the first time, I notice faint rusty stains scattered across his shirt. On Liam too, and Dylan, who has shed his blazer.

Dylan's voice is faint as he answers. "We wrapped him in the blankets off the bed back there and carried him up the stairs. It seemed shorter than taking the elevator."

"Then buckled him into one of the seats," Amir adds.

Silence hangs heavy over us, as if we're paying our respects to the dead. Finally, Liam glances between me and the others, and asks, "What did you find down here?"

My heart crashes along with my expression. I'd rather be the one to tell him. "Somebody hid—"

Taylor cuts me off. "Emily drugged the attendants."

"I did not!" I insist, doing my best to look as harmless as possible.

Liam's dark brows pull together, and Dylan cocks his head to one side, studying me.

"Somebody slipped a container of Ambien into my bag," I explain. "Ann has the bottle."

She holds it up for their benefit. "We found paper towels with dust from the pills in the kitchen trash."

"And this." Olivia leans back into the kitchen and snatches the whiskey bottle.

"I could use a drink of that." Blake holds out his hand, but Liam grabs his arm.

"The attendants were drugged?" He gives Blake a pointed look.

Blake seems to deflate as Olivia returns the bottle to the kitchen.

"So," Ann says, "we're keeping Emily under guard until we decide what to do about her."

"Like a reality TV show?" Liam glances between Ann and me. "Or is this a full-on criminal trial?"

"Does it matter?" Olivia huffs. "It's not like we can do anything besides buckle her into a seat and make sure she doesn't go anywhere."

I raise my hand. "I'd prefer not to be confined to a seat with a killer on the loose, personally. Even with guards."

Not much sounds worse than the shame of reaching Paris as the one all my peers have voted as the suspect. Even after the police sort it out and realize it wasn't me, what will the scholarship committee think? And worse, will the police investigation uncover what I did to get here?

Maybe whoever is framing me will achieve their goal regardless of whether anyone believes the evidence. The damage will be done, and they'll have one less person to defeat to win.

My shot at winning this thing has pretty much evaporated. *Unless* I can convince them it wasn't me.

"I think it's a good idea to regroup and review what we know, regardless," Liam says, his tone cool. He doesn't suspect me, not the way he did before, when he found me and Dylan together.

Otherwise, he'd be backing away from me rather than sliding closer.

"Back to the entertainment room, then?" Lily asks, and the others nod in agreement.

All I'm missing is a pair of handcuffs as they escort me forward. Simon stays on one side, Lily on the other, as we march up to stand in front of the big TV. Ah, poor naive Emily, who used to think we might sit around watching that television and relaxing on this flight.

"Can I stop guarding her now?" Simon asks.

Lily looks at Ann. "Do we have to make her stand?"

"For heaven's sake, let her sit already," Olivia says as she flops into one of the chairs.

When nobody objects, I perch on the edge of the nearest love seat. Simon slinks away behind the furniture to sit on one of the side benches and flips his book open. Tuning us out again. I wish I had his ability to detach from all the drama, but instead my heart skips like a speedboat over the waves.

"Can we please go over who else might have done it?" I ask. "I'm sure that will make it clear I'm not the only potential suspect."

"That's a good idea," Liam affirms. "And if we can rule out Em, maybe we'll be able to figure out who actually did it." His eyes catch on mine and linger. If only we could escape the others to talk again, just the two of us.

"First"—Ann taps her index fingers together—"we received the envelopes with the nasty notes."

"Any one of us could've found a way to slide them into the envelopes," Lily says, "but who had access to all that information about us?"

"Are you admitting yours was true?" Olivia says, shooting to her feet.

Lily holds up both hands. "I'm not admitting anything. I'm just pointing out that at least some of the accusations could be linked to reality. Taken out of context maybe, but plausible."

Like her stabbing her stepfather? I know that one's true because she confessed to me herself. But what about the others?

"That one about me spending a night in jail?" Liam says. "It was for stealing a rival school's mascot. We got caught, and the cops decided it'd be cool to teach us a lesson."

Blake laughs. "Dude, that's actually funny." He sobers, his face settling into hard lines. "Not like the stuff they were spewing about me and Paige."

"Did Paige carry narcotics on board?" Lily asks Blake point-blank. "Like codeine or something?"

He shakes his head. "No. No way. I know what the messages said, and maybe she used to have a problem, but she's clean now. *Was* clean." When he blinks rapidly, the rest of us go silent. While he could be lying, that pink powder points more toward the Ambien from my bag knocking out the attendants.

Unfortunately.

"So here's the thing," Amir says. "A lot of that stuff could be obtained. Or *invented*," he concedes when Blake stiffens, "from hacking into private records and monitoring social media accounts. It would just take some planning and either a little technical skill or cash to hire someone. Same with figuring out Taylor's allergy, unless that was a legit accident."

The thought of someone spying on me for the past several weeks makes me shiver. I tug my blazer sleeves lower with cold fingers. Amir certainly has the technical skills, but I'm almost certain it wasn't him. And plenty of people here have the cash. My gaze snags on Dylan, who's busy fiddling with his wristwatch, and I feel guilty for even considering him. But after everything that's happened, I can't help it. Not when I know how much he loves to win.

"That doesn't really give us anything to go on, then," Ann says.

I raise my hand. "Can I just point out that I don't have any hacking skills and I'm not exactly rolling in cash right now?" Confessing that my mom and I are currently living in an automobile might go a long way to supporting my case, but then I'd have an obvious motive for winning at any cost. Besides, if Dylan finds out, then my entire school will too before long.

"You attend a boarding school, Emily," Taylor states. "How hard off can you be?"

Of course, on one level she's right—I'm floating in privilege compared to so many others. But am I the only one here who's subsisting entirely on financial aid?

"Exeter does have needs-based scholarships," Dylan says thoughtfully, looking up from his watch. "But Emily doesn't need one of those. Right, Em?"

All eyes turn to me again, and I swallow. If I come clean about this, will everyone assume I'm desperate enough to kill to win? "Well, I just mean, um, my mom is single, and . . ." I hope people will infer whatever they want and leave me alone.

"School is expensive," Liam finishes for me. His lips tilt up into a little smile as his gaze meets mine.

"So what about the messages playing over the speakers?" Olivia asks. "That was preplanned? Rigged up in the electrical system? Or a computer virus or something?" Her cheeks tinge pink as Simon rolls his eyes.

"I guess we can rule *you* out as the culprit," he says. "It does take a certain amount of brains to figure out how to use an intercom."

Olivia's eyes narrow. "*You're* the one with a plan of this airplane downloaded on your phone."

"Would you like to study it?" Simon makes a face and offers her his phone. "There's nothing about electrical circuitry."

"Can we move on?" Blake smirks. "Or do you two need some time alone to work things out?"

I press a fist to my mouth to cover my smile as both Olivia *and* Simon turn bright red. I'm kind of surprised Simon even picked up on the insinuation. And Olivia . . . she doesn't exactly strike me as the type to get embarrassed about boys.

"So who could've done it?" Ann's face pinches into a frown. "Any of us?"

Liam shrugs. "I guess. I mean, unless somebody wants to come out and admit they're an electrical engineering genius, we'll have to assume whoever did it figured out how beforehand."

There *are* a few tech geniuses in the group, but neither Amir nor Simon volunteers to take my place on the stand.

"What about Paige?" Blake asks. "I'm telling you, she wouldn't have killed herself. After what happened to Evan, it's obvious someone else did it."

"Wasn't she in the bathroom the whole time, though?" Dylan asks.

"No, not when we first split up to look for the puzzles," Blake says. "She was sitting right here." He jabs at one of the love seats.

"But we were all coming and going," Lily says, "so there's no way to know who could've snuck back up front to do it."

"Or if anyone else even did do it." Liam's voice is so soft he's hard to hear. "People under stress will do unexpected things. Maybe she didn't see another way out."

Blake's face grows red, like he's about to object, but Ann places a hand on his arm and gives him a warning look. Probably thinking about James and how hard this must be for Liam.

"Was that the last time anyone saw the flight attendants?" Taylor asks.

I rack my brain, trying to picture one of those eggplant crepe suits and where I last saw it. "There was a flight attendant on the stairs. The one who couldn't help Taylor, because she was panicking. That was a couple of hours ago, before we gathered here to swap puzzle pieces, but after Paige. What about Evan? Did anyone see him?"

Several heads shake, and Dylan says, "Not since Hamlin set us loose. But I didn't pay much attention to where he went."

Because you were busy trying to hook up with me under the guise of watching a movie. Ugh, suddenly I feel like puking—especially when I think about how I'm going to confess all of this to Nikki.

Ann cuts into my unpleasant thoughts. "Who was alone? Who had the chance to sneak off and drug the attendants, and attack Evan?"

"Simon?" I blurt. "Where was he after we all split up?"

"Yeah, where *were* you, Simon?" Olivia's eyes narrow.

"Is there a rule against using the restroom?" His eyebrows lift over his dark frames. "Or escaping from the rest of you long enough to hear myself think? We don't *all* want to be around you constantly, Olivia."

She shoots him a nasty glare but doesn't argue.

"Besides," he goes on, "we've already established I didn't have time to kill anyone during the five minutes I spent finishing my team's puzzle."

He established that, not the rest of us. Though he does have a point—he wasn't back there alone for very long.

"Here's the thing," Liam says. "Emily was with me for part of that time, and then she went upstairs with Blake and the others to finish the puzzle. Right, Blake?"

He nods. "Until I got stuck in the lavatory. I don't know what she did after that."

"That's when the lights went out," I say. "I came straight downstairs to get help."

Liam starts pacing again, as if the motion helps him think. "But by that point, it was already a free-for-all. As in, any one of us could've found a way to sneak back, attack Evan, leave the nuts for Taylor, and stash the pills in Emily's bag." He pauses, rubbing his hand across the top of his head. "Though the attendants would've already been drugged. And maybe Evan was already dead *before* the lights went out."

Ann stops chewing on her thumbnail and points at Liam. "Right, the attendants must've snuck back to the kitchen for a drink after the video, while we were all doing our own thing. They felt sleepy, so they buckled in upstairs."

"But that means the whiskey could've been drugged anytime," I point out. "Unless, of course, this is all an elaborate scheme to mislead us, and they were drugged some other way."

Blake lets out a loud sigh and runs his hands over the short hair on the sides of his head. "So what you're saying is, we have no clue who did it."

"Yeah." Liam presses his lips together. "I guess that's what we're saying. But that means we can't place the blame on Emily." He places one hand on my back as he addresses the group, probably just to reinforce his point, but his fingers tangle in the ends of my long hair. I could swear his thumb rubs gently across my blazer one time before he pulls his hand away. My back suddenly feels cold.

Taylor shrugs. "Let's call a vote. If we decide it's Emily, she'll have to stay buckled in a seat under guard until we land and the police can take over. Otherwise, we won't hold any of this against her. Agreed?"

All I can do now is stare at this group of near strangers who hold my fate in their hands.

STANDBY

11:25 p.m. CDT

The show of hands doesn't take long. Taylor is the only aye, and the rest vote nay. All on account of there not being enough evidence, of course—which means if I can't stop whoever's out to frame me, things could do a 180 real fast. But despite everything, I'm carrying around this little warm bubble of hope that I could actually become friends with these people by the end of this trip. I feel lighter inside now than I have in hours. My peers have acquitted me, and as long as I keep an eye on Simon and Blake, nothing else suspicious should wind up in my bag.

"What now?" Amir glances at his phone. "We've got just under two hours left."

"I guess shut ourselves in here and wait it out," Taylor suggests. She covers her mouth as a wide yawn slips out.

Amir points aft. "Can we go back a compartment, at least? Those seats are way more comfortable."

"I need food." Blake edges toward the entry. "I'm starving here. Pretty sure nobody's going to be serving breakfast on this plane."

An excellent point. My stomach growls, as if to add an exclamation mark.

It's so easy at moments like this to imagine we're all just teens on an overseas trip. No death, no danger, no competition. The idea of staying locked up together in this compartment feels absurd.

Liam glances at me, a smile teasing his lips. "Moving around should be okay if we go in groups. At least three people together, and the killer can't do anything. Don't you think?"

His words fall like a heavy blanket over the mood in the room, which had been more positive than any time in the last several hours. An image of Evan bleeding out on the bathroom floor fills my mind again. I'd almost forgotten that note in his hand, and the very real possibility the killer could strike again.

As much as I want to think we're safe, somebody else *could* die.

But Liam's plan feels sound—and the only way we're going to make it through the rest of this flight. I mean, someone's going to need the bathroom eventually, and it's not like the one off this room is available.

Everybody nods or mutters, "Sure." I roll my shoulders, while Lily reaches toward the ceiling to stretch.

"Whose stomach growled?" Blake scans the room until his gaze connects with mine. He waves. "Come on, Emily. Get food with me. Who else is in?"

Most of the time, Blake strikes me as a big teddy bear, a guy who's tall and muscular and sweet. But between my earlier suspicions and his occasional unsettling flashes of temper, I'm glad I'm not supposed to go anywhere with him alone.

Of course, there *is* one guy I'd love to be alone with, and I can't stop myself from looking his way right now. Ann and Lily have him cornered already, but Liam towers over them, and his gorgeous blue eyes are focused on me. For a second, I forget the horrors of the day as giddiness bubbles in my stomach.

Maybe I'm not only sidekick material after all.

I raise my eyebrows, tilting my head toward the entryway in silent question. He shrugs, an expression of helplessness on his face, as Ann, whose back is to me, points aft. His gaze lingers on me, but our unspoken conversation is suddenly cut off by the tall form of Dylan. Olivia is with him, and Simon trails behind.

"Count us in," Dylan says. He glances between me and Liam, then raises one eyebrow slightly, as if he disapproves.

It's not like it's any of his business. I shift my weight from one leg to the other, then roll my eyes just for his benefit. "I bet Nikki is desperate to hear how the trip is going so far." We never exactly resolved the whether-to-tell-her question. Not together, anyway.

His brow furrows, like he can't quite pick up on the subtext. "She's never been the queen of patience."

We can't just ignore the issue, so this time I'm going to press my point. "Are you going to tell her all the details, or should I?"

I'm so not a confrontational person—where is this irritation coming from that's chafing my insides? Is it self-preservation telling me to move on? Or just my newfound resolve to be a better friend?

Keeping my internal drama off my face is hard, but from the way Dylan's eyes go all puppy-dog, I must be doing a decent job of remaining stoic. "C'mon, Cass, be reasonable," he begs. "We already talked about this. There's no reason to upset her."

Hold up.

That's the same name he mumbled earlier. My eyes narrow. Perfect time to ask. "Who's Cass?"

"Em," he corrects. "I said Em." But from the way *Oh crap* just flashed across his face, he did *not* say Em.

The dots connect in my mind like those drawings of constellations on star charts. The girlfriend back home. *She* must be Cass. Something sparks hot in my chest, flaming up like lighter fluid dumped on a dying fire as I think about Nikki and how she trusts him. How *I* trusted him. How could he do this to us?

But before I can make my brain cells pull together an appropriate response, Olivia grabs his arm and flashes a wide grin. "Let's go!"

Dylan shoots one last worried look at me before he lets her link her arm through his and tug him away. They follow Blake, who's almost to the door, leaving me to walk with Simon. A glance over my shoulder shows Liam, Ann, and Lily talking near the back of the salon. Amir and Taylor stand between the two groups, as if deciding who to join.

As much as I want to process what just happened with Dylan, now isn't the right time. I douse the anger smoldering beneath my ribs, force a smile, and wave at them. "Come upstairs with us. We won't be up there too long."

After exchanging a glance with Amir, Taylor shrugs, and they head toward us. We take the stairs to the second floor.

Blake, Olivia, and Dylan have already reached the top and disappeared into the upstairs lounge when someone calls my name from below. "Hey, Em?"

My heart does a little dance inside my ribs, cooling some of that angry fire Dylan stirred up. *Liam.* He's waiting at the bottom, a foot on the first step and a hand resting on the railing.

Simon lifts his eyebrows but keeps going as I float past Amir and Taylor down the stairs. Ann and Lily linger close by, talking softly as they examine the round entryway table that used to hold the basket of letters.

"Hey. What's up?" I stop on the step above so that my face is nearly level with his. The air between us sparks with an invisible charge.

He tips his head toward the other two. "They want to sneak back and see the hidden stairs. I thought we should tell you where we're going." That smile plays on his mouth, the one that makes me want to lean in closer and find out how soft his lips are. Heat singes up my neck as I realize I've been staring at his mouth a little too long.

I pull my gaze to his eyes to find they've softened, the bright laughter usually in them now subdued to something more serious. But I'm sure he didn't come over here to kiss me—did he?—so I force out words. "Cool. I want to see the stairs too." When my voice comes out hoarse, I clear my throat.

"How about we take a tour after you get a snack?" He glances over my head to the top of the stairs, then back to my face. Is somebody waiting up there? No way to check now, not with Liam's gaze searching mine. His eyes are the sky on a clear blue day, and I could stare into them for the rest of the flight and be perfectly content.

"It's a date." Wait, it's not a date—it's a deal. I meant to say, it's a *deal*, but I can't retract the words now, so instead I fidget with the pleats of my plaid skirt.

Across the entryway, Lily tugs open the mirrored door to the forward compartment to peek inside. Her reflection flashes a crooked smile my direction, and she speaks a little louder to Ann, as if trying to give us a tiny piece of privacy.

"Good." Liam grins, stretching that cleft in his chin into a perfect little valley. An essential part of him as much as his gorgeous eyes. "Well . . ." He says it as if he's leaving, but he doesn't move a muscle, like all he wants is to stay here with me. It takes serious effort to resist the urge to rock back and forth on my feet as my pulse picks up. "I just wanted to make sure you were okay. After finding those pills in your bag and all."

Right. *That.* I press my lips together and glance at my feet. There isn't much worse than being framed and having to wait to see if your peers believe you actually did it. "It sucked, but I'm okay now. Thank you for sticking up for me."

When I look up, concern lines his eyes, and he dips his head a bit lower to scan my face. "Em, I'll *always* stick up for you. I may not have known you long, but I know what kind of person you are. Beautiful, kind, honest, smart. The kind of person I want to be around. I hope . . ." His eyebrows lift.

I think back to my resolutions from earlier, to be honest about who I am. Now would be another perfect opportunity to come clean to Liam about how I cheated to get here. Or at least that I'm homeless and my whole life as a pretentious, elite boarding school student is a sham.

But as I look into his face, I can't make any of those words come out.

"Yeah?" I exhale the word as a mere breath, because Liam has stolen all the air out of my lungs.

A blush flits over his cheeks, and he swallows. "I hope you might . . . feel the same way about me." His eyebrows lift in silent question.

My voice would probably squeak like a mouse, so instead of trusting it, I nod and let my lips pull up at the corners the way they seem to want to whenever I'm around him.

He smiles back. Reaches out a hand to take a long strand of my hair and runs his fingers down it, like he did earlier. The touch is so light I only feel it as soft tugging at my scalp, but it's enough to send a little shiver of delight skittering up my back. "Is it because of the motorcycle?" he whispers, mischief glinting in his eyes.

"Hmm . . ." I pause, as if considering the idea. "Not only the motorcycle. We'd be kind of lost without you."

His shining eyes mirror the giddiness blooming in my chest. Somehow, we've drifted closer to each other, so that from my perch on the step above him our faces are only inches apart. He smells like clean cotton and warm skin, and my fingers itch to touch the sleeves of his gray sweater and feel the muscles underneath.

His gaze drifts from my eyes to my mouth, sparking a burst of fire under my ribs. I close my eyes as he moves closer, and my insides rage with a storm of anticipation and nerves, waiting for that moment when I'll finally feel his lips press against mine.

Will he be disappointed? Will he still be attracted to me?

Then all those anxious thoughts vanish as Liam's mouth meets mine in a soft kiss. Not a peck, but not a full-on excavation either. More of a restrained, gentle why-hasn't-anyone-kissed-me-like-this-before kind of kiss.

"Emily!" Blake calls from above. "You coming or not?"

My eyes burst open, and we spring apart. Embarrassment and amusement vie for my attention, and my shoulders curl as I turn back to Blake, who's standing at the top of the stairs with a can of Mountain Dew in his hand. Amir sticks his head out of the upstairs doorway.

My brain, which has been reduced to a pile of marshmallows, struggles to come up with an appropriate response. "Uh, yeah, I'm coming," I stutter, my fingers drifting to fix some imaginary problem with my shirt collar.

Blake lifts his eyebrows, glancing between me and Liam. "Sorry for the interruption, but, dude, you guys aren't supposed to be out here alone. Evan?" He raises his can of soda, as if he's toasting the dead.

Liam clears his throat. Rubs the back of his neck as he gives me a shy glance. *Busted.* "I clearly wasn't trying to kill her. Besides, we're not alone. Lily and Ann are down here."

At the mention of their names, they materialize from somewhere under the staircase and wave at Blake.

"*She* wasn't the one I was worried about," Blake deadpans. A smile cracks his face, and we laugh. "Nice move, though, bro, and good to see you're following the rules."

"Guess we'd better get going." Liam stuffs his hands into his pockets, chest caving, but the way he's looking at me makes my heart hammer. "Catch you soon."

"Okay." I shoot him a tiny secret smile.

I wish I could say something more—*I really like you, thanks for coming after me, kiss me again before I burst*—but he's already laughing with Lily and Ann as they leave the entryway, and the others are waiting for me.

The big football player quirks his eyebrows as I trudge up the stairs, a smirk lingering on his face. "What is it about class trips that makes people want to hook up?"

Fire explodes in my cheeks as Amir laughs, but there's no point trying to explain. Liam isn't Dylan—he's not after a lone make-out session or a third girlfriend or whatever that was. He actually wants something more, something longer-term than this trip. The possibility makes my heart soar, until I remember the harsh reality.

Will he still feel that way once he finds out all the things I've been keeping back? How many times can I hurt him and still expect him to trust me?

"Hey, I was totally joking," Blake says, concern crinkling his forehead as he looks at me.

"Oh, I know." I wave my hand, as if batting away his concern, and force my voice to sound casual. "How are you doing with everything? It's been a rough day. Night. Whatever."

Maybe it's dangerous ground to get close to talking about Paige. Who knows how razor-thin Blake's control is? But we're on our way to join the others, and the last thing I want is to keep thinking about how crushed Liam will be when he finds out the truth.

Blake knots a hand into a fist and cracks his knuckles. "I'm just ready to get to Paris and let the police figure out who's responsible for everything that's happened." The muscles bulge in his forearms, and I can feel the anger emanating off him.

When we reach the upstairs lounge, he walks around behind the counter as I approach the bar. "What can I get you?" he asks. He's not nearly as self-absorbed as I thought he'd be when I first met him—I'll give him that. If there's one thing I've learned on this trip, it's that first impressions aren't everything.

"Diet Coke," I say. "Just the can, no glass." Liam will tease me about it, but I need more caffeine.

Olivia sits on a barstool angled toward Dylan, shoes abandoned on the floor, dangling her long legs so that her bare feet nearly brush against his khaki pants. He glances at me, his face flushed, eyes not quite meeting mine.

Despite the anger festering in my gut, doubt pops up as soon as I'm around him again. What if he's innocent? What if Cass is someone else, like a friend or cousin, and I'm being totally unfair?

Taylor sits on Dylan's other side, and I plop down next to her. She offers a hesitant smile, and when I smile back, her grin widens. Maybe she truly meant it about not holding the bottle of pills against me. "Did you want to switch with me?" she asks, glancing between me and Dylan as if just realizing she's keeping us apart.

"No, I'm good." In fact, I need this space from him to figure out what to do.

Taylor arches her eyebrows, as if wondering what might be brewing beneath the surface, but she doesn't pry. When her diamond nose ring catches the light, I point at it.

"That's really pretty on you. Did it hurt?"

She laughs. "A little. Not as much as this one." She tilts her head and pulls back dark coils of hair to reveal her ear, where a piercing goes through the thick inner piece of cartilage near her cheekbone.

"I've always wondered," Amir says from across the semicircle, "if a nose ring gets in the way when you have a cold." He gestures at Taylor's face from where he sits on Olivia's other side. Next to him, Simon leans on the counter, both elbows on it, swirling a can of Cherry Coke. His downturned face bears marks of irritation. Conversation too dull? Or is he annoyed that we're making him stay with a group?

"Not really," she says, tapping the stud. "The backing is super small."

As we talk, Blake pulls a Diet Coke out of the refrigerator case behind him and slides the icy-cold can to me. Then he lays out a selection of airplane-size prepackaged snacks.

"I recommend the Funyuns," he says, shoving a neon-yellow bag toward me.

Ugh, the thought of eating those things makes me want to puke. Besides, onion breath? "Pretzels?" I ask. "Or is there cheese in that mini fridge?"

"Good call." Blake disappears out of sight for a moment, then stands back up with a platter of cheese and crackers on a shrink-wrapped clear plastic plate.

"Thanks." The plastic crinkles as I unwrap it.

Olivia leans around Dylan. "I wanted a nose ring for years, but my parents wouldn't let me." Her full lips tilt downward into a pout.

"Yeah." Taylor's face falls as she watches me select a piece of Swiss to lay on one of the crackers. "Mine didn't really care."

The words carry a subtle sting, like there's more to the story than she wants to share.

"Well, you're lucky," Olivia says. "Mine care way too much." Her jaw tightens, and she presses on an open Doritos bag on the counter, crunching the chips beneath her index finger.

We wait for her to say more, to explain, but she stays silent, and the only sound is the crinkle and crunch of the bag beneath her finger until Dylan whispers something that makes her laugh.

What was it the message said about her? That her father had bought her awards because she couldn't live up to her brother's achievements? I've been in boarding school long enough to know parents come in a full spectrum, from the super-controlling ones who want their kid to get into Harvard, down to the ones who couldn't care less and are only trying to unload the responsibility of their kid from their lives. Then there's my mom, who's stuck in the nostalgia of her own amazing experience.

Trust me, Emily, these will be the best years of your life. You'll form lifelong relationships.

Was she including her broken marriage to my dad in that list? Or whatever awful thing happened that he used to hint at occasionally? *North Hall, Elizabeth,* he'd say, usually when she had some harebrained idea he didn't like. That would clam her up real fast.

Funny how time glosses over the bad things in our memories. Does that mean one day I'll look back on this trip as a great experience?

Ha. My entire body aches with stress and exhaustion, a fact made all too prominent now that I'm doing something as normal as sitting down to eat.

I pop open the can of Diet Coke, savoring the fizzy burst of its scent. At the noise, Simon glances at me. Maybe it's time to see who *he* thinks the killer is. Before I've quite thought things through,

I wave him over. His eyebrows quirk above his dark eyeglass frames, but then he glances at Amir and walks behind the others. Amir follows, stopping on my other side to talk to Taylor.

Simon heads around the semicircle to the last stool on my other side.

Again, someone who has constantly surprised me—both with his sharp wit and the protective way he hovers near Olivia. Yet I can't help questioning what else lurks beneath the surface. He glances at her as he sits, then back at his drink.

"You're the brains around here," I whisper. "Who do you think is behind these attacks?"

Blake leans forward on his elbows to listen.

Simon shrugs moodily. "How should I know?" His gaze darts to Olivia and Dylan again, so fast I almost don't notice. Does he know something about her that I don't? Or . . .

An idea forms in my mind. "Are you *annoyed* at Dylan?"

"Dude," Blake whisper-shouts. "Do you *like* her?"

Simon's white face burns red, and he starts to stand, but I reach for his arm. Nearby, Olivia giggles at something Dylan said. When I glance back at her, she's oblivious to us, flirtatiously batting her eyelashes at my classmate.

"Wait, don't go," I say to Simon, and he settles onto the stool again.

Blake leans in even closer. "We won't tell her."

Simon shakes his head. "That's stupid. She picks on me all the time. Of course I don't like her." His words don't carry any weight, like he's repeating the same lines he's told himself for ages but maybe finally realizing they're not true. "She wasn't always like this," he mutters.

Sounds a whole lot like Nikki.

And me too, if I'm being honest.

"Have you guys gone to school together for ages?" I ask.

"First grade. Lancashire is ninth through twelfth, but we came from the same prep school." He glances at Olivia again, then back to his hands.

My mouth forms an O. "Wow. That's a long time. Exeter starts junior boarding in fifth, but I didn't know anybody when I arrived." Nikki and I were joined at the hip after two weeks.

"People definitely change." Blake sucks on his upper lip. His gaze darts to Olivia and Dylan, then back to Simon, and secret amusement dances in his eyes. "But don't throw in the towel yet. You've still got the fourth quarter."

"*What?*" Simon's face crinkles.

"You guys"—Olivia flips her long, wavy hair off her shoulder—"stop hassling Simon. He's got enough issues already."

Instead of his usual quick retort, Simon sighs softly and climbs off his stool, leaving his can on the counter. Olivia lets out a long huff, like she's annoyed by his reaction.

"Bro, you can't actually go anywhere." Blake's face grows serious. "Not without the rest of us."

"Unless you're the killer," I offer. Then I laugh, so he won't think I'm *completely* serious. But what better way to test his acting skills.

"Sorry, not this time." His mouth twists into a wry smile, and I can't tell if he's joking or actually serious. The question must appear on my face, because he follows up with, "I'm kidding. Obviously."

"What about the Two Truths and a Lie paper?" I probably shouldn't press, but at this point, why hold back? This is the best chance I've had to ply him with questions. "You read it off to our group like it was no big deal."

He flops back onto the stool, his shoulders slumping. "It wasn't a big deal. I told you, I like being alone. People don't hassle you with questions." His fingers push up his glasses, rubbing the bridge of his nose. "And after this trip, I can say there are more important things than scholarships or revenge. Like survival."

"I'll drink to that." Blake lets out one of his full-bellied laughs and holds up his can of Mountain Dew for a toast. When Simon only stares, I shake my head, grinning, and clink my can into Blake's.

"You seriously need some social skills," I say. Apparently, whoever killed Evan also managed to kill my mouth's filter, because I never would've bothered pointing this fact out to Simon six hours ago. And yet struggling for your life somehow puts everything into perspective. We're in this together—those of us who aren't killers, anyway. I hold my can up next to his, where it sits on the counter. "Come on, you can do it."

Simon shoots me a look of annoyance, but after a second it gives way to the slightest upturn of his mouth. He manages to look resentful, but he picks up the can and knocks it clumsily against mine, then does the same for Blake.

"I can't believe I'm saying this"—Blake shakes his head—"but you're okay, dude."

"And he's brilliant," I point out. The late hour is definitely getting to me, combined with the sudden hit of caffeine and that kiss with Liam, and I feel as giddy as a twelve-year-old at a slumber party. Plus, if we all stay together until we land, we'll be fine, won't we?

My good humor must even be rubbing off on Simon, because he manages an actual smile as he brings his can to his lips.

"Of course he's brilliant," Olivia says moodily, and I realize she and Dylan have been silently observing us for the last minute. "Even a moron can see *that*."

Was that an actual . . . compliment? I'm desperate to glance at Simon for his reaction but don't dare give away what we've guessed.

When nobody responds, Olivia huffs loudly and swivels on her barstool. "Can we go downstairs yet?"

Dylan shrugs. "I'm done. You guys?" His gaze passes over me as if I'm transparent, settling on Blake, who downs the rest of his drink.

"Yeah, I'm good."

"We're ready," Amir says, and Taylor slides off her seat.

The rest of us stand, and Olivia heads for the stairs, with Dylan hard on her heels. I hang back, as if waiting for the others, to give Simon space to tail them if he wants to. He stuffs a hand in his pocket, ducks his head, and follows in silence. Amir and Taylor stroll toward the door after him, a few paces ahead of me and Blake.

"That was kind of you," I whisper to him once Simon is hopefully out of earshot.

Blake scratches his head as he walks out from behind the bar counter. "It's too easy to believe the bad stuff and forget the good about people."

He's right. I can't help but think of Paige.

The others have vanished into the entryway stairwell ahead of us when the sound of footsteps from behind brings me and Blake to a halt.

A tall figure emerges through the shadows of the staff quarters doorway.

Liam, his face ashen.

And he's alone.

20

OBJECTS IN THE MIRROR

11:43 p.m. CDT

My eyes automatically run over his hands, his face, his limbs, checking for blood, as he walks toward us. But there's nothing, and he looks as whole as he did fifteen minutes ago.

Could it be Lily? Ann? Fear clutches at my insides.

"Liam?" My voice wobbles. "What happened? Why are you alone?"

He holds a finger to his lips and stops near the bar, waving us closer. I exchange a quick glance with Blake, who nods and follows me over to Liam.

Liam leans around us, looking at the empty exit to the entryway stairs. "The rest of them left you two alone?"

"Just now," Blake says. "We're supposed to be following. What's up?"

"What happened?" I ask impatiently. "Are they okay?"

His brow furrows for a second, then his face clears. "Oh, Lily and Ann? Yes, they're fine. They're with the senior flight attendant."

"O'Connor?"

"She's awake?" Blake asks at the same time.

"Yes, but . . ."

Blake pumps his fist, and I let out a slow breath. The tension releases from my too-rigid back so quickly I feel like a limp spaghetti noodle.

Finally, somebody who can deal with this situation. We're going to be okay.

Liam shakes his head. "No, you're missing the point. Here's the thing." He reaches into his pants pocket and pulls out a piece of cream-colored paper, thick and textured this time instead of a wide-ruled notebook sheet. What is it?

Apprehension ripples through my system as I stare at it, tucked in his strong hand.

Blake cracks his knuckles. "What'd you find?"

"So I took the other two back to show them the hidden staircase," he says rapidly, "and when we got upstairs, we checked on the attendants and found the one just waking up. When we told her about Evan, she wanted to see the body and where he was killed." He squeezes his fist around the paper. "While Ann was showing her the bathroom, I noticed Dylan's blazer on the nightstand in the bedroom."

Blake frowns. "Maybe he left it there when we went to move Evan."

"Maybe. Anyway, Lily thought we should check his pockets, and"—Liam holds out the paper to me—"we found this."

I take the folded paper. It's heavy in my hand, the same way my blood feels right now. *Dylan?* What does this mean? Does Lily suspect him?

Liam waits, his anxious gaze on my face, as I open it. Blake leans in next to me to see.

My mouth goes so dry that it's suddenly hard to swallow. It's not just any paper. It's from a sketchbook. *Mine.*

It's the picture of the house on the Cape—easily the best thing I've ever drawn—and it's ruined. Now there's a list of our names, written in the same handwriting we've seen again and again on this trip, right in the middle of the ocean, destroying the light dancing on the waves.

Evan and Paige have been crossed off in red ink. Two names are circled. Olivia's and—

Mine.

I think I might cry.

We're . . . next? Fear ripples through my system, mingled with sheer disbelief. Framing me didn't work, so the killer is going to bump me off instead?

But Dylan? It *can't* be him. I stare at the paper, struggling to make my brain comprehend, but the letters swim in front of my eyes and I blink rapidly.

When I finally look at Liam again, he pulls me into a fierce embrace. My cheek presses against the soft gray cotton of his sweater and the reassuring strength of his firm shoulder. For a second, wrapped in his arms, I feel perfectly safe, despite the awful list now crumpling in my hand.

"It's your artwork, isn't it?" he asks, rubbing one hand up and down my back.

I nod against his chest. "It was in my bag." It would've been easy for someone to find while stashing the pills, but Dylan didn't know about my clandestine hobby. I've never shown him my sketch pad before. And despite this new evidence, my brain fights against the idea that Dylan is the killer. There's no way he could know what I did to Nikki and keep it secret this long. And even if he did, he wouldn't kill people.

There's just no way. Is there? And am I willing to risk lives on that conviction?

"Dude," Blake says as Liam releases me, "are you sure this

wasn't planted? Or maybe . . . I know you guys are friends with Lily and everything . . ."

Thumps sound from the entryway stairs. "Hey, are you guys coming?" Taylor calls.

"Yeah, just a sec!" I holler back. We need a chance to unravel this mess and figure out what to do before Dylan finds out.

"No," Liam says to Blake. "Not Lily. I trust her. Besides, I watched her pull it out of his pocket."

"It's not his handwriting," I say. "I mean, not that I recognize. It could've been put there by someone else. Just like someone put those pills in my bag."

I know what it's like to be framed. Awful.

"O'Connor doesn't think we can take that risk," Liam says. "Dylan was alone in the back for a long time before we found Evan, and she says she found him skulking around the galley earlier too."

"She did?" I ask. What if I'm wrong about him?

He nods, his jaw tightening.

"One thing's for sure." Blake points at me. "*You* shouldn't go near him. Olivia either. Just in case."

"O'Connor wants both you and Olivia to go back and stay with her until she figures out what to do." Liam looks toward the shadowed hallway leading toward the tail. "She's trying to contact the foundation right now. Lily and Ann didn't want to leave her alone, so I volunteered to come tell you." His blue eyes find my face again. "She thinks you might have some inside knowledge on Dylan that could help too."

Amir's head pops through the entryway door. "Hey, quit stalling. We're supposed to stick together."

His gaze lands on Liam, and he frowns.

I hold up a hand to fend off his questions. "It's okay, Amir. We'll explain in a minute. Did the others go down?"

He steps into the room, followed by Taylor. "Yeah, Dylan, Olivia, and Simon did. What's up? Where are Ann and Lily?"

I point aft in answer to Amir's question as Liam glances between me and Blake, worry lining his handsome face at the idea of Olivia downstairs with Dylan. "At least Simon is with them," I say.

Amir starts toward us, followed by Taylor. "What's going on?" she asks. "Where are the other girls?"

Liam turns to Taylor and relays the good news about O'Connor, leaving out the part about the list.

Taylor presses a hand to her heart and lets out a relieved sigh, slouching against one of the lounge chairs near the door. "Oh, thank God. When is she coming up front?"

"As soon as she gets instructions from the foundation," he says.

Amir pumps his fist. "Let's go tell the others." He offers a hand to Taylor and pulls her to her feet. Blake moves to follow as they head for the entryway again, but Liam stops him.

"How do we get Olivia and Em back there without making Dylan suspicious?" he whispers.

Blake frowns. "We could escort Emily, then come back for Olivia. But then we'd be ditching Amir and Taylor instead of keeping to a group of three or more. And then everyone would wonder why we wanted Olivia to head aft too. Unless they just *all* want to go aft and see for themselves."

Liam shakes his head. "We should keep Dylan apart from O'Connor if at all possible. Just in case."

"I'll go by myself," I volunteer, hoping that my sense of relief isn't curdling my few remaining brain cells that are still functioning despite the sleep deprivation. "You guys can go downstairs with

Amir and Taylor and look for a way to extricate Olivia from Dylan without looking suspicious."

"No, you shouldn't go alone," Liam says. "I'll go tell her we couldn't get you back there without alerting Dylan."

"But he's downstairs with Simon and Olivia," I point out. "And the others are just a few compartments back, right? I'll be fine."

"Yeah, but still . . . What if Dylan made up some excuse and left them? He could be lurking somewhere back there."

"You guys come to the top of the stairs," Blake says, heading for the door. "I'll run down to make sure everyone is there, and we can all stay in sight of each other. Then if it's clear, Emily can go alone."

"I'll talk to Lily, Ann, and the attendant. Make a plan." I tuck the incriminating paper into my pocket, grateful nobody has leaped to the conclusion *I* planted it in Dylan's blazer to frame *him*. This whole thing is such a convoluted mess.

We head for the stairs. Liam and I pause at the top while Blake walks all the way down and stops in front of the short hallway leading into the entertainment salon. He leans sideways, probably trying to get a better view, then gives us the thumbs-up.

"You're good," he whisper-shouts up the stairs.

I turn to Liam, my heart rate suddenly skyrocketing like it's our last farewell or something. Which is stupid, because everyone—and Dylan, in particular—is accounted for at the moment. "Meet you in the dining room in fifteen minutes with Blake and Olivia? We'll go over the plan and get Olivia to safety. Unless O'Connor's ready to come up front sooner."

Liam takes my hand, wrapping his warm, strong fingers around my cold skin. He studies my face for a moment, as if he's memorizing every detail. The air crackles between us, like there's too much space. My breath catches, but instead of kissing me, he squeezes my hand gently. "See you soon."

I squeeze back, then let go. My knees go weak at the way his gaze lingers as he turns to join Blake downstairs. After they disappear, I press a hand to my chest and let out a short sigh, savoring this delicious feeling.

But walking through the dim space reminds me of the harsh facts, and my hand clenches around the ruined sketch now curled into my blazer pocket. It's a vicious reminder that whether or not Dylan was framed, there's still a killer on the loose. Targeting us one by one.

Is it him? Does that explain why he kissed me earlier? To try and build my trust?

And Olivia . . . Does this explain his behavior toward her?

As much as my brain rebels against the idea, in all the movies it's always the person closest to you. The person you're least likely to suspect. An image pops into my brain—my mom's side mirror, out the passenger window in our Subaru. The one I stare at for countless hours while trying to fall asleep at night. Tiny white print runs along the bottom: OBJECTS IN MIRROR ARE CLOSER THAN THEY APPEAR.

How many hours have Nikki and I spent with Dylan? Of course, even Nikki—how many hours have I spent with her? And yet reality has gotten distorted with each secret we keep, with each time we share what's easy, instead of what's true, until we don't really see each other anymore.

Habit makes me pause in the doorway to the first staff compartment, the empty one, with workstations and rows of seats. It's lit in here with the soft nighttime lights, same as the floor below, but there's no sign of motion. I listen for voices coming from the back—for Lily or Ann or O'Connor—but the air is silent except for an occasional distant thump. They must be talking softly enough their voices aren't carrying.

One of the window shades is cracked a couple of inches, and instead of black night outside, the sky glows a faint golden orange. Hope swells in my heart. If it's after dawn, we must be almost there. Despite my urgency to get to the others, my feet drag me over to the window, where I lift the shade the rest of the way in the hope of glimpsing the real world. A reminder that this airplane isn't the end of the story. Somewhere far below, the swollen waves of the ocean toss and churn, but soon the endless sea will give way to coastline and safety.

If we can just keep everyone alive until Paris, the police and the foundation can untangle this mess. Forget winning a scholarship— I'd give almost anything to be safe with my mom again in our car. *That* situation is temporary, unlike being dead. She's going to find a job—I know it. And I know Aunt Kacie will offer to help. At least we'll have each other.

And, hopefully, I'll have Nikki. Once we talk things through, she might decide she can't be my friend anymore, but even that would be better than the sham relationship we have now.

I dig out my phone and open my text messages as I keep walking toward the tail. I won't be able to send it until we land, but at least it'll be ready.

Hey Nik, we need to talk. My fingers pause over the keypad, but I force myself to keep going. **I've got some stuff to tell you. Love you, Em.**

Those last words aren't a lie. Deep down, beneath my resentment and the knowledge we're nowhere as close as we used to be, I do love her.

I slip the phone into my pocket as I approach the hallway at the rear of the seating compartment. An hour and a half to go in this flight.

It seems darker here than I remembered, lit only with floor track lighting and safety signs on the ceiling. My footsteps thump loudly in the eerie silence. Shouldn't I be able to hear someone by now? The door to the elevator is slightly ajar, probably from the guys using it earlier, but a little draft of recirculated air makes the hairs stick up on the back of my neck as I go past it.

By the time I reach the last compartment, with its smaller seating suites, my internal alarm is blaring full volume. The room is deathly still, no sign of Ann, Lily, or O'Connor. All the window shades are closed. I take a couple of deep breaths. There's probably a perfectly reasonable explanation. Maybe O'Connor already got through to the foundation and they went downstairs without waiting for me.

But why didn't they stay on this level and follow Liam? Wouldn't O'Connor need to find a way to talk to the pilots? Or did they dash downstairs to the bedroom suite for some reason while they were waiting for me?

I stand in the center of the room, gnawing the inside of my cheek and wishing I wasn't alone. Something definitely doesn't seem right. Maybe it's the stillness, like I should be able to hear them if they're just downstairs. That's ridiculous, of course—the engines are loud enough I couldn't hear anything from below. Or maybe it's just the thought that the killer could be up front right now, plotting some way to escape the others and come find me.

Swallowing, I shake off the oppressive feelings and force myself to focus on what to do now. Should I retreat the way I came? Or take the stairs back here, just in case they're below me in the bedroom? At the tail of the compartment, two doors are marked with glowing signs: LAVATORY on the left and EXIT on the right. That side must lead to the stairs.

My gaze catches on the glass doors concealing the other two flight attendants. Wait a second—O'Connor woke up, so maybe one of them will be stirring now too. Then I wouldn't have to keep going alone. *And* we'd have another adult.

Hope spurs my feet into motion, and after crossing the central area, I slide open the glass doors. The track lighting on the floor doesn't do much to illuminate the space, but my eyes have adjusted well enough to easily make out the motionless, dark shapes in the seats.

I blink. Once. Twice. Then clutch the door frame as the world rocks beneath my feet.

Because instead of two sleeping forms, there are three.

And O'Connor is one of them.

21

BLACK BOX

11:56 p.m. CDT

My stomach roils as the cheese and crackers I just ate try to force their way out. I step inside, prodding each one of the attendants, lifting O'Connor's hand and letting it fall back onto her lap, like she's faking it and I'm going to catch her in the act.

There *must* be some mistake. Liam wouldn't have—

He couldn't—

The cheese and crackers win, and it's all I can do to cross the compartment, slam the lavatory door open, and reach the shiny metal toilet before everything comes up. I kneel on the cramped floor, wedged between the toilet and the metal sink, sucking in deep breaths of reeking vomit mixed with the fruity smell of commercial hand soap. After I flush the toilet, it takes a long moment before my legs have the strength to stand, and I wash my hands and rinse out my mouth, scarcely thinking about what I'm doing.

If he lied about the flight attendant, then he must've lied about the paper too. *He's* the one who dug it out of my bag, after I told him I liked to draw. Wrecked the picture I had hoped to show him. Maybe at the same time he planted the pills and the wrapper. I squeeze the sketch through the fabric of my pocket, fire burning in my throat as it crumples beneath my hand. He set me up so thoroughly even now I can scarcely wrap my mind around this level of betrayal, a thousand times worse than if it had been Dylan. My lips still tingle at the memory of Liam's kiss.

The fire in my throat works its way up into my head, flaming in my sinuses and then into my eyes, until the tears prick and burn. I clutch my arms across my midsection, wishing I could shrink inside myself and vanish entirely.

What was the point, letting me come back here alone? Was he hoping I wouldn't check on the other flight attendants? Wouldn't figure out he'd lied until it was too late? My throat constricts. Maybe it was worse than that—maybe he'd planned on separating me from the others to kill me. He told me not to go by myself, but maybe that was an act to look innocent. Or he was hoping to find a way to come with me. If Blake and the others hadn't been there . . .

Tears stream down my cheeks now, and I make no effort to stop them. Bile creeps up into my esophagus, but my stomach is empty enough that I swallow it back down.

Then another thought hits me, and I cling to the lavatory sink as the room sways again.

What about Lily and Ann? Are they downstairs, or did he . . . ? Oh, dear God. No. *No no no no.*

I can barely see as I stumble out of the lavatory and run my fingers across the exit door, feeling for the latch. The door folds inward and slides open, revealing a narrow staircase. Tiny rust-colored stains decorate the taupe carpet like scattered confetti.

How could *he* be the killer? Liam? He's been so kind to everyone on this trip, so genuine, so levelheaded. Never blaming, never over-reacting. Was it because he was orchestrating everything all along?

Every cell in my body revolts against this wretched new possibility as I half run, half tumble down the stairs and burst into the empty bedroom from one of the doors I had taken to be a closet earlier.

I check the office first, which is empty, then the bedroom. No blazer on the nightstand. No Lily or Ann.

Not a surprise, though, is it?

Then I head back to the bathroom, fingers wrapped across my mouth to ward off whatever horrors lie in wait. Bloody shoe prints create a trail across the carpet leading out of the bathroom, dwindling to nothingness halfway to the staircase. A testimony of the guys moving Evan. His body is gone, but a huge swath of blood remains on the floor, now marred by scuff marks.

The lighting here is still dim, but better than before, when only the emergency lights were on. No dark shape looms in the shower, but my eye catches on the Jacuzzi tub, where a red blazer and a spray of black hair stand out against white plastic.

Ann. It's got to be Ann.

I force my feet onto the tile and pick my way around the lake of blood. Maybe she's still alive. Maybe I can stop her bleeding. Call for help.

But who would hear me? Who would come?

Pity and horror twist in my heart as I approach the tub. Ann sits slumped against the back wall, her pretty fishbone braid draped over the edge like she could just be taking a bath. Her hands are tucked in her lap, but her glassy eyes stare at the plane's ceiling. I press my fingers to her neck, vainly hoping to find a pulse. Her skin is still warm beneath my touch, but not warm enough. Like a forgotten cup of hot cocoa that's sat out for too long. She's gone.

I ball my fingers into a fist and press them against my mouth. The pressure against my lips feels solid and reassuring. Alive. Like it's going to keep me from screaming and crumbling apart into one of those panicking girls in a horror movie.

The button-down shirt beneath Ann's blazer is stained dark red across her chest like she was stabbed. With what?

And how long do I have before Liam extricates himself from

the group and comes to find me? He knows I'm alone.

I need to find a weapon.

And Lily.

Resolve strengthens my shaking knees. He won't catch me unaware.

I scan the bedroom for anything sharp, pointy, or heavy. Nothing leaps out at me, so I head for the closet, on the opposite side of the bedroom doorway. The doors slide open easily.

All the air whooshes out of my lungs at the sight of a crumpled body and tangled red hair on the carpeted floor beneath the shelves.

It takes a second for the utter shock to wear off before I have enough sense to drop to my knees next to her. "Lily?"

Her eyes are shut, not glassy and lifeless, and her face isn't deathly pale yet, not the way Evan's was. Is there a chance?

She's curled on her side, one arm under her head, the other flung backward at what looks like a painful angle. I scooch forward, partway into the closet, and move aside strands of her hair to expose her neck so I can feel for a pulse. Angry dark-blue bruises circle her throat, and I jerk my hand back in surprise.

He strangled her.

With his arm, or a belt, or . . . his hands. The smudges look like fingerprints.

Bitter tears wet my face again as anger and terror mingle in my churning stomach. I've got two fingers extended, reaching for Lily's neck again, when she groans. Her eyelids flutter.

"Lily?" I whisper. "Can you hear me?"

She groans again, fainter this time, and the arm on top twitches like she wants to move it.

They always say not to move somebody who's been injured until you figure out there's no damage to the spine, but I take her hand anyway, sliding it gently toward me and bending her elbow. The fingers are cold, but she's still alive. There's no visible wound beyond the bruising. Nothing I can fix with first aid.

"I have to get help." I hate to leave her here, but I've got to tell the others. Whether they think I did it or not, we need to move her into a seat for landing. Provide protection in case the killer figures out she's not dead. And if I stay back here alone . . .

I might be joining her and Ann on the victim list.

"We . . . were . . . wrong . . ." Lily coughs, the sound feeble and harsh at the same time, and my heart pangs with concern. Her eyes bulge, the whites gleaming in the dim lighting, and her breath comes in shallow gasps.

"Shh, I know. Save your strength. I'll be back soon with some of the others, and we'll take care of you." I push onto my feet, crouching next to her.

Her eyelids flutter again, and this time they stay partially open. Her gaze focuses on the floor, but her whole body trembles like she's trying to move.

"Don't move, Lily." I rest both hands lightly on her shoulder. "You might hurt something else."

"Liam," she moans, like every word costs her too much. Her hands shake. She must be utterly terrified of him.

"I'll find him," I say through gritted teeth. "Hang on, okay? You're safe for now, and I'll be back as soon as I can."

I leave the closet door partially open to make sure she has air, then turn away before I can change my mind. I *hate* leaving her like this. I hate that we're even in this situation. But as long as Liam thinks she's dead, he won't come back here looking for her again. Not before I find him.

The soft nighttime lighting bathes the office in a gentle glow.

Our puzzle sits untouched on the desk, its picture of the Eiffel Tower silently daring me to make it there alive. Then reminding me of who I wanted to share that moment with, and how all my hopes have been utterly crushed.

Sorrow threatens to take me out at the knees, so I clench my teeth and force my wobbly legs to search the room. I scan the bookcases first, looking for anything that could serve as a weapon. There's a hefty hardback Merriam-Webster dictionary—that might work, though it'd be pretty cumbersome. The other books are squeezed tight enough to rule out the need for bookends, and there isn't much in the way of decorative knickknacks. Probably to keep stuff from flying around during takeoff and landing.

Maybe the desk will have something. I rummage through the drawers first, checking for a letter opener or something equally sharp, but there's nothing but Bonhomme Foundation pens and stationery and envelopes. My eyes snag on a surprisingly beat-up white folder in the bottom drawer, tucked far in the back. It's not like I have time to explore, but I pull it out anyway.

A brown-and-green logo fills the lower right corner, and I run my fingers across the bumpy, raised *W* and *D*. Inside, the folder holds only lined notebook paper. Wide-ruled, and very much like the paper used for the notes we've found during the flight. Who put it here? Lined paper is a fairly ubiquitous office supply—is its presence here a coincidence?

I stuff the folder back into the drawer, then stand and examine the top of the desk. The glass paperweight sitting in its wooden tray gleams at me, and I realize the logo inside of it is an exact match for the one on the folder. Does it belong to someone on the flight staff? Or someone from the foundation who flies on this plane frequently? I wish I could remember where else I've seen it, but now isn't the time to stand around puzzling it out.

Instead, I pluck the smooth glass ball off the desktop, hefting it in my hand. It'll work, especially when combined with muscle memory from years of softball. If Liam's hiding somewhere ahead, waiting for his chance to attack me, I only need to hit him hard enough to knock him out. Then I can explain to the others, and we can help Lily and secure Liam under guard until we land.

Doubt gnaws at my insides, making my stomach skip around like a roller-coaster car as I work my way forward. There's no sign of him lurking back here, waiting to confront me. What if I'm wrong about his plan to get me alone? What if he's in the dining room with Blake and Olivia like we agreed, biding his time? Would they believe me if I accuse him?

Or would they think *I* hurt Ann and Lily, and now I'm going after Liam too?

None of it feels real until I pass through the narrow hallway between the kitchen and elevator, and step out into the dimly lit dining room to find Liam waiting for me at the other end of the compartment.

Alone.

22

FULL UPRIGHT AND LOCKED POSITION

June 22, 12:10 a.m. CDT

I'm only a few paces away from him when I decide my plan is utter trash. Voices drift back to us from the next compartment forward. A pair of arms—I can't see who they belong to—opens an overhead bin and pulls out a bag.

I can't attack him here. What if he yells, or even just drops to the floor with a loud thunk? They'll come running. They'll help him get free, and I'll be the one locked up instead. At least if I can contain him first, I'll have time to explain *before* they accuse me of being a murderer.

Time to think of something else, and quick.

Liam offers a lopsided grin as I draw near. "Hey," he says, low and soft, like nothing's changed, like I'm still the girl he wants to be with, not his next victim. It's like one of those complicated math problems where no matter how you try to solve it, you never get the right answer.

He looks past me, as if checking for Ann and Lily, and has the audacity to frown when he sees I'm alone. "Where are the others?"

It must be an act, and if he doesn't realize I've figured out what he did, I'm not going to give myself away. Though how could he expect I wouldn't have found them?

"I was going to ask you the same thing." I infuse as much forced affection into my tone as I can, but it comes out flat.

Thankfully, he doesn't seem to notice. "They're in the entertainment salon. We couldn't find a way to get Olivia apart from Dylan without looking suspicious, and I thought it was better for Blake to stay with them."

"They let you go alone?"

He shrugs. "Yeah. Well, Amir and Simon wanted stuff out of their bags, so not quite alone."

Why wouldn't they trust him, though? In many ways, he's been our leader, looking out for everyone, keeping calm in the midst of the chaos, protecting us.

Or so we thought.

In the semidarkness of the cabin, his brow furrows, like he can tell something's wrong. "Why are *you* alone? What's the plan?"

What's his endgame, acting innocent like this? Not making a move against me?

Maybe he's biding his time, hoping to lure me back into the big group. But why? Does he have the lights rigged to cut out again? Or—

With everything he's planted in my stuff, the peanut wrapper and the pills . . . maybe he's planning on setting *me* up to take the fall.

For all of it.

My stomach drops.

I can't go up front with Liam. The others would automatically believe him over me—he's seen to that already. And my pockets are loaded with incriminating notes. But how far is he willing to play along to get me to go with him?

"Actually"—I scramble to create a new plan—"I couldn't find them. The compartments back there were empty." Maybe if I keep playing along, acting like I didn't find another body in the tail, he'll come with me. "I thought maybe they came up here."

His brows squeeze together, and he shifts his weight, no doubt trying to figure out if I suspect him or if I'm just too dense to connect the dots. So much for Liam having a good opinion of me.

"No, they didn't. That's really weird." He glances through the doorway into the seating compartment. "We should get the others."

Right. So he can accuse me in front of them. I don't think so.

I shake my head. "No, we can't trust anyone else. Liam . . ." My voice quavers, an act that's easy to pull off when my friends are dying. "Somebody's planning this. First that list you found, and now more people missing? Maybe this is bigger than just Dylan."

"What do you want to do?" he whispers.

"Search for Lily and Ann." I wring my hands for effect. "I was too scared to stay back there alone."

When he throws an arm around my shoulders and pulls me against his side, it takes all my willpower not to stiffen. But there's no way he can kill me right here, feet away from where Amir is stuffing his bag into the overhead bin. And if he's truly planning on framing me, he can't kill me at all unless he makes it look like a suicide.

Like Paige.

Ugh, I think I might be sick.

Thankfully, he releases me and says, "Okay, let's go. But if we don't find anything, we have to let the others know." His voice is grim, determined. That same kind, brave leader I've come to appreciate this entire trip. Who I encouraged him to be.

Am I completely wrong about him?

That's not a risk I can afford to take.

"Of course," I say. "Do you mind . . . going first? I'm kind of creeped out."

"Sure." He smiles, blissfully unaware of the heavy paperweight in my pocket.

He leads the way as we retrace my steps, circling past the dining room table and its large chairs. The storage closet opposite the kitchen—it's got a latch on the outside. Probably to hold the door shut during flight, but hopefully it's sturdy enough to secure a muscular six-foot-tall teenage killer too.

My fingers tighten on the glass paperweight as we reach the hallway. I slide it out of my pocket. A blow to Liam's head is the only answer, even though the idea of hitting him makes me want to puke. Again.

I shuffle a half step closer—there's no room for error. If this blow doesn't land right, I'll be the one locked in the closet.

Or dead.

Gritting my teeth, I raise my arm and slam the paperweight into the back of his head. Tears stream unchecked down my cheeks as he lurches forward without so much as a groan, slumping against the wall and sliding to the carpeted hallway floor.

Panic rips through me—*What if I've killed him?*—so I run my fingers through his soft, thick hair and relax the tiniest fraction when I don't feel anything more than a growing lump. No obvious fracture. No blood. I stuff the paperweight into my pocket.

His legs stir, so I jerk open the storage closet and shove him inside, grunting with the effort. The door won't quite close, but when I lean against it, I can just slide the thick bolt into place.

Now what? My hands are trembling, my heart hammering, and I can scarcely force a full breath of air into my lungs. Lily needs help. I have to go tell the others what happened.

But doubts tear me apart as I linger in the hall. Three of our fellow competitors are now incapacitated or dead in the back of this plane, in addition to Paige and Evan, and I'm about to walk out alone with a story about how Liam deceived us all.

Sure, they voted earlier that I wasn't guilty, but now . . . ? Liam made sure to plant those Ambien pills in *my* bag so nobody would want to trust me.

I lean against the wall opposite the closet, tilting my head up and letting out a long, slow breath. How did things disintegrate so badly? A lump swells in my throat, and I blink as the contoured airplane ceiling goes blurry.

This trip has been one nightmare from start to finish. First, me cheating to get here. Then Dylan and the kissing. The murders. Now Liam, and the fact there's no way out.

Cheating is what started it all. And I've been more or less lying ever since, to myself and everyone else. Pretending what I did was justified because of my circumstances. Sure, being homeless sucks, but it was wrong to steal Nikki's place. And even *more* wrong to kiss her boyfriend. At every opportunity, I've kept my secrets hidden instead of telling the truth. I've dug myself into a hole so deep no one will ever believe me.

Maybe it's time to come clean anyway. How else can I become the person I truly want to be?

A tight band wraps around my rib cage, forcing me to take shallow breaths, but I dig into my blazer pocket and sift through the paper collection for the two pieces I need. The list of names, and the original Two Truths and a Lie message. Clutching the papers keeps my hands busy as I drag my heavy feet back through the dining room. Before I can second-guess my decision, I enter the seating compartment and press forward.

Olivia, Dylan, Blake, Amir, Taylor, and Simon sit in the entertainment salon. I stop short and blink. Somehow, they've gotten

Simon to play a game of cards with them, and he's actually smiling. In fact, with his dark glasses and spiky hair, he's kind of cute—in a nerdy way.

Taylor laughs as she reaches for the draw pile, and Amir gives her a playful swat. For one second, a sense of blessed normalcy settles over me. Then Blake notices me.

He leaps to his feet, and from the way his jaw loosens as his gaze sweeps from my feet to my head, I must look as disheveled on the outside as I feel on the inside. "What happened? Where's the flight attendant? Ann, Lily, Liam?"

"I'll tell you." My voice grates like a rusty door hinge, so I clear my throat. "But first I have to read this." Despite my shaking hands, I manage to unfold the lined piece of notebook paper.

"Wait—" Dylan stands too. "Emily, what's going on?" His eyes narrow, and I can't blame him. Not after how quick I was to assume the worst about him and believe Liam.

My insides deflate, all the resolve behind my decision fading like a spent flower at the end of summer. "Please just let me read this first," I say wearily. "Then I'll explain."

They stare at me, their faces a mixture of curiosity and fear and worry.

"*One: My mom lost our house, and now we live in our car.*" I keep my eyes on the paper so I won't have to see the horror and pity on Dylan's face. *He'll* never have to live in a car.

"*Two: I nearly failed math in ninth grade and have a 2.75 GPA.*" My voice catches, but I keep pushing on.

"*Three: The only way I managed to get into this competition was by cheating.*"

There. I said it. The awful truth.

I stop to swallow the lump in my throat, and Taylor fills in the silence. Her perfectly sculpted dark eyebrows pull together. "Why are you reading that to us?"

"Because . . . they're true. All three of them are true."

Silence settles like a heavy weight over the room, pressing down on my head until my knees shake. I let out a slow breath. Hard as this was, I haven't even come close to telling everything they need to hear. Not with Lily suffering in a closet.

Dylan's face falls. "You cheated?"

"Yes." My mouth feels like it's full of sawdust. "I switched the files and student ID numbers on my and Nikki's applications."

He leans back in his seat, eyes going wide as he connects the dots. "That's why you said you wanted to be a lawyer. You were using her bio. She *should* have been here."

I nod, though in all honesty, family law might not be a bad profession. I could work with a nonprofit that helps homeless families. If I live through this experience, that is.

When I open my mouth to go on, Blake holds up his hand to stop me.

"Mine were true too," he admits, his tone a low rumble. Something sparks between us—a moment of solidarity—then he looks at the others. "I spent two months in juvenile detention last summer. I'm trying to get off steroids, but it's tough."

Dylan sucks on his lower lip, focusing very hard on the floor at my feet. He doesn't look up as he says, "The dog was a mutt from the pound. I hated the way it barked constantly. But I didn't hit it on purpose." Finally, he looks at me, his hazel eyes rimmed with liquid. "And you know about the cheating. Cassandra's family is friends with mine back home."

I press my lips together, nodding my head a fraction. Somehow, I dig up the strength to ask, "Anybody else?"

Olivia raises a hand, then swipes at her cheeks. "The night of the car crash, my brother was drunk. So I drove us home, without a license. Only I lost control and went off the road. He wasn't wearing a seat belt. I pulled him out of the car to try to give him CPR, but I couldn't save him. When the cops came, I lied and told them he'd been behind the wheel. They declared it a drunk-driving accident."

Simon's eyebrows shoot up to his hairline at her admission, and when he squeezes her shoulder, she doesn't bat him away.

"How did someone find out?" Taylor asks, her voice thick. "And which one of us did it?"

"Liam." I nearly choke on his name, and I press a hand to my mouth to stifle the sob working its way out of my chest.

"*What?*" The others glance between each other and me, their faces twisted with confusion.

I hold up the other piece of paper. "I have more to tell you."

"Shouldn't we get Lily and Ann?" Amir asks, pointing aft. "So they can hear?"

The paper trembles in my hand. It's like I'm running on autopilot, with nothing in mind beyond the immediate goal of telling them what happened and waiting for the accusations to fly. They've been far more understanding than I expected so far. Maybe because they, too, have been wrestling with the guilt of having their secrets exposed.

I shake my head. "Not yet. I'll get to them."

Blake rubs his hands over his face, momentarily covering up the same dark circles the rest of us have. When he pulls his hands back, he frowns. "What about the flight attendant?"

"She's not awake." The words catch in my throat. "I'll explain everything. Please just let me talk."

Before I lose the tiny invisible thread of strength holding me upright.

But as I search for the right words, loud, screechy feedback bursts from the plane's intercom system—just like last time.

I hunch my shoulders up to my ears, as if tensing my entire body will somehow protect me from the hideous noise. It's not the pilots—not the calm announcement we're aching to hear about landing. No, this is the sound of somebody hacking their way into the system to play their own message. Again.

Did Liam rig it up earlier in the flight?

The soothing computer voice drifts from the speakers overhead.

"Have you solved the mystery yet?"

Blake groans, flopping backward on the couch like he couldn't care less.

"Which one of you is the killer?"

Dylan takes Olivia's hand but makes eye contact with me. I look at my feet.

"Look at yourselves. You all deserve what's coming. You know the things I said about you are true."

Haven't we just confirmed that ourselves? Is that it? Is Liam using vengeance as his excuse for taking us out one at a time?

"Have you ever heard of epoxy?" the voice goes on.

I glance at Simon. Anything science-related falls into his domain, right?

He shrugs. "It's plastic."

"The interesting thing about epoxy is that you can melt it and pour it into a mold, and it will harden into a rigid, strong cast of whatever shape you want. You don't even need a 3D printer. A long, pointy screwdriver. A knife with a blade sharp enough to draw blood. Use your imagination. And because it's plastic, it won't appear on a metal detector."

My breath catches. *That's* how he did it. Liam must've carried on an epoxy weapon. I sway slightly as the plane hits a patch of turbulence, and I brace myself against the nearest chair. Why is he revealing this to us now? Did he not expect me to figure out he was the killer?

"It's time for the final game, my friends. Who's going to die next?"

With another burst of static, the message shuts off.

Olivia inhales sharply, her face blanching even whiter. There's a momentary pause, a lull in which we all look at each other, holding our breath, silently asking the same questions: What happens next? And what on earth do we do now?

Then the lights cut out for the second time, plunging us unexpectedly into near-total darkness.

23

THE FINAL GAME

12:24 a.m. CDT

Olivia screams, ten feet away from me, so loud and shrill I clap my hands over my ears, and Blake swears. A half second later, another scream erupts from somewhere up front—the blood-curdling kind that chills you to your bones. It echoes through the entryway and into the lounge, where we stand frozen in the grip of instant panic.

"Who the hell was *that*?" Blake asks, his voice reaching a higher pitch than I've ever heard.

I work my jaw, struggling to overcome my sense of paralysis. Because we're all accounted for. Liam is in the closet, Lily and the attendants are in the back, and the rest of us are *right here*.

Unless—

"Maybe it was a recording," Amir says hopefully.

"Or a flight attendant who woke up," Simon offers, in a rare moment of helpfulness.

Ice runs beneath my skin until I'm covered in goose bumps. If that's the case, she's just panicking, right? Because Liam is in the closet . . .

"Didn't Emily say—" Taylor starts, but she cuts off as thumps sound close by.

It's impossible to tell where the noises are coming from—above us, or the forward stairs, or even behind us.

"If there's a flight attendant out there, why isn't she helping us?"

"Maybe *she* needs help."

"*Where's Liam?*"

"Stay away from me!"

The voices grow increasingly frantic. People scatter in a flurry of rustling noises, fumbling for their phones, light shooting randomly in blinding beams.

"Calm down!" Blake whisper-shouts over the pandemonium, attempting to take charge. He swivels his light across our panicked faces. "If it could be a flight attendant, we've got to check. Maybe she needs help."

"No way, man," Dylan snaps. "We need to hole up and wait it out. Maybe in one of those forward compartments where it'll be easier to defend ourselves. These other spaces are too exposed."

Everyone talks at once.

"But Lily needs help," I say over the racket. "She's injured in the back bedroom."

"All the way in the tail?" Amir asks. His voice wobbles. "We can't go back there. Where's Liam?"

"He's knocked out in a closet," I say, even though I never got to finish my explanation. Will they have any reason to believe me? And what if—my lungs freeze—he found a way to escape?

"We're taking Emily's word it's Liam, but how does *she* know?" Olivia shrieks. "What if it's somebody in this room?"

"What if . . ." In the light of someone's phone, Taylor wraps her arms across her chest and pins me with a cold gaze. "What if Emily made all that up?"

The words drop like whispered atomic bombs, igniting another round of chaos. Me vociferously defending myself, the others taking sides and pushing their own agendas. Dylan still wants to barricade himself in one of the suites up front, Blake wants to find out if an attendant is awake, and Taylor refuses to move from the seat she has installed herself in.

One thing's for sure: none of this is going to help Lily.

A dreadful realization settles over me as the others keep arguing, lights flashing around the room as if no one can decide what to illuminate any more than what to do.

These people aren't going to help me. Worse, they might turn on me and prevent me from getting back to Lily. There's only one solution, even though it terrifies me to the core.

I have to go alone.

Panic swells like an overinflated balloon inside my chest, about to burst, but I suck in a couple of deep breaths and force my brain to focus. Lily needs my help. If I think about Lily, I can do this.

"Fine," Dylan practically shouts. "If you all want to stand around and get killed, go for it. I'm going to find somewhere to hide where I have a shot at protecting myself." He swivels his light toward the entryway and stomps toward the door.

"Wait up. You can't go alone!" Blake insists, but he's lost the argument at this point.

Our group, which has held together so well under a ridiculous amount of stress, is starting to fracture.

Seizing my chance while the others are distracted, I drop low beneath the nearest chair and scramble toward the seating compartment, keeping my phone's light off. By the time another beam shoots my direction, I'm already slipping behind the bulkhead nearby.

I've got to get back to that storage closet and make sure the door is still locked. Then help Lily. As I work my way up one of the aisles, I desperately want to flip on my cell phone's flashlight. But there's no reason to make a public service announcement about my location. Just in case.

Attention, attention. If you'd like to kill Emily Walters, she's heading aft on the main level. Just watch out for that paperweight she's lugging around with her. She knows how to use it.

I bite the inside of my lip, to keep from laughing at my own pathetic humor, and drag my fingers lightly along each chair on one side of the dining room table. A couple of the window shades have been cracked open, letting in long streaks of new daylight.

Enough to see the dark form of the aft bulkhead, and the even darker hole of the hallway. The floor strips show me where to walk, but that's it. No indication of what's along each wall, or who might be hiding in the darkness the blue glow doesn't reach. I stretch my fingertips in both directions, feeling along the cool metal walls as I move. When I reach the entrance to the kitchen, I feel for the storage closet on the opposite side.

The door is still shut, the lock secured in place. Relief collapses my chest. He must have set up the recording and the lights going out in advance, not expecting he'd be locked in a closet.

As if to assuage any doubts I might have, a low groan issues from within, followed by the soft thump of Liam readjusting his position. Guilt pinches at me despite everything. It's tight quarters in there, and he's got to have a huge knot on the back of his head.

I pause to listen at the end of the hallway before I enter the workstation compartment. There's some soft noise just audible below the steady thrum of the engines. Or maybe instead of hearing it, I feel it—intermittent thumps vibrating through the floor. I hold my breath, listening, but the sound doesn't get any closer. Is it above me? Maybe whoever screamed earlier? *Please let there be a flight attendant awake.*

My palms grow slick as I creep past worktables and seats facing at odd angles. The high chairbacks could easily conceal anybody wanting to hide.

I wipe my hands on my skirt. My heart beats like a humming-bird trapped within my ribs.

Check on Lily, I tell myself. *Move her to a seat. Easy-peasy.*

The hairs stand on the back of my neck as I slip into the office. Air blows from vents high overhead, bearing the same recirculated scent of plastic and air freshener that it has the entire flight. When I don't hear anything else, I force my sagging legs onward to the bedroom, again pausing in the doorway. Listening to the silence.

The emergency floor strips end here, leaving the short hallway and bedroom in near-total darkness other than a couple of glowing exit signs on the ceiling. I have no choice but to fire up my phone as I tiptoe into the bedroom. A chill tracks across my shoulders as I creep toward the closet. The door is shut. Uneasiness tugs at my insides. I could swear I left it partially open. Did Lily close it?

I slide the door, a whoosh of air releasing from my lungs when it glides silently on smooth tracks. Then I freeze. Stare at the low-pile taupe carpet.

Lily's gone.

But—

What?

My brain scrambles to catch up as I stare slack-jawed at the empty floor. Where did she go? To find a new hiding place? Or did a flight attendant wake up and find her? Could Lily be the one who screamed? But then how did she get to the front of the plane without us seeing her?

Before I can make sense of anything, low-level vibrations set off a warning in my ears again, closer this time. Soft, rhythmic thumps—like footsteps. They sound like they're coming from above, on the second level. Heading for the staircase?

I dive for the back corner of the room and wedge myself between the bed and the built-in dresser. Digging the paperweight out of my pocket, I clutch it like it's a lifeline. My chest rises and falls too fast, and I realize I'm on the brink of hyperventilating.

Slowing my breathing gives me something to think about, something to concentrate on besides this nightmare of confusion and fear.

If Liam is the killer and still locked in a closet, and the screaming earlier was a panicking flight attendant like Simon suggested, why am I curled in this corner trying to keep my terror from taking over completely?

Where is Lily?

The doubts I've been pushing aside sweep in, mixing with my anxiety and horror, pushing at the seams of my self-control. I *hate* this. The indecision. The life and death hanging in the balance. The way I can't trust anyone. Pain flares in my jaw from how hard my teeth are clenched.

I have no idea what's keeping me together now, beyond the hope of seeing my mom again and the chance to reconcile with Nikki.

Picturing their faces grounds me a little, like glue pulling some of the cracks back together until I can breathe without shattering. I can do this—for them. Sucking in a deep breath, I stretch my jaw open. Roll my shoulders. Force myself to calm down. To think and to face the possibility my brain keeps avoiding.

Could the killer be . . . *Lily?*

The idea is so horrible I feel guilty for considering it. And yet . . .

I saw bruises on Lily's neck, but how closely did I actually look? The lights were dim, especially inside the closet. What if they were faked with makeup? She could've escaped to the front after I left her.

It'd be easy to avoid us if she used the second level. Cut the lights. Played the message. Attacked whoever screamed. Or screamed herself, just to throw the rest of us into chaos.

Lily's the *last* person I'd ever suspect—the most normal one of us all. But snippets of our conversations replay through my mind, making me second-guess my faith in her. The way she freely offered information about her past, how she gently encouraged me to evaluate the others' motives, or even how she stood up for me when I found the Ambien pills in my bag. All this time, I thought she was being my friend . . . but was she setting me up?

If so, I wasn't the only one she fooled tonight. If Liam really did see O'Connor awake, somehow Lily tricked her too. Got her back upstairs. Knocked her out again. Then came back down here to kill Ann and fake her own assault. She knew I'd find O'Connor asleep and buckled in with the other two attendants and conclude Liam had lied to me.

After which I smashed my would-be boyfriend in the skull with a paperweight and locked him in a closet.

The room around me spins, and I brace my head against the mattress until the wave of nausea passes.

Upstairs, the low steady thumps come again, and I tighten my grip on the makeshift weapon. Is there any point hoping more flight attendants are awake? Or is it Lily, on her way to finish them off? Is there any possibility, however small, that she just crawled off to get help? Or a flight attendant helped her?

And what on freaking earth am I supposed to do *now*? I almost wish I could recover that bottle of pills from Ann's pocket, slug one, buckle into a seat, and wake up in Paris. Or the afterlife. Either way, the emotional havoc would be over.

Not an option, of course. Because if he's truly innocent, Liam is counting on me, and so are my mom and Nikki. And being dead sounds so . . . final. Think I'd rather pass on that one.

I know there's only one thing to do, and it terrifies me to the depths of my soul. I have to keep looking for Lily. If there's even the slightest chance she's nearby searching for help, or buckled upstairs with the flight attendants, I have to know.

And if she's not close by . . . then I have to let Liam out and warn the others. *If* we can find them.

I delay in the corner for another minute under the pretense of listening for noises, but it's been a while since I've heard any of those vibrations above.

After a couple of steadying breaths, I crawl out of my hiding place and head for the workstation compartment before I can change my mind.

Each footstep reverberates too loudly as I tiptoe through pitch darkness. Maybe the morning sun is shining outside, but it doesn't reach this part of the plane, with its window shades drawn tight. Part of me wonders if the pilots know the lights are out back here, like they did the first time around, or if whoever cut the lights messed up their systems too. Maybe they can't communicate with us at all anymore.

With the dim glow of my phone wrapped in my skirt, I search beneath the big desk in the office and along the bookcases lining the walls. No trace of Lily.

The thought that maybe she's hiding, waiting to jump me, nips at the back of my mind as I search the workstation compartment too. There's no way to use a phone light in secret. But it's as silent and dead as a graveyard in here. If she'd gotten any farther forward on this level, I would've passed her when I first came to check on her.

Upstairs is the last option. I force my heavy feet to the bedroom, checking the closet one last time, just in case I somehow missed seeing a hundred-and-ten-pound girl lying on the floor. Still gone.

But then something catches my eye tucked inside the open door: a whitish-silver slip of paper illuminated by the soft light of my phone. Something I missed in the initial confusion of Lily's disappearance.

Wide-ruled notebook paper, ripped along one edge. The mere sight of it makes me clutch the door frame to keep my balance. I drop to my knees and snatch it up, risking a little extra light to read the hasty message scrawled across it in that handwriting I've come to loathe:

So trusting for a liar.

Five simple words, and the weight of the world crashes down on me.

It was Lily.

She set this whole thing up. She knows the truth about me, and she intends to frame me for it all. And I walked right into her plan, as tightly plotted as the novels she hopes to write someday.

Where is she now? Working her way back into the group up front? Explaining to them how she was wrong about me, how I attacked her and Ann and Liam? Was that thumping upstairs earlier her killing the flight attendants?

A bitter taste fills my mouth, but doubt gnaws like a hungry worm at my stomach. Is there any other explanation I'm missing? Some way that she could still be innocent?

Maybe she found this note somewhere, intending to show it to me. Or maybe Liam left it for me to find with her body.

Somehow, I know that's not what happened, but my feet insist on carrying me upstairs anyway, on that infinitely small chance that Lily is hiding from Liam, and I locked up the true killer in a closet down here. I have to *know* it's her. As much as I long to get Liam out of that closet, I can't afford to be wrong this time.

The door from the stairs makes the tiniest creak as I swing it open on the upper level, sending my already overworked heart into the red zone better than any aerobic workout. I freeze and silently count to ten, straining to hear any noise beyond the engines.

Is it my imagination, or is the plane angling ever so slightly downward? Pressure is building in my ears too—signs that *should* make me happy but only add to the tension knotting a noose around my neck. I'd really rather be buckled in when we land. And not worried about getting stabbed before I can grab my carry-on and disembark.

I creep out of the doorway and slink across the dark space toward the flight attendants' alcove. If Lily was truly injured and looking for a hiding place from Liam, wouldn't that be the most likely place she'd go? The door is open—did I leave it like that? I think so, but it's hard to remember.

None of the window shades are up in this compartment, and it's so dark I have no choice but to use my phone. I tuck it under a fold of my skirt, finger hovering over the power button. Farther forward, the steady thrum of the engines is joined by a whirring sound, so soft I almost think I might be imagining it. Could it be the elevator?

The hair stands up on the back of my neck.

A sudden noise behind me startles me so much I nearly drop my phone. Lily? I tighten my fingers and swivel around, raising the paperweight in my other hand.

A shape moves toward me—only visible because it's blacker than the surrounding darkness—and I bite down hard on my lip to keep from screaming.

Turns out to be a good decision, because a second later Blake whispers, "Emily, is that you?"

"What are you *doing* back here?" I whisper.

He edges forward until his outstretched hands bump clumsily into my shoulders. When he speaks again, he leans close enough his breath tickles my ear. "Hiding. Olivia and Simon are with me. In a compartment over there."

"What's going on? What happened?"

"I don't know. Dylan flipped out and went up front all alone, Taylor wouldn't leave the room, so Amir stayed with her, and Olivia wanted to hide."

I can't fault her for that, especially considering none of them know what I know.

"We've been back here for maybe ten minutes," he adds. "We never figured out who screamed."

"Have you seen Lily?" I gesture in the general direction of the flight attendants' alcove, though Blake can't possibly see my waving hand in the darkness. "Or any of the flight attendants?"

"No, but we didn't want to use a light. Plus, it's been dead silent." He makes some noise between a groan and a hoarse laugh. "Maybe not the best word choice."

I smile. I can't even help it at this point. Then I press my phone's power button. Like downstairs, the plaid fabric draped across the screen dulls the glaring light to a deep blue. Blake glances around, his broad face lined with exhaustion and worry. Gotta admit, when it's come to taking care of the others, he has really stepped up.

My insides are a jumble of apprehension and hope as I cross the couple of steps to the doorway of the alcove. It's risky, but I can't afford to be wrong again, so I ease part of the phone out from beneath the fabric to release more light.

Only two sleeping forms greet me—Allard and Kumar.

No Lily.

My forehead crinkles. But no O'Connor either. Only a trail of . . .

"Is that blood?" Blake's face contorts into a grimace as he surveys the dark stains leading away from O'Connor's seat.

I follow it with my phone light until it vanishes through the doorway into the narrow corridor. A shiver tracks down my spine. "I think so."

"What happened to the head attendant?" Blake's hands are stuffed into his pockets, and he shifts his weight from one foot to the other. "I thought you said she was asleep."

"She was." I swallow. "I'd say the killer got to her, to make sure she wouldn't wake up and talk. Then hid the body. You're sure you haven't seen Lily?"

"No." His face scrunches. "Why?"

"It's her. It's got to be her. Lily. It wasn't Liam after all."

Relief crashes through me so furiously my knees sag. I hadn't realized until this moment exactly how badly I wanted it *not* to be Liam. And yet . . . Lily? How can something be both the thing you most dreaded *and* the thing you hoped for so much you can scarcely breathe?

"I don't get it. She killed Paige?" Blake's voice wobbles as I let the phone's light die out. "*Why?* Does she need to win that badly?"

"I don't know." Misery tugs at my chest, tiny hands digging sharp nails with each heartbeat. She seemed so sweet, so ordinary. So concerned about her brother and her family's finances.

Enough to kill, apparently.

On impulse, I hold out the paperweight and break the darkness once more to show it to him. "Have you ever seen this logo before?"

His forehead crinkles, and he scratches the hair over his ear. "Yeah, my dad went there. Windsor-Dalton. He wanted me to go there too, but my mom said Florida was too far away."

Of course. *That's* why it looks familiar—Windsor-Dalton is where my mom went to school. I've only seen her wearing a sweatshirt with that logo in our old photo albums, the ones packed away now in a storage unit. Is that where the connection is? Through our parents? But what could that possibly have to do with Lily?

Then a worse and far more urgent thought occurs to me. If Lily set up Liam so I'd think it was him, does she know he's in that closet? Was that her in the elevator? Trying to stage O'Connor's body somewhere to implicate me, and sneaking down to kill him next?

"I have to go," I tell Blake as my feet start for the staircase.

"What about us? What should we do?"

My mind is a blank beyond the immediate problem of getting to Liam. Because the truth is, I have no idea. Lily is out there, and all I've done so far is play right into her hands. Who knows how many others she's attacked or killed while I've been back here?

"Stay hidden," I say finally. "No matter what you hear. And get into seats when we're close to landing. I think the audio feed from the pilots has been cut too. I'll get Liam and try to warn the others."

"You shouldn't go alone," Blake objects.

"I have to—it'll be easier by myself, and you need to stick with the other two. Somebody has to get off this plane alive to tell our story to the police." The words sound a whole lot braver than I feel, and it takes a concerted effort to keep a sob from bursting out of my chest and giving me away.

Blake squeezes my shoulder. "Good luck."

"You too."

In the darkness, I turn for the narrow hidden staircase, propelled by only one thought:

Get to Liam before she *finds him.*

24

EXIT STRATEGY

12:35 a.m. CDT

Despite how slow I'm moving, each step feels as loud as crashing cymbals as I fumble my way down the steep staircase. And my breathing—there might as well be a buffalo in here, snorting and pawing the ground.

Clamping a hand over my mouth doesn't help. It only makes me feel like I'm suffocating, and with the paperweight in my pocket instead of my palm, I feel vulnerable. But I'm already holding my phone, and having both hands full would leave no easy way to brace myself. Frankly, neither option is appealing.

But then what *has* been appealing about this flight?

Only Liam—and now that I've bludgeoned him in the back of the head and locked him in a storage closet, I guess I can kiss that relationship goodbye. Getting to him before Lily finds him will have to be enough.

I freeze at the bottom of the stairs, listening again. No telltale vibrations. Where is she? Slinking out of the elevator, looking for me or Liam? Or still in the front of the plane? My fellow competitors' faces float before my mind's eye—Dylan, Amir with his wide grin, model Olivia, stage-perfect Taylor. Somehow, Lily must've slipped back into the kitchen and put nuts into Taylor's dinner, trying to kill her and make it look like an accident. Then she stuck the wrapper near my bag and left the box for Taylor to find so everyone would suspect me.

How many of them are still alive? And how many will believe Lily when she claims it was me? Now that they know I cheated to get here, is it that big of a stretch to believe I'd be willing to kill?

The floor of the plane tilts noticeably farther downward as I enter the office, and when pressure builds in my ears, I yawn to try to release it. How much time do we have left? I slip my phone into my pocket and open one of the window shades a crack. A bright orange-sherbet rectangle shoots across the room and makes me jump.

My fingers fumble against the hard plastic to snap it shut again. If the killer is anywhere nearby, that light will draw her like a hawk to its prey. Cold sweat breaks out on my forehead and my palms as I tiptoe into the workstation compartment. My hand wraps tightly around the paperweight in my blazer pocket.

Is she here? Crouching behind one of the chairs, ready to leap at me? I can almost *feel* someone lurking in here, pressed against one of the bulkheads. A shiver tracks down my spine, nearly paralyzing me until I force my eyes onto the dark hallway opening ahead. The twin emergency strips glow like a set of runway lights.

By the time I reach the storage closet, my legs are so weak I nearly collapse. The elevator door is shut tight, and no rumbling issues from within. I imagine O'Connor's body crumpled inside, her blood steadily pooling around her until it dams against the door. My body shakes from head to toe, and I turn away.

Daylight drifts from the far end of the hallway through the partially open window shades in the dining room, bouncing off the metal walls. The welcome glow strengthens me like a bit of visible hope.

I fumble for the bolt to the storage closet, relieved to find it still locked, and pry it out of its latch. The door falls open, Liam groans, and his legs, released from their prison, spring out into the hallway and kick me in the shins. Wincing at the sudden pain, I step to the side and drop to my knees.

"Liam?"

He sits, groaning again as he knocks his head into the lowest shelf. I scrunch my face—that had to hurt.

"What happened?" he asks. The words slur slightly as they come out, spiraling my anxiety in a new direction. Did I give him a concussion?

And worse . . . now that I've gotten to him, what's next? He's not in any fit condition to help me warn the others. Maybe it would've been better to leave him here, safely hidden.

Too late now. Besides, what if Lily found him?

"Hey, how are you feeling?" I brush my fingers lightly along his arm until I get to his elbow, then I help pull him forward as he scooches out from under the shelf. A quick glance toward the dining room shows no trouble from that direction. The other way is still so dark I can't tell.

"My head," he says, loud enough the pilots could probably hear him. I shush him, and he lifts his face until the tiny bit of light reflects off his eyes as he looks at me.

As much as I don't want to, I've got to risk a little more light to see how he's doing, so I wrap the phone back in my skirt and press the power button. Dark-blue light illuminates us both. His eyes widen momentarily. Then he looks down at my lap until I say his name again.

"Liam, look at me."

He turns his gaze back to me. The bright blue of his eyes fades to deep sapphire in the darkness, and though he tracks my face as I lean first one way and then the other, he blinks several times, as if he can't quite focus. Like he's just a little bit lost. All the feelings that have drawn me to him this entire trip warm me from head to toe.

I rise up a little on my knees and stretch shaking fingers toward his thick tangle of dark hair. When he pulls back, eyeing me warily, I pause.

"Em?" His voice is grainy, like he's talking around a mouthful of sand. "You attacked me. Back to finish the job?"

His question yanks at the horrible emotions fighting inside of me—the anxiety and terror and stress—until a sob builds in my chest and I press a hand to my ribs. "Liam, I'm so sorry. When I went upstairs earlier, I found O'Connor asleep with the other attendants, so I thought—" My voice cracks at the memory, the utter shock of that awful moment.

When the light dies on my phone, I press the power button again. I need to see his face.

"You thought I lied."

Tears burn my eyes as I nod. "Yes."

He stares at his lap so long the hairs stand up on my arms, and I glance both directions again. We're sitting ducks right here in this hallway. How long do we have? But if I try to rush him, he might never believe me.

"You thought I killed Evan. And Paige." A statement, not a question, and it rips me apart. Had I ever *really* thought that, deep down?

"I didn't want it to be true, but I couldn't think of any other explanation. And I had to protect the others, just in case." Now the tears stream down my cheeks, and I suck in a ragged breath, attempting to stem the tide. The sound is alarmingly loud. I clap my hand over my mouth. "She's going to hear us."

"Wait." His eyes narrow as his face folds into intense concentration, but from the way he keeps blinking, he's still struggling to understand. "You said the attendant was *asleep*?"

"Yes, with the other two. Like she'd never moved. And Ann was dead, and Lily nearly strangled in the closet."

"Strangled? And Ann's dead?" His jaw tightens as he bites back a choice word, and his gaze falls to his hands, which he clenches and unclenches almost spasmodically. It takes all my patience not to yank him to his feet and at least tug him across the hall into the kitchen so we won't be directly in the walkway.

"Yes, but Lily was faking it, Liam. She's not in the closet anymore."

His shoulders stiffen, and he looks at me, the light from my phone reflecting in his eyes. "Lily killed Ann? How is that even . . . ?"

"I wish I knew. She's smart. She could've drugged them both before she killed them."

"O'Connor's dead too?"

"I don't know, but I think so. There was a trail of blood. Like Lily stabbed her and then dragged her away to hide her someplace. *And* Lily cut the lights."

"That's why it's so dark?"

"Yes. I'm afraid to use my phone or she'll see it." This time when I reach for his head, he leans forward like an obedient child. My heart swells at the second round of forgiveness, and I run my fingers lightly over the back of his head near the top. Beneath the thick, soft hair is a large knot. He winces beneath my touch as I press gently across his skull. "You've got quite a bump. Ice would help."

"No time for ice." He leans forward, looking around me toward the dining compartment, then peering around the door to the workstations. "Where are the others?"

"Blake, Olivia, and Simon are hiding. I don't know about the rest. The pilots haven't announced how long till we land, but Lily might have cut the comms from the flight deck. Liam, she's loose on the plane."

He stiffens, his muscles growing taut.

"She played another message," I go on, "about how we all deserved to die, and she's got these epoxy weapons, and . . ." Tears distort my voice, and I swipe viciously at my eyes. I'd thought being homeless was bad enough. Driving around to a new deserted parking lot each night so nobody would notice and give us a ticket. Paying for showers at the state park campground. Making peanut-butter-and-honey sandwiches for half our meals so we didn't have to spend valuable cash on fast food. It's only been a couple of weeks since school let out, and every single one of those days has been *eternal*. Like, how could I survive another minute of it?

But after the hell of this flight, I'd give my right arm to be safe with my mom again. Because even though it's miserable living in a car, it's not forever. Not like dying. I can't stop the sobs choking me, making it hard to pull in a normal breath, and somewhere in the back of my mind I know how loud each gasping breath sounds.

Attention. If you'd like to kill Emily Walters, she's crying her eyes out in the hallway near the kitchen. She's with Liam Scott— special two-for-one offer.

"Hey, hey, shh." Liam wraps two strong hands around my shoulders, pulling me into his lap. He's injured—I shouldn't—and the noise . . .

But whatever feeble willpower has kept me going for the last seven hours is gone, and I collapse into his arms, curled up against his soft sweater while the tears and snot flow down my face.

Thirty seconds. That's all I can allow myself.

He tucks my head beneath his chin, his fingers tangling in my long, messy hair. It's like being wrapped up in a cozy citrus-scented blanket next to a crackling fire with a hot cup of cocoa, and I'm fairly sure Lily will find us like this and kill me on the spot because I can't make myself move.

But there's more I need to tell him, isn't there? The thought shoots through my body like ice water. I've betrayed him twice already—will this third confession be the final straw?

The fear and discomfort are enough to make me push away from him and scramble off his legs. "Liam, I have to tell you something." The original paper is a wrinkled ball by now, but I dig it out of my pocket and push it into his hand.

"What's this?"

"My two truths and a lie. They're all true."

He clenches his fist around the paper. Doesn't open it. "Mine were too, you know."

"Here's the thing." I stare at my hands, the shape of them just visible in the growing light from the dining compartment. "Your truths were out of your control, other people's fault. But mine . . ."

He leans forward like he's ready to shush me again, but I shake my head.

"I stole my best friend's application to get here. Nikki's." The admission doesn't cost nearly as much as I thought it would, not after the way I've emptied myself already. "It was a stupid thing to do, but my mom made some bad financial choices, and then the bank foreclosed on our house, and this summer I'm living in her car until she can get back on her feet. There's no way she'll be able to pay for college. And my grades, they were stellar this past year, but freshman and sophomore years . . ."

I'm rambling. We both know it. This time, when he leans forward, he places a hand behind my head and pulls me toward him until our lips touch. A small contented sigh escapes my chest. And I realize, as he kisses me despite all of the garbage I've just spewed, that maybe being homeless doesn't mean there's something wrong with *me*. Or even Mom. Sure, she could've made some better choices, but she gave up years of working to be home with me when I was little. No wonder it's hard for her to get a well-paying job. Society doesn't make it easy for former stay-at-home moms. Or for a lot of people struggling to get by.

Maybe the problem is far bigger than us. Suddenly, the idea of finding a career where I can help people in my situation makes a whole lot of sense.

The plane begins a banked curve, sending me tumbling sideways with a thump that's way too loud, and my heart rate shoots into the red zone again. I glance both ways up the corridor. My career choices will be irrelevant if I die in this hallway. No sign of movement yet, but the natural light peeking in from the dining compartment windows creates white-hot diagonal slices across the floor out there.

It's enough light I can see Liam's face without the phone.

"We've got to warn the others," he says as the plane's course flattens out. He yawns to clear his ears, then presses his fingers to his forehead and rubs. "How much time do you think we have until touchdown? Thirty minutes?"

I shrug, only half listening. "Maybe?" Something's bothering me still, and I suck my lower lip. After all the effort Lily has put into tormenting and killing us, there's no way she's going to kick back and relax while the plane lands, taxis to the terminal, and the pilots pop out of the flight deck to call security. Not after she's been so careful this entire flight to cover her tracks.

I hate feeling like this, like I'm constantly one step behind, and every failure results in somebody new dying. Something buzzes deep in my bones. This isn't over yet. And then it hits me, because she's been setting it up all along—

"She's going to frame me. Maybe us. It'll be our word against hers." A sense of urgency builds in my chest, and I tug at Liam's sleeve. "They'll believe her too, because she's probably got an impeccable record, and the rest of us are a bunch of liars. Except you. But half the group still thinks *you're* the killer."

His eyes slip out of focus for a second, like he's struggling to make his brain follow everything I've said, but I keep going. "We already found the pills in my bag. All she has to do is stick a blood-coated weapon in there and wait out the landing. Or schematics for the plane, or—"

"Well, regardless, we can't stay here. Help me up." Liam slides his arm around my shoulder and squeezes tight, then releases me. While he's digging out his phone, I scramble to my feet. Then I take Liam's hand and pull gently. He stands, swaying slightly.

He presses a hand to his head. "Whoa."

Alarm flashes through my system. "You okay?"

"Yeah, just wobbly. I think you might've actually given me a concussion." Is that a note of *pride* in his voice? "Good arm, girl. You've gotta play softball again next year. Rethink your life choices."

My insides flush with warmth. "I'm planning on it." *If we live that long.*

"Let's go t—" Liam cocks his head toward the workstation compartment farther aft.

"What?" I ask. He presses a finger to his lips, and I strain to listen. There—soft intermittent thumps, barely audible over the engines, coming from the tail. Louder one moment, muffled the next. Somebody shuffling around. Or—

Being attacked. Did she find Blake and the others?

Our eyes lock, and Liam's eyebrows rise in silent question.

"Let me go first," I whisper. "You're injured." Besides, it's a lot easier to walk into the unknown with Liam at my back.

"What if she's not there?"

I take a deep, steadying breath. "Then we let her know *we* are. We can't let her keep killing people until we land. We've got to stop her. Prove it wasn't us."

"*Do* you have any proof? Beyond your testimony?"

A slow smile stretches my lips. "I will."

Lily left me that note, like a cat toying with a mouse before it makes the kill. She knows I'm on to her, but she doesn't know what I'm going to do about it. Will she expect me to hide? Try to warn the others? Either way, she can't just outright kill me unless she makes it look like a suicide. Otherwise, all the groundwork she's laid to frame me will go to waste.

Which leaves me just enough wiggle room I might be able to confront her and get her to talk. To confess to the brilliance of the convoluted plot she's pulled off.

I type my idea on my phone in Evernote, just to make sure nobody overhears. Then I hold it out for Liam to read.

She knows I'm on to her. If she's back there, I confront her to get confession and u record w phone. If not, u hide and I lure her back.

His brows pull together, and he gestures impatiently for my phone. **U against her. :(What if she kills u?**

I shake my head. **We get her to confess, then u help. If ur ok.**

He rolls his eyes at me. "As if I'd lie around complaining about a headache while somebody kills you."

We have to get the confession 1st!!!!!!

I hope that string of exclamation marks is enough to get my point across. Because we'll be back to where we started if Liam jumps out and attacks her the second we find her. In fact, that would be downright incriminating.

He holds up both hands. "Okay, I get it."

"Keep your phone out. Just in case she's already back there . . ." Attacking somebody. I shiver.

One last walk through the terror, one last confrontation with a killer, and if we survive, we'll be free.

That thought keeps my feet moving as the darkness swallows me.

25

FINAL APPROACH

12:44 a.m. CDT

Where is she?

Beneath the thrum of the engines, beneath the hammering of my heart and the steady, slow rhythm of my feet, the question pounds over and over again.

Where is she? Where is she?

The sound we heard has died away, and now I'm left wondering if it was nothing. Blake and the others shifting their positions.

Or a trap.

Maybe it was another recording, and she's really *behind* us. Stalking through the darkness, ready to pull Liam into a dark corner, kill him, and blame me for that too. Or maybe she's way up front, tracking down Amir and Taylor and Dylan, planning to kill them one by one, not worrying about me at all.

If only we could open these window shades and let in the morning light. *Not yet*, I remind myself. Not until we're ready to reveal where we are.

Something brushes against my back, and I have to clap my hand over my mouth to keep from screaming. It's only Liam, sticking close as I pause at the entrance to the workstation compartment. Just this one room to cross, and then we'll be back in the office. Back to the bedroom suite, where we'll finally get the upper hand.

At least that's what I tell myself to stem the shaking in my limbs.

I listen closely for any extra sounds—the rustling of fabric, the soft whoosh of stifled breathing—but I can't hear anything over the jackhammer beneath my own ribs.

I reach back and feel for Liam's hand, then slip my fingers into his. He grips mine tight, and only then do I dare tiptoe across this great open expanse of darkness.

This plan is going to work, isn't it? All the possibilities for failure keep pushing at the edges of my mind. What if that noise wasn't her? What if she's found a way to get down below, in the cargo hold, and doesn't hear or see me?

I shove the questions aside, because we're out of options. And time. A darker level of blackness indicates the bulkhead walls up ahead, but the glowing strips on the floor mark the opening into the office. As I reach the doorway, the plane turns again, and I clutch on to the thick plastic walls to keep my balance. Liam squeezes my hand tighter, stopping right behind me. The warmth emanating from him feels solid against my back.

Wordlessly, we cross the short distance through the empty office to reach the bedroom. The paperweight and phone in my blazer pockets bang reassuringly against my hips. I keep one hand out in front like a blind woman, feeling for the edge of the desk so I don't crash into it. I've walked this path enough now that I manage to catch the corner with my fingers, right where I expect it to be.

Once we've passed the desk, I release Liam's hand and extend my arms to feel for the walls. My fingertips brush against plastic faux-wood paneling. It's as silent as a crypt, no hint of a struggle. The tension knotting my insides ratchets a degree tighter, until I can scarcely draw in a decent breath. Are we walking into a trap? Maybe I've got it wrong. Maybe all Lily wants is two more victims before we land? Perhaps this has nothing to do with setting me up. Maybe she only wants to kill, to control, to frighten. To create the most elaborate story. To play a game she can win if she doesn't have what it takes to land the scholarship in Paris. It's a story a writer like Lily might want to pen. A plot only she could weave.

But we've made it back here without being attacked. Only a few more feet through this corridor, and we can tuck Liam into a hiding place and flip up the window shades until the place is glowing like the sun itself. Then at least I'll see her when she shows up. Whatever her plan might be.

Only a few more feet.

My fingers run lightly against both sides of the hall, feeling the bumps in the decorative paneling as I tiptoe forward. Smooth plastic passes beneath my fingertips one slow inch at a time, my breath frozen in my lungs.

Then fabric, thick and textured against my right hand. Beneath it, heat: 98.6 degrees Fahrenheit.

There's a split-second gap between the moment my fingertips register the change and when my brain makes the final computation, and in that span—

She moves.

A scream rips out of my throat, and I throw both hands up—crisscrossed in front of my chest and face.

She slams into me, shoving me sideways into the paneling, with a thud that echoes through my body and into my brain. How did short, compact Lily get so strong?

A light flicks on somewhere behind me—darting across the walls like a strobe—and Liam calls my name.

"Emily!" His voice rings with panic.

For a second, the light catches my attacker full in the face. My stomach drops into my knees.

It's *not* Lily. It's O'Connor.

Her lips are pulled into a grimace, and her once-tidy bun is a disheveled, lopsided mess. A swollen, dark bump protrudes from her forehead. She looks like she's been through the wringer. But why is she attacking *me*?

I jerk away, instinctively, but she's whiplash-fast as she hooks one wiry arm around my neck and with the other jabs something sharp into my left side. It digs into my blazer, into my shirt. With just a little more force, it would puncture my clothing and skin to slip between my ribs and reach the blood and bone beneath.

"Hold still, girl," she says. "Liam, are you all right?"

Liam? "How do you know his—" I say, but she cuts me off by tightening her grip around my neck.

"Quiet," she warns, relaxing her arm a bit. "I know all your names. That's part of my job."

Liam's light slams us both in the face this time, and I'm a raccoon caught in headlights as I blink furiously.

"Let her go," he commands. His voice wavers ever so slightly, but what matters is that he's here. I'm not alone.

"I'm afraid I can't do that. She's not who you think she is. She's the one hurting your peers. She's fooled us all."

26

WHAT GOES AROUND

12:49 a.m. CDT

Wait, *what*? The world flips upside down yet again at O'Connor's words.

"I didn't hurt anybody!" I protest.

"Sure, you didn't," O'Connor scoffs. "But you're the one telling the story. Why should we believe you?"

Liam drops the light to our knees, so that I only see a vague outline of him raising his other hand, palm toward us. "Hold up," he says. "There's obviously some mistake. When I left you with the other two back here earlier, I went to get Olivia and *her*. That's Emily."

"I know who she is," O'Connor says calmly. "The question is, do you? What happened after she came back here? What did she tell you?"

"Well . . ." The light flickers across our legs, and in the dim light I can see Liam touch his head. "She knocked me out, actually. Thought I was the one who did it."

"Did what?"

"Killed Ann, obviously," I splutter. We don't have time for this, not when Lily could be off murdering the rest of our group somewhere in the front of the plane. "Didn't you look in the bathroom? But it wasn't Liam. It was Lily, and she's still loose on the plane."

"Didn't Lily attack you?" Liam asks O'Connor. He scratches his head, like he's struggling to get his concussed brain to keep up.

"I mean, how did Emily find you upstairs again with the other attendants? And . . . and there was blood. I didn't see it, but . . . she said it's up there."

I hold my breath, waiting for the inevitable moment when O'Connor sees her mistake and releases me. She probably has no idea how tight her grip is around my neck.

"Is that what she told you?"

I freeze. Like literally every cell in my body stops.

But nothing holds O'Connor back. "Liam, she joined us back here. Me, Lily, and Ann."

Words have utterly abandoned me. Maybe because my stomach is hanging somewhere down by my knees, and I can't for the life of me make sense of what she's saying.

Why she's *lying*. The one person I've been counting on this whole time to rescue us from this madness. It's like the universe's sick attempt at payback for all the cheating I've done.

"I was still in the bathroom," O'Connor says, "about to go back upstairs and examine the body you boys carried up. She attacked me, hit me in the head with something, and when Ann tried to intervene, she stabbed her. I blacked out while she was wrestling with Lily, then came to and managed to run up the stairs, but I wasn't fast enough. Obviously."

She tips her head forward, catches the light. That's when he sees it. Liam's eyes flicker to O'Connor's forehead, where the purple lump resides. One that matches his perfectly.

Damn.

"I tried to run," O'Connor says. "Tried to lock myself in with the others, but she's fast, Liam. She attacked me with some kind of blade. Hit me again. Dragged me to . . . to . . ." She starts to tear up, then her face shifts back to anger in a heartbeat. "I just came to a few minutes ago in the service elevator. Bleeding." She says it so matter-of-factly—in her soothing, professional I've-got-everything-under-control voice—that *I* almost believe her.

She rotates the arm wrapped around my neck, revealing the spiderweb of scars and, beneath them, her wrist bound tight with white cotton, blood seeping through.

More evidence—against *me*.

So it's no wonder that Liam's phone light wavers again. When he asks, "Em?" in a quiet, childlike voice that slices straight to my core.

"None of that is true," I insist. "She's lying."

"But why?" Through the darkness, Liam's form shakes his head.

I feel like my brain has turned to thick pea soup, but through the sludge I grope for any reason he should believe me. "Blake— ask Blake. He's upstairs. He was with me when I checked for her and she was gone. He saw the blood."

"I've been gone the entire time since Liam last saw me." O'Connor's tone is gentle, like I'm a fragile china doll that might shatter. It's infuriating, especially given how hard she's got her arm clamped around me. "Who saw me asleep?" she asks me. "Just you?"

Was it only me? I sift through my tangled memories from the last hour, a span of time that feels like it stretches over an eternity. "It . . . I . . ."

The words die on my tongue as I give up. She's right. No one else *did* see her up there. I was alone.

Did I imagine it? A trick of an overactive, stressed-out imagination?

My insides cramp into a hard knot, and bile rises into my throat. I think I might puke.

Wait, what about Lily? I didn't imagine *her* vanishing out of that closet.

"Look for Lily," I order.

O'Connor's grip tightens ever so slightly, but then she relaxes. "Go ahead if it makes you feel better. Check the closet. We can wait."

Liam's phone light bobbles and swells as he steps nearer. O'Connor lowers her arm from my neck to my collarbone and drags me backward. Recirculating air hits my face as she pulls me into the bedroom, giving him space to walk past us and over to the closet. The door is partway shut, and he slides it open, taking his light off us to shine it on the floor.

Where Lily lies curled on her side, her hair glowing bright red in the artificial glow of Liam's phone.

My mouth hangs open, the air painfully dry against my parched tongue.

Am I losing my mind?

"Emily?" The way Liam's voice cracks nearly breaks me.

He swings the light back to my face, and I blink in the bright spotlight. Tears spring into my eyes as my confusion and fear and frustration fight to escape.

He doesn't believe me.

27

DO OR DIE

12:54 a.m. CDT

O'Connor tightens her grip, hard enough that something digs into my shoulder. I manage a sideways glance at her hand, where a class ring gleams, its green stone shining in the light inches away from my face. And etched around the stone: the words WINDSOR-DALTON.

The folder in the desk drawer. The paperweight. They're from Windsor-Dalton too, the same school my mom went to. And Blake's dad.

A connection between us and O'Connor.

Thoughts fly rapid-fire through my brain, the fog giving way to sudden clarity, aided by the something sharp digging into my side. *Where did she get a weapon?*

"It's you, isn't it?" My words fly out, practically in a hiss. "*You're* the killer."

She barks out a short laugh but at the same time shoves the sharp point harder into my side, close to my back, where Liam can't see it. "Getting desperate enough to blame the flight attendant?" Her voice is taut, like a cord that might snap any second. "Come on, Emily. Give it up. Let me secure you in a seat for landing, and we'll let the authorities sort out this mess. Liam, you can bring the injured girl."

He stands frozen, his light waffling between Lily on the floor and our feet. An eternity passes in mere seconds.

My chest is so tight I can't breathe.

"No." He swivels his phone back to our faces, the movement decisive. My knees sag, but O'Connor tightens her grip to keep me from collapsing. "You told me to check the closet, but how did you know Lily was there? By your own admission, you blacked out before seeing what happened to her. And Emily never told you."

"Wrong choice, Liam," O'Connor snarls. The arm around my shoulders slips up to my neck and tightens. I twist furiously, trying to break the viselike grip—the same one that nearly killed Lily—but she shoves the sharp point harder into my skin.

Hard enough that there's a popping, swishing sort of sound as my clothing tears, and a hot flash of pain explodes up my side.

An awful, screeching wail escapes my lips—it's like it's coming from somebody else, like I'm merely standing here observing the scene. My mind fills with the most pointless questions.

Did she use an epoxy screwdriver? Or a knife? Is it coated with Evan's and Ann's blood?

Will Liam come to my funeral?

Is he recording this?

Does dying usually feel so . . . normal?

"Stop fighting, girl," O'Connor rasps. "And you'll survive a little longer."

Good, I'm not dying yet. But I gotta admit, this *not dying* is still pretty darn painful.

I stop struggling, mostly because my side is on fire and I need a moment to regroup. She's still got a death grip on my neck, but now the other arm wraps around my waist.

"What'd you do with Lily?" I ask O'Connor. "Where'd you take her?" I think back to that noise I heard earlier, and then it hits me. "The elevator. You hid her in the elevator, didn't you? So you could convince everyone it was me."

"*That's* what I heard from the storage closet," Liam says. "But why? Why are you doing this to us?" His phone light is now steady, directed right at our faces. Doing his job of getting the confession.

O'Connor laughs, harsh and bitter. "It's almost funny how identical you all are to my generation as teens. The details shift, but the vices stay the same."

"What are you talking about?" It's a struggle to get words out with the pressure of her arm around me, but if she's willing to talk, we have to keep her going.

"The petty, cruel teasing. Emotional abuse. Lying. Violence. Cheating. Being so selfish you're completely unaware of the despair of those around you." She flings the words like a barbed stinger at Liam.

I can't see him behind the light, but I know how badly it hurts him. *Be strong*, I want to say. All I can hope is that he sees my concern, that he knows I'm here for him.

"So, what, you were spying on us?" Liam asks. His tone is hard. Flat. "How did you come up with all that stuff?"

"Apparently, you've underestimated the resources available to someone like me with means. But the job was easy enough. Private investigators, record checks, social media trails. I barely had to snoop into your lives to dig up enough dirt to make you all come unglued," O'Connor goes on. "And you lived up to your roles perfectly."

I draw in a shaky breath. "We've messed up. You're right. But who appointed you judge and executioner? Are you so perfect?"

"Who appointed me judge? How about Miss Flawless, Elizabeth

Ashby?" O'Connor's voice rises until she's practically screeching in my ear. Her arm tightens too, and I dig my fingers in enough to protect my throat. "Perhaps you'd know her better as Elizabeth Walters?"

Ice fills my veins. "Mom?" My voice falters.

"Is that what this is about?" Liam asks. "Your own twisted sense of revenge?"

"It's not twisted at all." O'Connor's voice levels out, and she relaxes her grip enough that I can at least breathe properly. "It's quite logical, actually. When I was reviewing scholarship applications and found Emily's, I realized I'd found the perfect opportunity to let Elizabeth know exactly how I feel about what she did to me all those years ago. A little bit of advance research, pulling a few strings with Hamlin, pushing some of my ideas through with the rest of the committee . . . and here we are. The rest of you were more or less collateral damage, but thanks to the intimate nature of the boarding school world, I managed to find a few of you with Windsor-Dalton connections."

"But I cheated to get here," I object, as if that'll suddenly fix everything. "I never would've gotten chosen if I hadn't."

"Recommending applicants to the committee was my job, and I would've picked you regardless. The cheating only gave me more ammunition." Her voice goes sickly sweet. "And removed any qualms I might have felt about using you for revenge. You're obviously cut from the same cloth."

How can everything I thought I knew flip upside down so rapidly? Nikki wouldn't be here, no matter what I'd done. Not that it actually matters, because the competition this year was never real. O'Connor never intended to let us reach Paris intact. She probably never reported any of this either, instead stringing us along this whole time. "You've never contacted the outside world this whole flight, have you?"

"Of course not. I cut the intercom to the pilots after takeoff, then faked the calls to the foundation so the other two attendants wouldn't figure it out. For all the foundation knows, all twelve of you are alive and eagerly competing for your futures. I guess you are, in a way. Who will reach Paris alive?"

"What does my mom have to do with you?" I press. "You went to school together?"

"Oh, honey, has she never mentioned me to you? Her dear friend Jennifer, the one she blamed for burning down half the science building? She was a lot like that little cheerleader, the one who was so easy to isolate and kill when she wanted a shoulder to cry on. Popular and cute and used to getting whatever she wanted."

"Paige?" Liam's voice has a painful, raw edge to it.

I stiffen, both at what she did to Paige, and at what she's saying. "What happened?"

"Elizabeth always wanted what she didn't have," she says. "After she stole my boyfriend sophomore year, she dumped him and decided she wanted Rob Walters."

"My dad?" I say. I knew they met in high school, but . . . "He didn't go to Windsor."

"No, he went to the all-boys' school down the road. He was a year older than us, best friends with Mitch Adams—Blake's father. One Friday night, when they came over to hang out at our school, she decided it'd be fun if we all snuck into North Hall, the science building, through the old underground tunnel system. We were goofing around in one of the chemistry labs and accidentally started a fire. I got third-degree burns that *still* itch to this day."

North Hall. The scars on O'Connor's arms.

"What happened?" Liam prods.

"We got out and called 911, but half the building was gone by the time they put the fire out. It didn't take long for the police to figure out we'd been inside. When they interrogated us . . ." When O'Connor keeps going, her voice comes out like she's talking through gritted teeth. "Elizabeth and the others told them it was *my* fault. My idea. They let me get expelled from school, and my family had to pay the insurance deductible for property damage. Then the insurance company sued us, and we had to pay even more. Enough that it broke my family apart."

"No." I try to shake my head, but her grip around my throat is too tight. Each movement sends pain shooting up my side. "My mom might not have been a good student, but she wouldn't have done that."

"Really? Don't act so shocked. Look at what you did to *your* supposed best friend. Elizabeth got what she wanted in the end, but how'd that marriage work out for her, anyway? On the positive side, if it weren't for the community service I had to do, I might never have decided to go into nonprofit work and ended up at the Bonhomme Foundation. We would've missed this lovely chance to get to know each other."

She's pressing harder against my neck, whether she means to or not, and stars twinkle at the edges of my vision. "What . . . about . . . the others?" I gasp.

"Em?" Liam's voice rings with alarm. He calls to O'Connor, "You're choking her!"

"Oh, I'm *sorry*. I wouldn't want to kill anyone," she taunts, but she relaxes her grip enough that the stars fade. "Like I said, collateral damage. We needed twelve candidates."

"How'd you kill Evan?" I ask. "The body just . . . appeared."

"Easy enough to offer him a spiked drink, then keep his unconscious body hidden until I was ready to slit his throat and let someone find him."

"You used the sleeping pills?"

"What do you think this is, amateur hour?" O'Connor scoffs. "That Ambien was entirely for your benefit, so the rest of them would blame you. I used my own drug cocktail."

"And Taylor?" Liam asks. "Did you contaminate her meal?"

"Of course. A simple task when you're on the flight staff. Too bad the girl from your school was so quick on her feet with the EpiPen."

My stomach twists. Ann saved Taylor, but she couldn't save herself.

"I didn't know who out of this group would emerge as the leaders," O'Connor goes on, "but I have to admit, I'm delighted it's you two."

"My parents didn't go to Windsor-Dalton," Liam says quietly.

"No, sweet, handsome Liam, they didn't. But your uncle Chris did. Two years ahead of us. When I asked him to the spring formal my freshman year, he laughed in my face and made sure to tell the rest of the school. I never would've done it if my so-called *friends* hadn't talked me into it. They knew he didn't like me. That should've been enough to warn me away from Elizabeth Ashby, but apparently, I was too forgiving back then. I've learned my lesson." She laughs, a hollow, bitter sound.

Maybe this is pointing out the obvious, but . . . "How exactly is this supposed to stop the cycle of hate? Taking revenge on me won't undo the past."

She squeezes my throat again, painfully tight for a second before letting off the pressure. "Don't you get it? Once *you've* been wrongfully convicted of killing your classmates and sent to jail for eternity, your mother will get to enjoy the exquisite pain of knowing every single day that your life has been stripped away and it's *all her fault*. What better revenge could I ask for? There's poetic justice in it, don't you think?"

Liam's light keeps shining the entire time, getting this whole diatribe on video, and while I know this for a fact, I wish beyond anything I could see his face. The strength and care radiating from those blue eyes.

"You need counseling," he says. "Or jail would work."

O'Connor laughs again, slow and soft and condescending. "Poor children. I won't be heading to jail. It's hardly my fault you drugged me and killed each other. The evidence is sufficiently planted around the plane, and when you combine that with the confusing finger-pointing testimonies of the survivors and Emily's own history of lying, the police will have no reason to suspect me. Not when it's obvious you did it. Who would believe her over me?" She tightens her grip on my stomach. "Now, it's time for you to hand over that phone, unless you'd like to watch your girlfriend die. I can make it look like you killed her, if necessary, though I'd rather let her live out her life in jail."

No. I shake my head. Adrenaline scorches through my veins, overriding the cloying fear of death. She's lying. She has no intention of letting either of us live. "Liam, you can't. It's the only proof we have."

He shuts off the phone's blinding flashlight, leaving us in the dim blue glow of the screen, and finally I can open my eyes without painful squinting.

"Get out of here," I urge. "Don't worry about me. Make sure they hear the truth."

"Aren't you noble all of a sudden?" O'Connor sneers. "Go ahead, Liam. I'm betting I can still find you before we pull up to the gate. As soon as I finish with this one, of course." She pivots her hand on my stomach, and my breath catches as the sharp edge bites into the thin cotton fabric of my shirt. "Or you could hand over that phone, and after I delete the video you recorded, I'll release Emily. Give you two a chance to face the police together. Maybe they'll let you write letters to each other in jail."

He hesitates. Tips the phone back up so he can see the screen.

"Uh-uh-uh . . ." O'Connor squeezes her arm tighter around my neck, putting painful pressure on the tender tissues, and a horrible strangled sound flies out of my mouth. "Don't even think about trying to send that to somebody," she tells Liam. "Give the phone to Emily. Now."

Liam sucks his upper lip. His eyes, twin gleaming blue marbles reflecting the screen's light, dart to mine. I shake my head again, holding my breath. He stares hard at me for a fraction of a second, like he's trying to tell me something, but I can't understand.

Don't let O'Connor have it. I want to shout the words at him, but I can't speak. All I can do is stand here wishing he could read my mind.

The moment passes, and my insides deflate as he clenches one hand into a fist, his shoulders slump, and he holds out the phone.

"Take it, girl," O'Connor orders.

I pry my hands off her arm, leaving my neck totally exposed, and open them, palms up. My injured side aches at the motion. Time slips into slow motion as a thousand possibilities fly through my mind. Can I drop the phone? Somehow switch it with *my* phone instead? Slip the paperweight out of my pocket and attack her?

Risky—it's all so risky, with her weapon in my stomach and her arm around my neck. Could Liam take her out in the dark if she kills me? Or would she kill him too?

If we let her delete the video, is there a chance we'll walk away unharmed?

No. The answer is no. And I know it deep in my core. A person this warped, this bent on revenge, can't be trusted to keep her word. She'll make me delete the video, and then she'll kill us too. Or maybe just one of us, leaving the other to take the blame.

Liam's hands, so strong and warm, enclose mine as he sets the phone in my open palms and wraps my fingers around the edges. The light from the screen dims as it filters through my fingers, casting giant shadows on the ceiling. He looks at me, eyes full of invisible strength and reassurance in one brief glance, before flicking his gaze to O'Connor's hand on my stomach. Gauging the distance from his hands to hers.

He wants me to do something. Expects me to—now, while he's still close enough to wrestle that weapon out of her hand. But what?

Then my finger rubs against a button on the outside of his phone. The power button.

That's it. If I press it, the screen will go black. Liam already shut the flashlight off.

There's no time for a deep breath, or any breath at all, with O'Connor's blade jabbing into my stomach. So I can only hope for the best as I press the button and the world descends into pitch blackness one more time.

28

TIME RUNS OUT

1:04 a.m. CDT

People always talk about how time slows and everything happens at once during intense moments. I never understood how that was possible, when so much of life flies by in a blur.

Not now, though. Somebody presses the pause button, and we become actors in a slow-motion action scene—one where a single wrong move means death.

Liam's fingers dig into my stomach as he wraps them around O'Connor's arm and drags it off me. The feel of the hard, spiky weapon vanishes in a glorious burst of freedom—*I can breathe*. But then there's a wet, suction-y sound, like someone just got stabbed, and my heart stops as Liam groans in pain.

Thumps echo across the space as if he's falling backward. I latch on to O'Connor's other arm—the one around my neck—with my free hand, and bite with every bit of force I can muster.

She cries out, her grip loosening, and I cram my elbow into her ribs. Something clatters to the floor. O'Connor's weapon? But before I can twist free, she brings her other arm up and locks it behind my head in some sort of freaky MMA choke hold.

Liam's phone falls with a thunk to the floor as both my hands go for her arm, trying to drag it away from my neck. She applies pressure behind my head, forcing my windpipe against her arm. Stars flirt with the edges of my vision. I yell, but only a squeak comes out. Like stepping on a mouse. Or a dog's chew toy. O'Connor isn't big, but she's strong, and the last time I took martial arts was *never*.

"Emily!" Liam rips open one of the window shades. Blinding sunlight pours into the room.

He lunges toward us, but O'Connor pulls me back, slamming us against the edge of the bed. I dig my fingernails into her sleeve, kicking at her shins with my feet. The plane tilts again, farther and farther as it banks in another deep curve, sending the three of us stumbling across the shifting floor. But also loosening O'Connor's grip enough that the stars recede. The paperweight bangs hard against my hip, and with sudden inspiration I pull out the heavy glass ball. The movement sends pain shooting up my injured side.

O'Connor regains her footing and squeezes harder, using all her wiry strength to cut off my airway and snuff out the life in my chest. My legs are stone columns, heavy and immobile. The blackness returns—did Liam close the shade?

No, he's there, he's coming, a dark shadow against the brilliant morning sun. With what's left of my strength, I hold out the heavy glass ball. O'Connor claws for my arm, but Liam reaches it first. His fingertips scrape my palm as he takes the weight. Switches it to his other hand. Draws back in the fluid motion of a baseball player.

My legs give way, and the darkness explodes with stars as I slip down, down, down . . . Somewhere in the distance, far away, a woman shrieks, loud and piercing. A heavy thud.

Then silence.

Is this what death feels like?

I never expected it to be so still. So empty and dark.

Then air rushes into my lungs in a burning, fiery whoosh, and for a second I think maybe I *am* dead and I've ended up in hell.

"Good girl," I hear. "Another breath, nice and easy."

I'm pretty sure that's not the devil talking. Not unless he's turned into a hot teen guy who I'd really like to live to kiss again.

I force in another breath, despite the ragged pain running up my throat and along my left ribs.

"Em? You with me?"

Definitely Liam.

My eyelids object, but I pry them open anyway. Everything is hazy, and I blink a few times until the room comes into focus. He's crouching over me, his face blanched white and lined with worry. What I want more than anything is to see him smile, to see that cleft in his chin pull tight as the laughter dances in his blue eyes.

I stretch unwieldy fingers toward him, and he clasps my hand in his, then presses my palm to his lips. The smile I've been longing to see lights his face.

Beneath us, something rumbles, not like the thin vibration of footsteps, but something that shakes the entire floor. Liam drops my hand and looks over his shoulder toward the window.

"The landing gear." Alarm spikes his voice. "We've got to get you buckled. Lily too, if she's still with us."

He slips his hands beneath my back and under my knees, then hoists me into the air.

"You don't have to carry me," I protest, but my throat hurts so badly the words barely make it out.

"Yes, I do," he says, holding me securely against his chest.

Footsteps thud down the stairs, and Blake sticks his head out of the door. His gaze widens as he takes in the scene. "The flight attendant?" His voice goes high-pitched, like he doesn't believe his eyes.

"It's a long story," Liam grunts. "Lily's in the closet. Hopefully, still alive."

Blake nods and walks around us to get Lily.

I glance over Liam's shoulder as we head toward the office. O'Connor lies facedown on the carpet, the paperweight glittering in the sunlight not far from her head. A few feet away, what looks like a six-inch white screwdriver rests abandoned on the floor. Its tip drips with red.

I close my eyes and dig my face into Liam's chest. He holds me tight as he carries me through the office and into the workstation compartment, then sets me in one of the window seats and pulls up the shade.

Land looms awfully close, a patchwork of mottled green-and-brown fields.

I reach for the seat belt to buckle myself, but my arms are as useless as jellyfish tentacles. Liam chuckles as he locks the belt into place for me, then presses a soft kiss to my forehead. It's only then that I notice the blood crusting his hand. A circle of red stains the thigh of his khaki pants.

"You're hurt."

He glances at his leg, then presses the crusty palm against it. "Yeah, she stabbed me. Twisted that screwdriver around as soon as I grabbed her arm." When he pulls his hand away, the blood on his palm still looks fresh. He glances around, as if looking for a first-aid kit. Then he gives up and presses his hand to his leg again. "I'll have to deal with it later. Right now, I have to move O'Connor into a seat."

"Don't go," I say. "There's no time." Not to mention she tried to kill us.

"I'll be fast," he assures me.

The intervening moments feel eternal as the ground outside my window grows closer and closer. I strain for a glimpse of the

Eiffel Tower—anything to keep myself occupied—but the airport is too far away from the Paris city center, and we're coming in at the wrong angle. The trees swell and roads stretch like black ribbons decorated with tiny cars as the plane descends.

Blake appears with Lily, carrying her the same way Liam carried me. She stirs as he buckles her into a seat opposite mine. Gratitude floods my heart. She's alive.

"Hey," she says, blinking at the bright morning light. "Are we landing?"

"Yeah. Finally." Blake disappears into the back and returns a minute later with Liam. Together they strap O'Connor's limp form into a seat on the other side of the room, before returning to sit with us.

"Is she . . . ?" My voice trails off.

Liam collapses into the seat beside me and shakes his head. "Not dead yet. I hope the others made it into seats."

"Me too." It's too late to warn them now. The plane bounces and wobbles as the pilot makes tiny adjustments. The ribbons of black are turning into actual roads, with near full-size cars.

"Simon and Olivia did. They're upstairs," Blake says. "We all heard somebody scream, but I told them not to come."

I clutch the armrests of my seat as the plane dips lower and lower. Liam presses one hand against his thigh, then places the other over mine, squeezing gently. When I glance at our hands, and then up at him, he gives me a sheepish grin.

"Sorry about the blood."

I smile. "No reason to worry about it now." My white dress shirt is already splattered with patches of red, and from the crusty, crinkling feeling over my aching ribs, I'm sure my skin is too.

The runway appears outside the window, a vast, welcoming

expanse of striped asphalt. I hold my breath in that liminal space where the plane seems to hover just above it. Then with a reassuring thump, we land.

My seat belt digs into my waist as the plane brakes and a burst of pain from the screwdriver wound wraps around my middle. Loud whirring fills my ears. The world stops racing by, and soon we're merely driving along the runway, then turning to taxi to the terminal.

I collapse with relief into my seat. Lily's staring out the window, tears glistening in her eyes. Liam squeezes my hand, and I turn to meet his gaze.

His lips hitch slightly on one side, and his blue eyes gleam. "Welcome to Paris," he says softly, pressing a slow, soft, safe kiss to my forehead.

I smile and take his hand.

We made it.

29

WELCOME TO PARIS

June 30, 2:11 p.m. CEST

It takes a full week before I get my first glimpse of the Eiffel Tower.

The aftermath at the airport was like a scene out of a movie where a bomb goes off and all the survivors creep dusty and disheveled out of their hiding places, eyeing each other with a how-did-we-live-through-that look on their faces.

We stayed in our seats, exhausted, bleeding, until the plane finally lurched to a halt. Olivia and Simon found us downstairs. With help from Liam and Blake, Lily and I hobbled through the compartments toward the front.

By the time we reached the entertainment salon, Dylan, Amir, and Taylor were sitting on the entryway steps, thankfully whole and intact. Dylan frowned as he looked me over, his eyes lingering on the patches of blood on my shirt. "I'm glad you're okay, Em."

"Thanks to Liam. Who is *not* the killer," I emphasized.

Liam tightened his arm around my shoulder. "No, I'm okay thanks to *her*." And he looked at me with the kind of smile that makes me want to melt. We must've stared at each other a little too long, because after a moment Dylan cleared his throat and turned away to somebody else.

The pilots, oblivious and laughing, traipsed down the stairs, then stopped dead and stared at us slack-jawed. After a split second of utter silence, the whirlwind began.

Medical personnel and airport staff and police officers soon arrived. Lots of people talking in French, so fast that my five years of language study couldn't make a dent in anything they were saying.

An ambulance ride to the hospital. Interviews. Nurses bustling over us, cleaning and patching our injuries. O'Connor carted off to the hospital, and eventually to jail.

Email volleys with my mom. It's okay, Mom. Calm down. Yes, she went to school with you. Jennifer O'Connor. Blond hair. Yes, she told me about the fire. No, you don't have to explain now. We can talk later. They're keeping us in Paris for now. No, I don't know yet what will happen. But it's going to be okay. We'll be all right. And I'm calling Aunt Kacie, so don't argue.

My mom finally swallowing her pride and talking to her sister. Aunt Kacie is taking us in until Mom can get back on her feet.

Texts from Nikki. What on earth, girl? Worried sick over here. Luv u.

A phone call to Nikki to begin the slow process of restoration. "No time like the present," my new mantra. A bitter moment of pain and betrayal, followed by tears and the hope of forgiveness and reconciliation. Dylan most definitely in the doghouse. Our friendship course-corrected so we at least have a shot at getting to where we could be.

Then Liam—sitting beside me, holding my hand, checking on me constantly. Making my heart swell until it might burst.

More interviews. With the police, with reporters, with Sir Hamlin and the scholarship committee, who had no idea O'Connor had taken over the competition for her own ends.

Days blurred into nights into new days, until today, the first day we've been set free to see the city. There was talk early on of sending us home immediately, but the foundation gave us the option of finishing out our time if our parents agreed. In fact, they even offered to fly all our parents out to join us. Nearly everyone who had a passport came. Mom couldn't, but that's okay, because it gives her a chance to settle in with my aunt. Blake returned home right away, on account of Paige and her funeral.

But the rest of us who made it, we're here, staying in a luxurious Parisian boutique hotel and enjoying every minute of the foundation's efforts to make up for its errant employee. Today, we're strolling the city streets, taking deep breaths of flowery summer air, nibbling croissants, savoring the freedom of being alive beneath a brilliant blue sky, and generally acting like a bunch of teenage tourists who've never been to Paris before.

"There." Liam stops on the sidewalk in front of me at the intersection of Avenue de la Bourdonnais and Rue de l'Université and points down the street.

My heart leaps—with excitement for once, not fear or anxiety or panic. The others stop around us, taking in the beautiful old buildings framing the tree-lined street. At the end, cobblestone gives way to benches, flower beds, and green trees, and above the park stands one of the world's most famous monuments. We've caught glimpses of the tall metal spire over the tops of the buildings, but this is our first full view, and it's spectacular.

"The Eiffel Tower!" I squeal, hands clenching at my chest. I'm a kid on Christmas morning, where the rest of the world washes away, pale and inconsequential compared to the vivid splendor of this experience.

Liam slips an arm around my shoulders and pulls me close. That adorable smile quirks his lips, and amusement twinkles in his eyes at my delight over finally being here. But it's not like I'm the only one standing here gawking.

"Stop laughing at me!" I swat at him, but it's impossible to scowl when he's looking at me like this, like I'm the prettiest girl he's ever seen.

His expression sobers, though a ghost of the smile still lingers. He glances at me, then back to the Eiffel Tower. "I'm so glad I get to share this moment with you."

I slide my arm around his back and squeeze tight. "Me too."

Bittersweet sadness tugs at my heart as I watch the others. Olivia snaps a picture and rolls her eyes at Amir and Simon, who's actually laughing. Maybe he'll even work up the courage to tell her how he feels one day. A huge smile lights up Lily's face as she says something to Taylor and Dylan. The parents and foundation chaperones chatter softly together behind us.

I'm grateful we made it. But too many didn't. I think of Ann and Paige and Evan, the ones we lost. "I wish all of us could've been here."

Liam's eyes glisten until he blinks the moisture away. "So do I." He presses a kiss to the top of my head, and we stroll down the street after the others.

The future is out there waiting for us, with all its unknowns—both the good and the terrible. I don't know what's going to happen, but I do know this one thing:

We're going to be okay.

EPILOGUE

BONHOMME FOUNDATION RESTRUCTURES GOODWILL MERIT AWARD, OFFERS SETTLEMENT TO SURVIVORS

PARIS, FRANCE—The world-renowned Bonhomme Foundation made headlines earlier this year when the chair of its Goodwill Merit Award selection committee, Jennifer O'Connor, was charged with planning and executing a horrific attack on a group of 12 high school students aboard a transatlantic flight during its annual scholarship competition, resulting in the deaths of three of the teenagers. Despite O'Connor's attempts to cast blame for the incident on the students, evidence from both the crime scene and O'Connor's personal records, in addition to video footage recorded by one of the teens, has shed new light on her involvement and led to a scramble within the foundation's board to reassess the nonprofit's hiring practices and the structure of its scholarship program.

Although the foundation has contributed greatly to many global projects under its stated purpose of "bringing goodwill to humankind," its Goodwill Merit Award scholarship has repeatedly come under criticism during the 20 years since its inception. "Offering a scholarship only to boarding school students, who are already some of the most privileged teenagers in the country, is, frankly, ridiculous," stated one critic after the recent events. "And now we see the fallout."

A source within the foundation, who has asked to remain anonymous, claims that O'Connor had mentioned on a few occasions how "delighted" she was with the pool of merit award applicants, and how this year in particular had brought back "nostalgic memories" from her own school days. As chair of the selection committee, she was given near-total control over which applicants were selected to participate.

According to our inside source, CEO Sir Robert Hamlin was aware that O'Connor had boarded the flight as a member of the staff but claimed that "that was always the plan." The source quotes Hamlin as also saying, "The scholarship committee and I needed some eyes on the plane to keep track of the contest. How else were we supposed to monitor the competition and provide chaperones? When she volunteered, we had no reason to object. How could we know she was planning a gruesome killing spree?"

Before the incident, O'Connor had logged 15 years working for the foundation, the last 6 of which she'd served on the scholarship committee.

O'Connor, who was struck in the head with a paperweight by one of the victims, survived the flight and was apprehended after landing. She was treated for minor injuries and then released into police custody, where she now awaits a criminal trial.

In light of increasing negative publicity and the likelihood of civil lawsuits, the Bonhomme Foundation announced yesterday that it will be restructuring its scholarship program and undergoing a complete re-evaluation of hiring practices. The organization has also committed to fully funding each surviving student's undergraduate studies at the university of their choice, in addition to paying a settlement for damages to each of their families. The settlement numbers haven't been made public, but our inside source claims the amount is "very generous," further stating that "the foundation is making sure those students won't have to worry about finances for a very long time."

ACKNOWLEDGMENTS

It's hard to wrap my mind around the fact that I get to write these words. Publishing is a long and hard journey, not for the faint of heart, and this book was no exception. I wrote *Thin Air* in 2020, in the heart of the pandemic, when it was far too easy to imagine the sense of claustrophobia and the fear of an unknown killer that propels the story forward. Maybe it was my way of processing what was going on in the world. When you pour yourself into a book, you don't know what will happen to it—writing is an act of faith. I couldn't be more grateful that this one has found its way into your hands.

So first, thank you, Reader, for giving this book a chance. I hope Emily's story entertains you and gives you a little measure of the strength and hope I found writing it.

I can safely say this book would never have existed without Ali Herring, my brilliant agent. Thank you for your publishing wisdom, editorial insights, and constant support. I can't imagine navigating this process without you.

Thank you a million times over to Julie Rosenberg, my former editor at Razorbill, for taking a chance on an unknown author and championing this story. I'll be forever grateful to you for your faith in me and this book. Also to Julie, Simone Roberts-Payne, and Tiara Kittrell, who picked up this manuscript partway through the editorial process—together you managed to extract from me a far better book than I believed I was capable of writing. Tiara, I can't thank you enough for your patient guidance through this process and your support of this story. Thank you too to Casey McIntyre,

Rūta Rimas, and the rest of the Razorbill team for believing in this book and for your help during the transition between editors.

To the many others who helped polish this manuscript until it gleamed and who assembled it into a gorgeous book, you have my endless gratitude. Thank you to Elizabeth Johnson, Ana Deboo, Misha Kydd, Lisa Schwartz, Tony Sahara, and Jayne Ziemba.

Jessica Jenkins, thank you for your incredible vision for *Thin Air*'s cover and your work to make it happen. To talented artist Nicole Rifkin, thank you for your spectacular artwork and for bringing Emily and friends to life.

Thank you to my publicist, Sierra Pregosin, for your work on this book's success and for your lightning-fast email responses. You've been a delight to work with! Also to Bri Lockhart, James Akinaka, and Felicity Vallence, thank you for all your help with marketing and publicity.

Writing may be a solitary pursuit, but I never would've gotten here without the support of so many others in the writing community. Kerry Johnson, your willingness to read whatever heap of words I send you means the world to me. Thank you for your encouragement, sharp editorial eye, and brilliant suggestions. To the rest of my fellow #TeamSpencerhill Ali-ens, I'm so glad we can cheer each other on. And to so many others on Twitter and in my #2023debuts Slack group, you've been a fountain of answers for my endless questions and provided a good laugh when I needed one.

Mom, Dad, and Matt: who knew all those Nancy Drew books would lead to me writing my own mystery stories one day? Thank you for reading to me, for buying me books, for taking me to the library whenever I wanted, and for letting my imagination run wild while we played. Dad, thank you for "cheating death" with me on all those flights to exciting places and for inspiring me to love travel. I love you all!

To my husband, Jason: thank you for your tireless support as I tried to do the seemingly impossible, and for all those writing sessions where you let me vanish to get work done. I couldn't have done this without you. And to our kids, Isaiah, Nate, Ella, and Luke: look, here's a book for you! I hope when you hold it in your hands, you remember how much I love you. Never give up on your dreams.

Last of all, to my Lord and Savior Jesus Christ, who gifted me with the desire to create: You are the Word who gives me my words. "In the beginning was the Word, and the Word was with God, and the Word was God" (John 1:1). May all the glory go to You.